# What I Lost

# WHAT I Lost

## Alexandra Ballard

SQUARE
FISH

**FARRAR STRAUS GIROUX · NEW YORK**

SQUARE
FISH

An imprint of Macmillan Publishing Group, LLC
175 Fifth Avenue, New York, NY 10010
fiercereads.com

Square Fish and the Square Fish logo are trademarks of Macmillan and are
used by Farrar Straus Giroux under license from Macmillan.

Our books may be purchased in bulk for promotional, educational, or business use.
Please contact your local bookseller or the Macmillan Corporate and Premium
Sales Department at (800) 221-7945 ext. 5442 or by e-mail at
MacmillanSpecialMarkets@macmillan.com.

Library of Congress Cataloging-in-Publication Data

Names: Ballard, Alexandra, author.
Title: What I lost / Alexandra Ballard.
Description: New York : Farrar Straus Giroux, 2017. | Summary: When sixteen-year-old
Elizabeth is sent to the Wallingfield Psychiatric Facility's Residential Treatment
Center, she encounters girls whose problems seem much greater than her own
anorexia. | Description based on print version record and CIP data
provided by publisher; resource not viewed.
Identifiers: LCCN 2016035895 (print) | LCCN 2017013642 (ebook) |
ISBN 9780374304645 (ebook) | ISBN 9781250158420 (paperback)
Subjects: | CYAC: Anexoria nervosa—Fiction. | Psychiatric hospitals—Fiction. |
Self-perception—Fiction. | Interpersonal relations—Fiction.
Classification: LCC PZ7.1.B358 (ebook) | LCC PZ7.1.B358 Wh 2017 (print) |
DDC [Fic]—dc23
LC record available at https://lccn.loc.gov/2016035895

Originally published in the United States by Farrar Straus Giroux
First Square Fish edition, 2018
Book designed by Rebecca Syracuse
Square Fish logo designed by Filomena Tuosto

1   3   5   7   9   10   8   6   4   2

LEXILE: HL590L

*For Chris, Callie, and Eliza*

# 1

**NO ONE TOLD ME THAT WHEN I GOT SKINNY I'D**
grow fur. Tiny, translucent hairs, fine like white mink, appeared on my arms, my legs, and even, to my horror, my face, giving me downy blond sideburns no girl should have. When I looked it up, the fur had a name—*lanugo*. Babies are born with it. Anorexics grow it.

My first thought? *What a pain in the butt.*

My second thought? *So far, so good.*

After all, you had to suffer to be beautiful. Of all the things Mom ever said to me, I knew this one was true. If you wanted people to notice you, want you, admire you, envy you, want to *be* you, you had to sacrifice. Easy? No. But that's why people call it suffering.

And even when it seemed like it was getting me nowhere—well, nowhere except the Wallingfield Psychiatric

Facility's Residential Treatment Center—I tried to remember this: There is always success hidden in failure. I might have been locked away, but I was still a size 0.

It was just past ten on a cloudy morning when my parents and I first pulled up to Wallingfield. The treatment center was only fifteen minutes from my house, but might as well have been in another country. It sat atop a rolling hill in the old-money part of Esterfall, where houses overlooked the Atlantic and the families who lived in them had ancestors who came over on the *Mayflower*. "Elite and Discreet Mental Health Care, tucked away in a scenic part of Massachusetts." That's what the tiny box ad in the back of my parents' *New Yorker* magazine promised.

Dad parked in front of a large brick building. A burnished brass sign read *Wallingfield Psychiatric Facility Residential Treatment Center. Building Two.* The other buildings, I'd learned online the night before, were for the patients with schizophrenia, bipolar disorder, and other psychiatric illnesses.

I opened my door and willed my legs to move, but they felt like cement.

"Brush your hair before you go in." Mom passed me her purple travel brush from the front seat and touched up her lipstick.

In the rearview mirror I caught Dad's eye by accident. The skin around his eyes was the color of a bruise, like he hadn't slept in weeks.

"You okay, Elizabeth?"

I glared at him. "I'm *great*." I knew I sounded like a jerk, but the moment I walked through those big wooden doors, I'd forever be known at Esterfall High as the girl who'd gone nuts. So no, I was definitely not okay.

Inside the waiting room, a man in a gray suit sat on a green couch, bent over a laptop. Next to him, a dark-haired girl with a messy ponytail and a hospital ID bracelet scrunched in her chair, scowling. Her purple hoodie and black leggings hung off her like clothes on a hanger, and her legs, folded beneath her, were so thin they made her feet look too big for her body.

My cheeks burned. I felt inferior. She was so much skinnier than me. I held out my hand and tried to look friendly. "Hi. I'm Elizabeth."

"Lexi." Her fingers were cold and her handshake weak, but her eyes were angry. I shivered and pulled away as fast as I could. She didn't seem to notice, though.

Dad cleared his throat as he approached the front desk. "We are here to admit . . ." He couldn't finish.

Mom spoke up, her voice strong and all business. "Our daughter, Elizabeth, is here to be admitted to the eating disorder unit. Are we in the right place?"

I wanted the receptionist to say no, to say, *I'm sorry, but we don't have an Elizabeth on the list. You must have made a mistake.*

But she didn't even have to look me up. "Yes, here you are," she said, glancing at her computer. "Please sit down. Someone will be with you shortly."

When Lexi spoke, it startled me. "Where are you from?"

"Here," I said. "Esterfall. You?"

"Long Island. Massapequa. But I go to Smith in Massachusetts now."

I'd never been to Long Island, but Smith was at the top of my list of colleges to apply to next year. It was supposed to have a great psychology department, and I wanted to be a psychologist someday. "Oh, that's cool," I said.

"Yeah, I guess." She turned away, picking at the chipped red polish on her fingernails. We sat in silence until, a few minutes later, an older, crunchy-looking woman about Mom's age entered the room through double doors. She wore a gray top draped over her shoulders, flowy black pants, and black clogs. Vaguely gold-colored bracelets clinked on her arm. Mom looked her up and down, a slight frown on her face. She wasn't impressed.

The woman walked over and stuck out her hand. "Elizabeth? Hi, I'm Mary, your therapist." I hoped she didn't notice my clammy skin. "I'm going to help you get settled. Follow me." I looked back at Lexi and waved, but she was gazing out the only window, staring at the parking lot, and didn't see me.

Walking through the wooden double doors, I expected to see 70-pound girls in hospital gowns hobbling through cold, linoleum-lined hallways. Instead, Mary led us into a cozy space that smelled like cinnamon, not medicine, and was full of sofas, slouchy chairs, and soft carpeting. Windows looked out onto a lawn, which stretched down to the woods, the trees in full October reds, oranges, and yellows. Across from them was a line of bedroom doors, each decorated with photos, drawings, dry-erase boards, and letters fashioned from construction paper. It looked like the Boston College dorm I saw with my parents last summer.

On the closest couch, a little girl who couldn't have been older than ten sat hunched over her journal, one ear pierced all the way to the top, her arms covered with soft pink scars I assumed were self-inflicted. A pair of taller girls sat across from her, quietly talking, their jaws sharp and distinct. They giggled. I couldn't imagine ever giggling in a place like this. They all looked thin, but not life-threateningly so.

"It'll be snack time soon," Mary said, sniffing the air. "Smells like Chef Frank's famous coffee cake muffins." We all inhaled. The room smelled like the Cinnabon stall at the mall. I looked at the girls on the couches. *They* were going to eat muffins?

"Well," said Mom, her voice full of relief, "isn't this cheery!" I wondered if she'd pictured a hospital, too. The girl with the scars looked up and watched us, her face blank.

Mary turned to me. "Elizabeth, if you'd like to eat the snack with your parents, they can join you in the guest dining room."

*Eat? Already?*

"Thanks, but I'm not hungry," I said.

Mary smiled like she'd heard this excuse a hundred times. She probably had. "I understand, but we eat all our meals here, hungry or not."

Of course "we" did.

Mary continued. "So, every day we gather in the dining room for breakfast, lunch, and dinner. There are three snacks scheduled throughout the day—morning, afternoon, and after dinner. Meals last forty-five minutes, snacks twenty. For the first few days, your nutritionist, Sally, will set your menu, but after that you'll work together to create your food plan. At each meal you'll find a menu check sheet on your tray. A nurse will make sure you've eaten everything. Any questions so far?"

I shook my head. She didn't say what would happen if I didn't eat, and I didn't ask. I'd read about places like this online, how they required you to eat every single thing they put in front of you, how they punished you with super-fattening nutrition shakes if you didn't.

Mary kept talking. "Weights and vitals is every morning from six to seven. Since it's your first day, we'll also do a medical intake, like a physical, later today. Oh, and at some point we'll take you to get a bone density test."

A bone density test? I didn't need one of those. My bones were fine. I ate yogurt. And why did they need to weigh me so soon? They knew my weight already. They wouldn't have admitted me otherwise. I shook my head. *No. No weighing.*

Mary watched me, her face soft and knowing. I recognized that look. It was the same look my friends Priya and Shay always gave me at lunch at school. They felt sorry for me. Sometimes, when I left the table, I saw them bend their heads together and whisper.

Mary put her hand on my shoulder. I flinched and she dropped it. "I know this is hard, Elizabeth, but we weigh everybody. Every day. It's an important part of recovery."

Mom piped in, "Does she get to know her weight each morning?"

"No," Mary said. "We don't reveal numbers."

Mom frowned. She probably wanted me to know so I wouldn't gain too much.

Once, at lunch, Priya asked me if I was anorexic. I didn't know what to say. I'd hoped that maybe I was, because of the lanugo and all, but to have someone else actually say it? I felt like dancing right then. But I couldn't

9

admit that. No one was supposed to *want* to be anorexic. So I'd said, in as sarcastic a voice as I could muster, "Obviously, no. Have you seen my thighs?" Priya didn't push the issue after that, and I spent the rest of the day smiling.

". . . alarm clock?"

"Sorry?" I'd completely spaced.

"Did you bring a cordless alarm clock?"

We'd bought one at CVS on the way; everybody I knew, including myself, used our phones' alarms, but Wallingfield didn't allow anything that got Wi-Fi. Or had cords. I guess so we wouldn't strangle ourselves. I nodded.

"Great. So lunch is at noon," Mary continued. "I'll give you your daily schedule after lunch, but it goes pretty much like this: group therapy three or four times a week, individual therapy with me twice a week, family therapy— either in person, on the phone, or in a group setting— once a week, and various other types of activities, such as dance and art, scattered in as well. We do meal support therapy after lunch and dinner. Oh, and we got another admit today—did you meet Lexi in the foyer?"

I nodded.

"Great! She's going to be your roommate."

I shrank into myself a little. No one told me I was going to have a roommate. And Lexi? The angry girl? I shot a look at Mom. I bet she'd known. But her face looked as surprised as mine.

How could my parents leave me here?

Mary continued on. "Now, I haven't seen your schedule, but my guess is that you'll likely start with a group session today. Our first individual therapy session is set for the day after tomorrow. Tonight we have free time. On other nights it varies; there might be activities, or arts and crafts, or group sessions. It will all be on your schedule. Any questions?"

"Are there boys here?" I hoped not. I'd read that some programs were coed.

"No. This adolescent and early adult program is for girls only. We have a coed program in Building Three for ages twenty-five and over." She paused. "We've talked about including boys, though. Their rate of anorexia is rising. But for now it's just girls."

"Oh," I said, relieved. Being here was bad enough. Being here with boys? I couldn't even imagine it.

We followed Mary around the facility until we ended up back at the common room, with its line of bedroom doors. She stopped in front of the only bare door on the hall, number 16. Bits and corners of Scotch tape littered the dark brown wood, the only sign of the girls who'd come before me.

Inside were two normal beds stripped down to the plastic mattress pad. Morning sun filtered through the curtains on the single window; outside, I could see our maroon

Honda in the parking lot. A nightstand with a beige lamp stood between the two beds, and across from it was another door, closed. Mary pointed at it, her bracelets clinking. "Bathroom," she said. "You share it with the room next door." The whole setup reminded me of a hotel, which, weirdly, made me feel better. I didn't need a "real" bedroom. Wallingfield's website said that the average stay was a month, but there was no way I'd be here that long. I wasn't that sick. I was just a little bit anorexic. All my body needed was a rest. I'd be out of here in a few days—a week, max.

The room had gone quiet. Everybody stared at me. "Okay, Elizabeth?" Mom asked. I nodded like I had a clue.

"I'll give you a minute to get settled," Mary said, closing the door on her way out.

When Mary left, Mom dove in. She rolled up her cashmere sleeves and opened my suitcase just like when they sent me to sleepaway camp in middle school. She pulled out my favorite sheets, my gray wool blanket, and my purple-and-blue-pinstriped duvet. She stretched the sheets tight and snapped the duvet up and over the bed. The room filled with the smell of our fabric softener, a scent I loved. After she fluffed the duvet, she reached into her purse, brought out a gray stuffed dolphin with only one plastic eye, and leaned him against a pillow. Flippy. My favorite from when I was little. I thought I might cry. I looked at her, questioning.

"The 'What to Bring' list said a stuffed animal," she said defensively.

Our eyes met, mirror images of each other. We'd always looked alike—the same straight brown hair, the same cheekbones—except she'd been the thin one. I got my dad's genes, my grandma liked to say, which meant I vacillated between average and chubby, depending on whether it was cross-country season or not. Now, though, I was skinnier than Mom. Even in this room, I was proud.

She reached out to touch my cheek, her hand soft on my always-cold skin.

Mary knocked and entered. Mom's hand fell to her side.

The room felt crowded now. "You look settled," Mary said, then smiled at Dad. "Will you be joining us for snack?"

Of course he'd stay. He'd stay until Mary told him to leave. I knew it.

"No, thanks," he said.

*What?*

He didn't look at me. "Elizabeth's mother and I both need to get back to work, and I know we still have some paperwork to complete."

My heart flew into my throat. He was abandoning me?

I'd had this whole scenario worked out in my head that when my parents saw the other girls here, they'd realize I was basically fine and take me home. They'd say, *Elizabeth, we've made a terrible mistake. This place is for sick girls. Not you.* Then we'd sweep through the front doors and jump back in the car and all go to Starbucks, and over coffee we'd laugh about how they almost had me committed.

Instead, Dad took me by the shoulders. "I love you so much, kiddo," he said, voice gruff. "I'll miss you." And then he held me so tight I could barely breathe. He grabbed his coat and tried to leave before the first sob but didn't make it, his shoulders heaving. "You are a wonderful daughter. I love you so much." And then he was gone.

Mom smoothed her skirt and adjusted her sweater, clearing her throat like she always did when she was nervous. "Well, do you need anything else?" Her voice was brisk and professional.

I shook my head, not trusting myself to speak.

"Okay, then. Don't forget to call us, all right? You're going to be fine." She looked me up and down and nodded. "Yes, you are going to be fine." She said this more to herself than to me. We hugged. We never hugged. Mom wasn't the cuddly type, but all of a sudden I didn't want to let her go. I inhaled her perfume, realizing for the first time how much I liked it. And then she too slipped out the door, a cloud of Chanel No. 5 lingering behind her. Without thinking, I walked through it, hoping a bit of her would stay with me.

With everybody gone, the room felt lonely and too quiet. I tried to make myself as small as I could. I sat on the corner of the bed. It crackled.

"All set?" Mary asked. I'd forgotten she was there. I nodded.

"Let's go, then." She led me into the hall, where a row of girls waited in front of double doors that read *Dining Room*. The tiny girl from the couch was at the end of the line, picking at a scab on her arm.

"I'm going to leave you with Willa," Mary said. "She'll be in your cohort." The girl barely looked up at me.

I was confused. "Cohort?"

"Your cohort is the group of girls you'll be doing the majority of your therapy with. You have six in yours. Willa, here, is the youngest." I looked at her. A tiny gold Winnie-the-Pooh, a silver Ariel, and an orange-and-black enamel Tigger clung to her earlobe. "Willa, this is Elizabeth. Take care of her, will you?"

Willa smiled then, and as she did, her face changed. Became friendlier. "Welcome to the crazy house," she said in a smoker's growl. How old *was* she?

Mary frowned. "Willa," she warned.

"Sorry." She grinned. "Welcome to paradise."

# 2

I WAS STILL TRYING TO UNDERSTAND THE STRANGE creature that was Willa when the dining room doors flew open. A woman dressed in baggy jeans and a plaid shirt straight out of the nineties stood just inside the door, greeting each girl as she entered. "That's Kay," Willa whispered. "The food police." I looked at her, not understanding. "She's the meal monitor, the one who makes sure you eat what you're supposed to and makes you drink Ensure if you don't."

"What's Ensure?"

"A high-calorie nutrition shake. The chocolate isn't so bad."

Oh, those. *I'll never drink one of those,* I promised myself. *Ever.*

"Hello, Willa." Kay smiled. "And are you Elizabeth?"

I nodded.

"Welcome! Come on in."

I followed them through the doors into a room the same size as the classrooms at school. Big windows overlooking a stone patio lined the wall opposite the entrance. Off to the left, a door led to a kitchen, where girls entered in a long, slow line. Willa grabbed a tray. "So, the rules in here are simple: Eat. No matter what." Then she whispered, "And don't even try to stick the food down your pants. They'll see it, I promise." I had a feeling she was speaking from experience.

Kay appeared holding a sheet of paper. Her reddish hair looked frizzy, like she'd had an unfortunate run-in with a curling iron. "Your menu plan is a basic one today. Here's your list—one muffin, one apple, and one milk. Not too bad. You go through the kitchen line for snacks here, but for your meals, the kitchen prepares your tray before you arrive. When you finish, raise your hand and I'll check you off. Got it?"

"I, um, I'm sorry, but I don't like milk," I said.

She didn't even blink before responding. "Well, once you can design your own menu, you can discuss that with your nutritionist. But until then, I think you're stuck."

I couldn't drink milk. I'd throw up. With a pang I wondered what my parents were doing, if they'd stopped for coffee on the way home or if they'd driven straight to their offices. I stared at the floor, blinking to keep back the tears.

Kay noticed and touched my shoulder. "It'll be okay," she said. "You'll see."

I doubted it. Being here was like a permanent stain. No matter what I did in the future, I could never erase the fact that, once upon a time, I'd been locked up like a crazy person. The eating disorder unit was separate from the rest of Wallingfield, but it was still a part of a mental institution.

Five tins of muffins, straight from the oven, filled the counter. The cinnamon crumble on top of each one made my stomach growl and my mouth water. I hadn't eaten that morning, and I ached for one. That was what anorexia was. A constant battle with the ache.

At home I wouldn't have gone near them, but here I didn't have a choice. Gingerly I picked out the tiniest muffin I could find, the grease from it making my fingertips shiny. I shuddered and wiped them on my pants.

My brain spun, calculating. I'd never been good at math, but when it came to calories I could add like Stephen Hawking. Dunkin' Donuts coffee cake muffins had 590 calories. That's right. Five hundred and ninety calories. Oh, and 24 grams of fat. I knew because I'd looked it up once. These were smaller, but still. Three hundred and fifty calories at least. I'd put the grams of fat at 16. Maybe more. My stomach rumbled. No. I was not hungry. No way. Not allowed. Not for a *muffin,* anyway.

I felt a nudge from behind.

"Sorry," I mumbled to the girl behind me.

"It gets easier," she said sympathetically.

I nodded. *I doubt it*, I thought.

I took an apple from a basket. I saw other girls reaching into a refrigerator and grabbing low-fat yogurts and cheese sticks. Others helped themselves to little containers of pre-measured granola stacked like a pyramid on the counter. Granola was a calorie bomb—up to 280 calories for half a cup. Would I have to eat that someday, too?

Milk was next. The carton was wet and made my hand smell sour. I wished I had some Purell to get rid of the smell. Willa came up behind me. "All set?" she said.

I nodded, numb, and wiped my hands one at a time on my pants.

"Great. Come on." She led me to a table next to the toaster in the corner. Her tray looked like mine, except she had a cheese stick, too. "Let's sit."

I sat.

"So." She peeled the paper liner off her muffin. "Don't get Kay mad at you. She'll force Ensure down your throat faster than you can say 'anorexic.'" She placed her muffin carefully on her tray and cut it in half. Then she halved it again. And again. She continued until the muffin was nothing but a pile of crumbs.

"Are you going to eat that?" I asked. Willa gave me a sly grin. "Of course." She popped a crumb in her mouth. Then

19

she did it again, except this time, she let a second one fall on the floor. Then she smashed it with the bottom of her fake black UGG. It stuck to her sole and disappeared. For her next bite, she let the extra crumb fall not on the floor but behind her, into the hood of her sweatshirt. It was remarkable, really, that she managed to aim right every single time. She proceeded this way, alternating between floor and hoodie, until she'd destroyed over half her muffin and hidden most of the crumbs in her sweatshirt or under her shoe on the floor.

"You better start eating," Willa said, reaching down to scratch her foot. She dropped a hunk of cinnamon topping into her jeans' cuff.

"Oh, right," I said. I broke off a tiny piece of muffin and held it in my hand. It was still warm.

"Where are you from?" Willa asked. "I'm from Worcester. That's about an hour and a half from here."

"Right. I'm from, um, Esterfall." This girl was so chatty. How could she be so chatty?

She brightened. "Here? You're from here? That is so cool!"

I wasn't sure I agreed. "I guess," I said. "How long have you been here?"

Willa shrugged. "Three weeks."

"How long do you think you'll stay?"

Willa shook her head. "I don't know. They keep saying

my insurance is going to run out, but Mary—she's your therapist too, right?"

I nodded.

"Anyway, Mary said that I'd probably be able to get a scholarship and stay longer."

"A scholarship?"

"Yeah, isn't it funny they call it that?" Willa secreted a muffin chunk in her hood. "It's like, I'm so good at my eating disorder they are going to give me a scholarship to get rid of it. Funny, right?"

I didn't get a chance to respond because Kay stopped at our table. "Elizabeth," she said, "please get started." I brought the chunk I was holding to my mouth, but my throat closed and my taste buds shut down. It tasted like rubber. Kay stood by, watching.

Willa slid her napkin over the remaining crumbs on her plate. "Sometimes water helps," she said, and poured me a glass. Kay marked something on my sheet. Why would she do that? Water doesn't have calories. Why did it matter if I drank it?

Snack was supposed to be twenty minutes, but it felt like forty. By the time girls started to clear their trays and leave, I'd only eaten about a fifth of my muffin and taken one sip of lukewarm milk, which tasted like the carton.

When snack ended, Kay said, "Because it's your first day,

I'm not going to make you drink an Ensure, but starting tomorrow, you will be expected to eat your full portions."

Willa picked up her tray. "She's got it. Let's go, Elizabeth," she said. "Later, Kay."

Kay stopped her. "Not so fast." She picked up Willa's napkin. Crumbs stuck to it and fell to the floor. "Willa, lift up your shoe."

"No."

Kay said it again, her voice steady. "Willa, lift up your shoe, please."

"No!" A couple of girls turned around.

"Willa," she said, her voice still calm but also with an edge. "Please lift up your shoe. Now."

"Fine!" The entire bottom was coated with muffin.

Kay sighed. "Willa, we've talked about this. I'm sorry, but you're going to have to have a supplement."

Willa's impish, little-girl face contorted. She stared at Kay for a few seconds and turned bright red. Then she lost it. "I don't want an Ensure! I hate you, Kay!" she said, kicking at the crumbs on the floor. "I hate everything!" And then she pushed out of the room, past the other girls waiting patiently to get checked. I just stood there, mouth open bigger than my muffin, wondering how the hell I ever got myself into this mess. And, more importantly, how the hell I was ever going to get out.

# 3

AN HOUR LATER IT WAS TIME FOR MY MEDICAL
intake. In a small room off the main hall, a stone-faced
woman made me take off all my clothes except for my
underpants. I put on a hospital gown and stood on the
scale, the rubber surface cold on my bare feet. She shielded
the paper with her hand when she wrote down the number. I tried to tell what it was based on her scribbling, but
I couldn't. Then she took my pulse lying down and standing up. I peed in a cup. She measured my height. She
checked my blood pressure. And then she asked me questions about my weight that I didn't want to answer.

"Lowest weight?"

I paused. "This morning. Ninety pounds."

"Highest weight?"

*Shameful,* I wanted to say. *That's what my highest weight was.* "A hundred thirty," I muttered.

"When was this?"

"Eight months ago. Last February."

"Do you purge?"

"Purge?" I stalled.

"Make yourself throw up after eating?"

I knew what she meant. I'd done that a few times to correct mistakes, like when I'd let myself have a spoonful of Dad's ice cream in August. The worst time had been in June. Nobody else was home. I let down my guard for a minute and my brain shut off, and I stole a chocolate from the box of See's Candies Dad had gotten for his birthday. They were my favorites—fat circles of marshmallow perched on caramel disks, the whole thing covered with dark chocolate.

I didn't stop there. I ate the whole box—nine chocolates—wolfing them down so fast that after the third or fourth I didn't even taste them. Afterward, my stomach bloated, and I looked up the candies online to see just how much damage I'd done. Each one had 80 calories and 4.5 grams of fat. That meant I'd just stuffed 720 calories and 40.5 grams of fat into my face. I was horrified. I ran to the bathroom in a total panic, stuck my finger down my throat, and puked into the toilet until my eyes watered and my mouth was sore. But I knew I hadn't gotten rid of all of it. A hard ball of chocolate and caramel and marsh-mallow remained and was slowly dissolving in my stom-ach and turning into fat on my thighs.

Afterward I called my boyfriend Charlie and told him I needed to get a present for my mother and would he please come pick me up. He drove me to the mall and I marched right into Lord & Taylor and up to the candy counter. When the saleslady asked if I wanted a free sam-ple, I said, "No. Thank you. Definitely not."

Charlie perked up. "I'll have hers," he said, and ate two.

Once home, I replaced the empty box and no one was ever the wiser. From that point on, I made sure I didn't go near food I really liked. Too dangerous.

I'd never told anyone that story, and I wasn't going to start now.

"No," I said. "I've never purged."

Back in the common room, I caught a glimpse of my re-flection in the mirror above the fireplace. A narrow-faced girl with long, dark hair and arms that looked skinny only because a shirt hid the flabby bits stared back at me.

*Leave me alone,* I told her.

That girl made me sick. I hated catching glimpses of her. It didn't matter where—whether in a mirror, or a window reflection, or on my phone screen after a group selfie.

And right now, I had no patience for her. *She* was the reason I was here. If she'd been able to keep it together a little bit more, maybe I'd be at school right now, trying to text my friends during pre-calc.

Then again, if you know anything about anorexia, you know a lot of things mess with your head. Like TV, and fashion magazines, and skinny jeans, and social media, and the Internet, and pro-ana websites, and Diet Coke, and *People* magazine's diet issue, and peer pressure, and every tabloid with celebrity cellulite on the cover. I mean, I could even blame Caroline, the super-skinny senior at school with the kick-ass body I coveted, and on and on.

But mirrors are the worst. One reflection lifts your spirits and another crushes them. A good one can make you feel like the most beautiful girl in the world. But a bad one can make you burst into tears.

Sometimes, walking down the street, I'd catch a glimpse of myself in a mirror or window and there would be this millisecond before I realized the girl in the glass was me. I'd think how she looked as thin and graceful as a ballet dancer. But then I'd come to my senses and realize that it was just me, and I'd look down at my real-life thighs and get pissed at myself for falling for such crap. That's why I only trusted the fat mirrors. At least they didn't get your hopes up.

Last February, my best friend, Katrina, wanted me to

go bikini shopping with her in preparation for a trip to Florida she was taking with her parents in April. I put her off for a month and convinced her to diet with me, saying how much cuter the bathing suits would look if we were 10 pounds slimmer.

I knew we'd go to Target. Target had fat mirrors. Every time I tried something on, I left wanting to sob on the handle of my red plastic cart. "How does Target expect to sell clothes if their mirrors make everybody look like Honey Boo Boo's Mama June?" I'd joke if I was with a friend, but deep down a tiny part of me was grateful that the person staring out at me wasn't at all distorted. At least then I knew what to work on. And if forced to choose between the truth and a lie, I'll take the truth every time.

This time I decided to beat the fat mirrors at their own game. I cut out carbs and ate things like cauliflower mashed potatoes and noodles made from seaweed. I told Mom I was dieting and she said, "Let me know what I can do to help. I think you'd look great if you lost a few pounds."

By March I'd lost 10. Katrina had given up after the third day and looked the same. When we got to Target, I marched into the dressing room with the teeniest bikinis I could find, convinced that this was going to be the best day of my life.

I looked like crap in every single one of them.

Katrina didn't fare much better than me, but she wasn't

worried. "Everything looks better with a tan," she announced as she plunked a pink-and-blue bikini down in front of the cashier.

I left mine on the dressing room floor.

People say anorexics don't see themselves as they really are. But what if anorexics are the *only* ones who do? What if we are the clear-eyed ones, and everybody else out there sees some brain-altered version of themselves, a massive mind trick designed to make them feel better?

Katrina went to Florida and came back with tan lines and crushes on all the lifeguards. I went back to Target. Four times. Just to try on bikinis. But even after I lost 40 pounds, when I looked in those mirrors, I saw something shameful.

A fat cow.

# 4

ON MY FIRST NIGHT AT WALLINGFIELD, I AWOKE TO loud thumps and heavy, tortured breathing. I'd had trouble falling asleep—the heater was loud and I shivered under my duvet. The room was full of weird noises, and even before Lexi started doing whatever it was she was doing, I'd heard her breathing, rustling, and smacking her pillow as she twisted and turned.

The rest of the day had been overwhelming and exhausting and a big blur. We'd had some sort of therapy session where we'd written bad thoughts about ourselves on balloons with black Sharpies and popped them. I'd taken a nap. There was snack, where I ate two tiny chunks of granola, and at dinner I'd shared a table with Willa, who acted like her whole outburst at snack had never happened, and Lexi, who sat with her arms crossed, refusing to eat anything. Kay told Lexi that if she at least tried, took a bite or two, she'd avoid the supplement. Lexi didn't move. At the end of the meal, Kay brought her an Ensure and told her that she had five minutes to drink it. "That's the rule around here," Willa whispered. Lexi didn't touch it.

And now, apparently, she was having sex. Or trying to dry heave. Or doing . . . burpees? We used to do burpees sometimes as a warm-up at cross-country practice, and they always killed us. You had to jump in the air with your hands raised, then go down in a squat, do a plank, and then spring back to a squat, then stand, jump in the air again, and start over.

I turned on the light, but she didn't even pause. Jump, squat, plank, up. Jump, squat, plank, up. *Boom-cha-boom-thump.*

I needed to stop her. We'd both get into trouble. This had to be against every Wallingfield rule.

*Or maybe you should join her, you fat ass.*

"Lexi?" I whispered.

She didn't answer.

"Lexi!" I hissed louder.

Startled, she let her knees hit the carpet.

"Lexi, what are you doing? You know if you get caught you're going to get in trouble."

She lifted her head and went into a cat stretch, staring at me the whole time. She looked a little ridiculous in her PJs, which were light blue and covered with dogs knitting sweaters. "Are you going to tell on me?"

"What? No! Sorry, that's not what I meant. I just don't want you to have to drink Ensure or anything."

"That's my problem, okay?"

In the shadows Lexi's eyes were just sockets. She was so tiny her pajamas looked more like a blanket.

"Okay, sorry." I turned off the light and rolled over, face hot.

I waited for the *boom-cha-boom-thump* to start up again, but it didn't.

"Elizabeth?"

"Yeah?"

"Do you want to get better?"

"What?"

"Do you want to get better?"

"Of course." We all did, right?

"No, I mean, do you really?"

Maybe it was because of the dark, or maybe it was that I'd already caught Lexi doing something worse. I don't know. But I told the truth. "If I have to gain weight, then no. I don't. I totally don't."

"Me either," she said.

She climbed back into bed. "Thanks for being honest." Her blankets muffled her voice. "It helps."

"You're welcome."

And just like that, we were friends.

# 5

**THE NEXT MORNING MY ALARM CLOCK BEEPED AT** 6:55 for weights and vitals. I shivered and started pulling on a pair of leggings. Lexi, from under her covers, said, "Just wear your bathrobe over your pajamas. That's what everybody does in these places." Sure enough, when I peeked out my door, a long line of girls in brightly colored flannel and terry-cloth robes snaked down the hall.

"Told you," she said.

In line, Lexi turned to me. "Oh, and tomorrow, set your alarm for six. That way, we can beat the line so the whole thing will take two minutes and we'll still be sleepy enough to go back to bed after they weigh us."

Apparently I was in charge of waking us both up. Everyone in line seemed to be trying to cling to sleep by leaning against the wall with their eyes closed, so I whispered, "Okay."

"By the way," Lexi whispered back, "you know that today, we're going to have to eat everything."

I nodded and gulped. "I don't know how I am going to do that."

Lexi shrugged. "Even if they force an Ensure on you, you still can say no. You just have to be okay dealing with the consequences."

I nodded. How did she know these things? "Lexi, have you been here before?"

"No," she said, twisting a strand of black hair between her fingers. "But I've been at a place just like this. And this is what I know: They're going to try to make you eat whether you like it or not. If you refuse, they give you Ensure. If you refuse Ensure enough times, they'll make you go around in a wheelchair or make you get a feeding tube. At least here they make you get an NG."

"NG?"

"A nasogastric tube—the one they cram down your nose to your stomach. But an NG isn't as bad as the stomach one I had a while back. That one really sucked. Oh, and it scars." She undid her robe and hiked up her PJ top to reveal what looked like a second belly button above and to the left of her real one.

I cringed.

"I know. Gross, right?" She pulled her robe closed over her shirt. "You basically have two choices when you're here. You can either refuse to do everything, and then eventually they'll kick you out. That's what happened to me at my last place. Or you can do what they tell you, get fat, and go home when your insurance runs out and do it all over again. It's up to you."

*What about girls who want to get well?* I almost asked, but then she might think I was one. "Thanks for the intel."

Lexi fussed with her top. "Anytime."

Breakfast was a nightmare. It was so bad, in fact, that I can't even talk about it except to say just imagine someone putting ten times the amount of food you'd usually eat in front of you and then telling you to finish every bite. I cried. A lot. Lexi refused to eat again and sat with her mouth glued shut in front of the resulting Ensure. She amazed me. I wasn't as brave as she was, so I left with a bowling ball for a stomach. Then I got nauseous and barely made it to the bathroom before it all came up, burning my throat the whole way: two scrambled eggs, two slices of buttered toast, another carton of milk, and three orange wedges. I didn't throw up on purpose, but Kay, after handing me a paper towel for my mouth, still made me go to group therapy. "Once your stomach settles," she said, "that will be one Ensure."

Fantastic.

# 6

GROUP WAS HELD IN THE THERAPY WING ON THE far side of the building. Once again everybody queued up in the hall. I joined them after I brushed my teeth, my stomach still queasy. I was beginning to think all girls did at Wallingfield was eat, wait in lines, get weighed, talk about themselves, and wait in more lines.

A big picture window at the other end of the corridor displayed a clear view of the entrance. "Check that out," said a girl with a blond ponytail. She sounded just bitchy enough that I wished I had the willpower not to look. A couple more girls, on their way somewhere else, stopped and looked too.

Outside, a girl hauled herself out of a black Mercedes idling in the middle of the driveway. She crossed the gravel slowly, her blue wool peacoat straining across her broad shoulders, her suitcase wheels getting stuck in the tiny rocks. Her mouse-brown hair hid her face. At one point she turned around, as if to wave goodbye to the person who'd brought her, but the Mercedes was already half-way down the driveway, brake lights winking. Shoulders slumped, she opened the front door and wrestled her suitcase and backpack through, the door closing on her the whole time. Then she was gone, and the parking lot was empty again.

A couple of girls snickered. A tiny girl with a pixie cut who looked a little like a real-live fairy called out, "Thar she blows!" and the girls nearest to her laughed nervously.

"Who is that?" I said quietly to Willa, who'd slipped in next to me.

"Her?" Willa made a disgusted face. "That's Coral," she murmured in my ear. "She's evil."

"Oh," I said.

"She used to run this intense pro-ana site before she came here, Thinsporgasmic. Have you heard of it?"

"*She* ran Thinsporgasmic?" I'd gotten great tips on how to avoid eating from that site. Her most popular feature was "How Thin Am I?" where girls posted their photos and others rated them on a scale of one to five skeletons— one being "Lard Ass," five being "Totally Dedicated." It was pretty sick. But motivating, if you want to know the truth.

"Yeah. Her parents shut it down when she was admitted."
That's why it had disappeared.

"A whole posse of girls followed her around. Some were in her cohort, so they mixed up the cohorts last week to separate them. It was a big scandal. Allie, who's in our cohort now, was one of them. Coral was pissed. But whatever." Willa shrugged. "She deserved it."

I snuck a glance at Coral, who was still snickering. This place was getting more like high school every minute.

We'd all settled into our seats when the girl who'd just been dropped off walked into the room. She sat hunched over like a lump next to Marcia, the twentysomething counselor in charge.

"Group therapy," Willa told me from our spot on one of the three neutral-colored couches arranged in a triangle, "is basically the same every time, except that what we talk about and do is different."

"Wouldn't that make it different every day?" I asked.

"Well, yeah, but it's the same, too."

I raised my eyebrows. "I'm confused."

"Just wait. You'll see. Marcia will introduce you guys, and then she'll do a check-in with everybody else," she said.

Sure enough, the first thing Marcia, who was pretty, skinny, and wearing the brown leather Frye boots I'd coveted for months, did was smile at me and the lump on the chair next to her. "Everybody, please say hello to Margot, Elizabeth, and Lexi."

I smiled and tried to look like someone the other girls would want to be friends with. The lump/Margot didn't respond. I felt guilty thinking about her that way, but I couldn't even see her face. She really needed to sit up, at least a little.

"Let's do a quick check-in," Marcia said.

"See?" Willa mouthed. As we went around the circle, girls said things like "fine," or "cold," or "anxious," or "sad." One girl, Beth, said, "Excited! I got my feeding tube out yesterday."

I said "nervous." Margot said nothing.

The baseboard heaters creaked and groaned, but I was freezing. I should have worn another layer. I had goose bumps practically all the time, which made my lanugo stand on end. I sat with my knees curled up to my chest to stay warm. Most of the other girls did too, except for Margot, who sat with her arms across her chest, head down, legs splayed out in front of her. I'd never sit like that. It made my thighs look fat.

"A couple of days ago," Willa whispered next to me, "we sat behind cardboard walls made from boxes and talked about what parts of ourselves we wanted to hide. That was the worst. I hope we aren't doing that again."

We didn't. Instead, we filled out a worksheet to help us

identify any emotions that might be hiding when we felt mad. Then everybody talked about it. It wasn't so bad.

About forty-five minutes into the hour-long session, Marcia asked if Margot had anything to say. She looked up for a second, and our eyes met. My stomach dropped. Oh my God. I knew her. Her name was Margot Camby. She lived in Esterfall and went to boarding school. We'd taken ballet together when we were six. In the performance, we'd both been shooting stars, twirling each other in our light-blue tutus and silver ballet slippers as our parents took pictures.

Her eyes were desperate, trapped. *Do something*, they seemed to say. *Help me.*

What did she want me to do? I didn't want to talk. At home I always went with the smile-and-nod approach, which I'd developed in my old support group. I'd joined after Dr. Brach, our family doctor, told Mom during my annual physical that I'd lost too much weight over the summer. He was the one who told her to sign me up. It met once a week in a plain room in the one office building in town. He'd also told Mom I needed to quit cross-country, at least until my weight stabilized. Even though Mom told him she thought I was fine, she obeyed him because, as I overheard her say to Dad later that day, "I didn't want him to think I was a bad mother."

Smile-and-nod was the best way to show you cared without having to contribute. The smile was key. It had to be upbeat, but not too yay-everything-is-awesome cheery, because the person talking might feel laughed at. It had to be sympathetic, but not wow-that's-totally-how-I-feel, because group leaders lived for that stuff and would definitely call on you to "share your thoughts." And you definitely couldn't zone out, because that was rude and you'd get a reputation for either being self-absorbed and bitchy, or on too high a dose of antidepressants.

"Margot?" Marcia's voice was a little more demanding this time.

"I hate this hair," I blurted out, plucking at the thin layer of lanugo on my arm. I blushed. Of all the things to say, I chose that? I looked toward Margot, expecting a thank-you, but she'd gone back to looking at the floor.

Everybody waited for me to continue. I cleared my throat. "It doesn't seem fair, you know, that you work so hard and you get *this*," I said, holding out my arm as evidence. "I would have shaved it off, but the only thing weirder than too much arm hair is none at all. And now, here, I don't even have the option." Razors were sharp, and sharps weren't allowed at Wallingfield.

*You owe me, Margot.*

A couple of girls in the room nodded, and I was relieved that they didn't think I was crazy.

Beth raised her skeletal arm. You could still see the tape residue on her cheek from her feeding tube.

She smiled in my direction. "I totally agree, Elizabeth. This fuzz sucks."

Willa leaned over and in my ear said, "Beth never smiles. She must be in a good mood because she got to walk to group. Up until now, she's been pushed around in a wheelchair so she'd burn fewer calories and gain more weight."

With her white-blond hair, Beth looked like a cross between an angel and a ghost. Her skin was so pale I could see the blue veins on her wrists.

Lexi spoke then. "Kids called me Amy Winehouse." Ouch. Amy Winehouse was a rock star who died from alcohol poisoning. She'd been anorexic, too, with an unfortunate whorl of black hair right below each ear, like Lexi.

"I wore so many layers people called me a bag lady." This came from a girl named Jean, who smiled at me as she spoke.

Willa leaned in. "She's twenty-two. She's from *Canada*." Willa said this like it was a miracle or something. "She's been here for eleven weeks. Everybody calls her a lifer because she's been here for so long."

Jean was tall and awkward, like a female Abraham Lincoln.

"She's really nice, though. Maybe the nicest," Willa said.

Then, without missing a beat, Willa turned to the group

and held out her arms, which were covered with downy hair and parallel scars. I looked away. "I didn't know . . ." She stopped herself midsentence. "I tried to shave mine off," she said.

Everybody nodded. Suddenly the grubby, white-painted cinder-block walls, folding chairs, fluorescent lighting— even the whiteboard, which someone had ruined by writing *YOLO* on it with a Sharpie—felt warmer. For the first time, I felt understood. These girls got me. And yet . . . a part of me wanted to cry. This wasn't normal. I wanted to be home, listening to Spotify with Katrina, studying for my SATs, reading *Hamlet,* and training for states with my cross-country team.

Marcia looked around. "Does anybody know why people with low body weight see more hair on their bodies?"

Practically every hand went up except mine. "Jean?"

"We grow lanugo because our bodies are trying to keep us warm."

"Yes, that's right," Marcia said. Then she glanced at her watch. "Oh, darn it. I hate to do this, but unfortunately, our time is up. Please put your chairs away as you leave. Lunch in five minutes. Thank you, and I'll see you all on Thursday."

I sighed with relief. So far, the minutes passed slowly at Wallingfield. It felt like nothing moved fast, including us. When you moved fast you burned calories, and the goal around here was to expand, not contract. Willa had told me that if you moved too much or, God forbid, ran somewhere, the nurses made you drink an Ensure.

As I walked to the door, Willa slipped in next to me. "Hey," she said under her breath, her voice so soft I could barely hear it. "I thought the hair was part of, you know, puberty . . ." Her voice trailed off.

"Yeah, well," I said as nicely as I could, "it's not."

She leaned into me a little bit.

"Don't worry," I said, "everybody here has hair like that." Margot pushed past us and disappeared down the hall. "Well, almost everybody."

"Okay," she said, and right then she seemed young—too young to be in a place like this. She looked like Becky, a nine-year-old I sometimes babysat.

"Willa," I asked, "how old are you?"

"Twelve. Why?"

"No reason." I blanched, but only for a second. Twelve. A baby. Figures my first friend would be the only middle schooler here. But twelve was better than nine. I hooked my arm through hers and smiled. "Come on. It's time for lunch," I said.

# 7

**TO GET TO THE DINING ROOM, WE HAD TO TRAIPSE** back through the depressing, white cinder-block therapy wing and down a little breezeway lined with arched windows and white rocking chairs. As soon as we passed the first rocking chair, everybody sped up like we were in a race or something. Willa turned to me. "Come on! This is the only place you can walk fast. The nurses can't see your speed here." I didn't ask questions. I just booked it with the rest of them.

At first, my lunch didn't look so bad. A veggie burger patty, one round pita, an apple, a tub of peach yogurt, a carton of milk, and a curiously plain bowl of lettuce waited for me on my tray. I didn't notice the little plastic cup of ranch salad dressing until I sat down.

When I did, I panicked. There was no way I could put

that in my body. It was like eating straight butter. Unhealthy. Disgusting. My throat closed just thinking about it.

But if I didn't, I'd have to drink an Ensure.

I pushed the salad dressing as far away from me as I could. Then I shoved my veggie burger into my pita, picked up my knife and cut the sandwich into strips. Next I cut each strip into eight tiny pieces, which was hard since it was a sandwich and the top layer of pita kept falling off the little squares. But I managed somehow. After that, I cut my apple in half, then into quarters, then eighths, and then cut each one of those eighths in half again, making sixteen thin slices.

Kay walked by. When she saw what I was doing, she stopped. "Elizabeth, no ritualistic behavior is allowed in the dining room."

I looked at her blankly. *What?*

"No cutting up food into tiny pieces. That's an eating disorder behavior."

*Oh.* But I cut my food up like this all the time. How was I going to eat without doing it? Cutting up my food stretched out meals, and eating the resulting tiny pieces made me feel like I'd eaten more. At home, I could often convince myself I was full after six half slices of banana. Throw in a few glasses of water and I could cut my intake from six bites to four.

I'd managed to choke down the pita, the burger, and

the yogurt, and was on bite six of my apple when I heard Kay's voice behind me. "Elizabeth?" she said gently. "You have six minutes left. Don't forget your salad."

I stared at the white nastiness in its tiny plastic tub. I hadn't touched anything like it in over eight months. Little black specks of pepper floated in the creamy white fat. I gagged at the smell of it. My throat clamped shut and my body froze, just like the time Katrina dared me to stick my fingers in a candle flame when we were eight. Instinct stopped me then and it stopped me now. "I can't eat it. I'm sorry, but I can't."

Kay walked to the little fridge near the entrance and picked out a bottle of vanilla Ensure. "If you don't eat your salad, you'll have to have one of these," she said, not unkindly. "So try. Trust me, vanilla isn't good. The first time reintroducing a food in your diet is always the hardest. You can do this, Elizabeth. I know you can."

"But I ate everything else," I said, begging.

Kay nodded. "I know," she said, "and I'm sorry. But you have to eat the dressing, too."

Willa put her fork down and took my hand under the table. "You don't want an Ensure," she said. "That's more calories than the dressing. Come on, I know you can do it."

I heard a quiet voice in my ear. "Take one bite, and then wash it down with a big gulp of water. Then a few more, and you are done." I turned around. Jean. She smiled a little. "It's just dressing. The faster you eat it, the faster it will be over."

By this time I'd attracted quite the crowd. Willa, Beth, Jean—even Allie came over. Then Lexi, who'd watched this all in silence, said, "If I take a bite, will you?"

*No* was the response I wanted to give. But I barely knew these girls. I didn't want to disappoint them.

So I dipped my fork into the dressing and stabbed a piece of romaine lettuce with it. Opening my mouth, I choked it down. Lexi cut off a tiny corner of her veggie burger and did the same. I'd liked ranch dressing once, but now I gagged on the nasty, oily, putrid-smelling white foulness that coated my gums. I swallowed, a slick of grease remaining on my lips and a sour, peppery aftertaste permeating my mouth. I sucked down water, hoping to get rid of the taste. No luck. I promised myself that when I was in charge of my own eating, I'd never, ever eat ranch dressing again.

Lexi and I looked at each other. I swear we were thinking the same thing. *This is torture.*

Kay patted me on the back. "I know this is hard, but someday you'll look back on this meal as the first step toward victory," she said.

For a second I imagined myself shooting a glass bottle of ranch dressing into a million pieces, and that made me smile a little until I thought about the aftermath—how

48

the dressing would explode everywhere and I'd likely be covered with the greasy stuff.

I leaned over to Lexi. "What do you think our victory medals will look like?" I whispered.

"Fat and round, that's for sure," Lexi replied.

"No body talk, girls," Kay said.

Lexi smirked and took another bite. I couldn't let her suffer alone, so I took one, too.

# 8

AFTER LUNCH I FOLLOWED THE HERD OF GIRLS TO
the common room for mail call. A frowning, gray-haired
woman in a nurse's uniform stood in front of an old mar-
ble fireplace, a bunch of letters in her hand. She'd stacked
a pile of packages next to her on the thick, dark-green wall-
to-wall carpet.

"That's Nurse Jill," Willa said as we sat down. "She's
the head nurse. I call her Nurse Pill because she always
seems so annoyed."

The girls pressed in close, eager to read the names on
the packages. Nurse Jill picked up the first one, which was
shoe box–sized. She said my name twice before I realized
she was calling me. And then, as if one wasn't enough, she
stooped down and picked up another. "Elizabeth again?"

I stood up and Willa grabbed me. "Wow! You haven't

even been here for two days. That's amazing! After Ray opens them, show us what you got, okay?"

"Okay." I didn't know who Ray was. And showing off my boxes? That was the last thing I wanted to do. Willa must have read my mind. "Everybody shares," she said, her voice firm.

Nurse Jill handed them to me. "Take these to the nurses' station to get checked. Everybody who receives a package needs to get it cleared." I nodded and tried to cram them both under my cardigan, hoping no one would notice. Unfortunately, my attempt to hide two boxes in my cardigan just made me look like I was trying to hide two boxes in my cardigan. I picked my way around the girls and walked to the nurses' station.

A man stood at the counter. It had to be Ray. He was tall and looked like Idris Elba. Total crush material. "Well, what do we have here?" he asked. I dumped my packages on the counter and shrugged.

He smiled at me with perfect teeth. "I'm Ray. And you are?"

"Elizabeth."

"Elizabeth! Right! Well, hello, Elizabeth! So, you got two packages?" he said. "People must really like you!" He picked them up. "You want to know what's in them?"

I shook my head. What I wanted was to open them myself. Opening them was the best part.

Ray seemed like a nice guy. I took a chance. "Ray, would it be okay if I didn't look while you opened them? I sort of like the surprise."

He nodded. "No problem. Turn around."

I turned. I heard him slitting the tape on the boxes and easing at least one thing in and out of them.

"You can spin back around now. You're going to love 'em," he said, and then he directed his attention to Allie, who was behind me in line.

As I walked away I heard her squeal with excitement. I glanced back to see her holding what appeared to be a stuffed animal. A seal. "From my boyfriend, Hugh," she gushed. "He knows I collect them."

While she giggled, I snuck off to my room. The waterproof plastic cover under my sheets crackled like it always did when I sat on the bed. I picked up the second package first because I recognized the handwriting—Katrina.

I could have cried. A week earlier, Katrina had confronted me in the school cafeteria. It felt like a year ago. I'd planned to skip lunch and hide in the library, but Katrina found me and hustled me to our table, where Priya and Shay were already sitting, munching away. I didn't have a lunch, so instead I put my backpack on the table to fill the empty space.

"Why aren't you eating?" Katrina had never asked me that point-blank before. Every once in a while she'd ask if

I wanted something when she went up to the lunch line, but I'd say I was full or make some joke. She always let it go. But she'd been acting funny the last couple of days.

"I'm full," I'd said.

"From what?"

"What are you, the cafeteria food police?" I froze my face into a smile.

Katrina didn't respond. "Guys, don't you just want to make her eat a cookie?" She looked across the table to Priya and Shay. They shrugged and didn't look at me.

Why should they have cared if I opted out of lunch? The three of them had inhaled their pizza. Only the standard-issue school Jell-O, red with Cool Whip on top, quivered on their blue plastic trays.

"Seriously. You're going to make us self-conscious!" Priya spoke with her mouth full, the words muffled by pieces of a still-warm chocolate chip cookie she'd bought from the à la carte line. Priya ate everything in sight and always complained she couldn't gain weight.

"Um . . . I bought a blueberry muffin during the study hall before assembly," I said.

Katrina studied me. "Okay, if you say so. Except that today is Wednesday, and the Wednesday muffin is corn, so I guess you were lucky they made a blueberry one just for you."

Crap. Wednesday. It had been so long since I'd bought

anything from the cafeteria. Wednesday was corn. Of course. Monday was blueberry, Tuesday was apple, and Thursday was . . . what was it again? I couldn't remember. Friday was chocolate chip. Damn. I sucked at lying.

"Just remember, Elizabeth." Katrina balled up her lunch bag. "Starving yourself is so *emo*." She turned on her heel and headed toward the trash can.

Emo. Melodramatic. Drama queen. Is that what Katrina really thought? I looked around at the stream of kids leaving the dining room. They laughed, chatted, and flirted. Only my skirt, purchased two weeks earlier and already loose on my hips, made me feel better. *Katrina's just jealous,* I'd thought at the time. *She's never been a size 0.*

We'd made up, but it was still weird after that.

But now here was proof that she didn't hate me. I'd just stuck my hand in the box when Lexi entered, a big, soft package in her hand. Before I could ask about it, she tossed it on her bed like it hurt to hold and said, "Who's yours from?"

"My best friend, Katrina." Inside was a mangled Beanie Baby stuffed cat, most likely destroyed by her puppy, Lance. It came with a card covered with lots of *BFF*s and hearts, but they were all dripping red colored-pencil blood and looked drawn by some deranged creature. Inside, Katrina had written, *Put this on your wall. The crazies will love it. Seriously, though, we miss you. Eat and get out of there! Love, Katrina, Shay, and Priya.*

It was perfect. I laughed out loud.

"That's sort of a disturbing present," Lexi said, confused.

"No, it's an inside joke," I said.

The afternoon before I'd checked in, Katrina had come over. I couldn't tell if she felt obligated or really wanted to say goodbye. "What can I send you?" she'd asked.

"I don't know," I'd replied. "Just promise me you won't send me anything cheesy, like flowers with one of those tinfoil balloons, or anything that comes with a stuffed animal or has the word 'BFF' on it, okay?"

"Okay," she'd promised.

Now, telling Lexi, I worried I might piss her off. I sort of doubted it, but what if she harbored a secret love for flowers, balloons, or teddy bears?

She wasn't and didn't. "I think Katrina is my new hero."

I could have kissed that girl.

Her eyes lit up. "Are you going to put the card on our door? Please say yes. I love it so much."

"Maybe." But I knew that I wouldn't. I wanted to keep it just for me.

"You got a package, too! What is it?" I asked, stashing mine under the bed and trying to ignore the thick knot of homesickness in my stomach.

Sighing, she looked at the box like she wished it would disappear, and then picked it up halfheartedly, pulling out a purple NYU T-shirt. "From my friend Molly."

"Cool," I said.

She shrugged. "I guess." She frowned at the T-shirt, fiddling with the XS label inside. The muscles in her jaw flexed, and she sucked on a chunk of her hair.

"Lexi, are you okay?"

"I'm fine." She tossed the T-shirt into the closet. It landed on the floor in a pile. "My best friend, Laura, who goes to Yale, sent out a group e-mail last week telling our high school friends that I left Smith and was coming here. Now, just like last time, they're all going to send me care packages. I don't know why anybody would think a T-shirt, mug, or bumper sticker from whatever college they're at is a good gift for someone like me. All they do is constantly remind me that I'm not at school. But nobody thinks about that. Last time I was in treatment, I got stuff from Boston University, Skidmore, and Brown."

"How do you like being a Smithie?" The words were barely out of my mouth before I cringed. What I'd meant to say was, *What's Smith like? Is it amazing?* but instead I sounded like one of those people who uses slang nobody actually uses, like my uncle Rodney, who lives in Atlanta and always says, "What's happening in Beantown these days?" when no local I know has ever called Boston Bean-anything.

Lexi scowled. "I can't really say since I was only there for two weeks."

*Crap*. I'd said the wrong thing. "Oh. Sorry. So when did your eating stuff start?"

"When I was eleven. I spent three weeks last year in a hospital being fed through a tube. My organs were at risk of failing. When I stabilized, I went to New Hope, which is just like this place but in New York."

I'd read about how you could only come to places like Wallingfield if you were medically stable enough to eat and not in need of around-the-clock medical care. Otherwise, you went to a real hospital, where you just sat around hooked up to a feeding tube.

Lexi avoided my eyes as she continued. "The good news was that all this happened after college applications were due. Mom talked the guidance counselor into not telling Smith about my medical leave in the spring. I got out just in time to graduate."

"Is Smith going to let you go back?"

She sighed. "I think so. I'm hoping for January. I should be better by then. It sucks, because I really thought I'd be okay this time. But as it turns out, transitions are hard for me. I fell apart pretty much the minute my parents dropped me off. The dean of students made me leave after I ended up in the hospital. I fainted and hit my head." Her whole body slumped and she looked like she might cry.

"I'm sorry." I felt terrible for asking. "That does suck."

"Thanks. But enough about that. It's so depressing." She gestured to my second package. "What else did you get?"

"I don't know."

She studied the paper-wrapped box. "That's a ton of stamps." The box was covered with at least twenty Janis Joplin and Jimi Hendrix postage stamps. "Hurry up and open it! I've got to go to therapy in, like, two minutes."

"Okay." I ran my finger over my name, written in blue pen. I didn't recognize the handwriting, which was cramped and small, and there wasn't a return address.

When I shook it, something thumped inside. I scrunched up my eyebrows and immediately heard Mom's voice in my head—*Stop! You'll give yourself wrinkles!*

Ray had broken the seals, so it was easy to slide out the tissue paper inside. A silver dollar–sized brass ring, strung on a red satin ribbon, fell into my palm. The surface was worn and smooth, and it glowed like dull, tarnished gold. Holding it, I felt calmer, like how I felt with Flippy, my stuffed dolphin. I put it around my neck, the ring swaying gently back and forth against my chest.

"Who sent you that?"

"I don't know." I lifted the ring over my head and carefully hung it on my bedpost, where it clinked before settling against the metal frame.

"Really?" Lexi didn't believe me, I could tell.

"I'm not kidding. I seriously have no idea."

"You know, it looks like one of the brass rings you get on the Flying Horses," Lexi said thoughtfully.

"Flying Horses? The carousel on Martha's Vineyard?" My heart beat a little faster. Martha's Vineyard is an island off the coast of Massachusetts. Lots of kids I knew went there on vacation in the summer.

"Yes. Have you been there?"

"No, but I've heard of it."

Lexi nodded. "It's pretty cool. I went once when I was little. When you ride the carousel, you pull rings from this metal arm when you go around. The last ring right before the music ends is a brass one. If you grab it, you win a free ride."

"Right." I'd learned about that carousel from my ex-boyfriend Charlie. Charlie, officially Charles Winthrop Abbot III, used to ride it all the time when he was a kid. His family had a house on the Vineyard. From the photos he'd shown me, Charlie spent most of his Vineyard time sailing, playing tennis, or wearing reddish-pink pants or shorts that were must-haves if you were a guy and your favorite store was Vineyard Vines or J.Crew. My family had never been to the Vineyard, and I don't think my dad owned a pair of pink-colored anything.

Now, though, I perked up. One night over the summer, at a bonfire on Chorus Beach, Charlie and his friends traded stories about their wild parties on the Vineyard, especially on South Beach. In the middle of one story that involved fireworks, dune grass, and the police, Charlie drunkenly promised that he'd take me there. He told me about the carousel and promised that when we went, he'd win me the brass ring. His friends made fun of him for being so romantic.

That night, lying in bed, I'd pictured us riding the horses together, sharing cotton candy and leaning in to kiss as the carousel went round and round. Cheesy? Sure, but awesome, too. I still thought about it sometimes. I'd assumed that Charlie had forgotten all about that. Beer— and breaking up—has a way of wiping memories clean. But now? Maybe he hadn't forgotten after all.

"Do you go to Martha's Vineyard a lot?" I asked Lexi. Maybe she knew Charlie. He'd said the island was small.

"What? Oh, God no. I'm a Long Island girl. I prefer the Hamptons." Lexi gathered a notebook and black sweatshirt into her hands. "I've gotta go," she said. "I have a phone therapy session with my dad." My brain flashed back to the man I'd seen on the first day, completely buried in his laptop. He hadn't seemed like the talkative type.

"Good luck," I said, sending her a sympathetic glance.

"Yeah," she said. "We'll see."

Willa walked in as Lexi left, the two slipping around each other like they were made of air.

"Elizabeth!" Willa said. "Tell me what you got!"

I hesitated, already half wishing Lexi didn't know. It felt good to have a secret here. But it was Willa asking, and she was so excited I didn't have the heart to disappoint her.

"It's just a little thing. I'll show you, but you can't tell anyone, okay?"

"I promise." She sat on my bed and I had to hold my tongue to keep from asking her to sit somewhere else. When I buried my nose in my comforter, I could still smell the fabric softener Mom used, a smell that was already fading.

I carefully lifted the ring from its perch and held it out, the brass warm on my palm.

"Who sent you this?" Willa took it from me, put it on her finger, and then tried to slide it over her wrist. It almost fit.

"That's the thing. There wasn't any note."

Maybe Charlie hadn't sent a note on purpose. Maybe he'd wanted to make this like a game. That was totally something he would do.

Willa's eyes darted from me to the ring, as if trying to decide if I was putting one over on her.

"Seriously? That is so awesome!" Willa spun the ring in a circle and dropped it on the comforter. The ribbon was twisted. I snatched it back and smoothed the satin with my fingers.

"It's, like, a total mystery. Maybe it was sent by someone who secretly loves you or something." Right then, Willa seemed very twelve.

"Sorry," I said. "But secret admirers don't exist. We're at Wallingfield, not in fairyland."

"Well, I think you're wrong. I just know it's from a secret admirer," Willa said. "I bet there are a ton of guys out there in love with you."

*I only want one,* I told myself, still thinking about Charlie.

Not that I'd ever admit that out loud.

That night, lying in bed with the brass ring resting on my chest, I found myself reasoning with the universe. Because I did want Charlie back. I missed him. *Please,* I whispered to the air. *I promise, I'll do anything. Just make it be from Charlie.*

# 9

**THE NEXT MORNING I WOKE UP TO FIND MY HANDS** clamped around the red ribbon and the ring pressed into my leg, leaving a round, red, itchy imprint on the inside of my thigh.

*Charlie wants me back.*

He couldn't. He wouldn't. Not after—

*Don't get your hopes up, Elizabeth!*

But I couldn't help it. Maybe he wanted to make up and get back together.

Next to me, Lexi groaned as she pulled herself out of bed and fumbled around for her robe.

"Lexi," I said as I wrapped myself in my pink one, "do you have a boyfriend?"

She let out a snort. "Yeah. His name is Rex."

"Rex?"

"Yeah, as in ano-REX-ia. That's the only boyfriend I've got. Last time I checked, guys weren't exactly dying to go out with me. Why, do you?"

I didn't see why any guy *wouldn't* go out with Lexi. Aside from the fact that she looked a bit skeletal, she was still pretty, with her layered black hair, clear skin, and big dark eyes. "No," I said. "Totally not."

But I'd had one. The best one.

I'd gone out with Charlie for the first time nearly four months earlier, one week after school let out for summer, back when life was still relatively normal.

On that day in June, Charlie showed up at Scoops, the ice cream shop where I worked, wearing his board shorts, his hair still damp from the beach. When he asked me out, I'd thought he was kidding. Me? The Scoops girl? I didn't even belong to the country club. He ordered a blueberry ice cream cone, crammed five dollars in my tip jar, slid a piece of paper with his number on it across the counter, and told me he'd seen me at a couple of his lacrosse games. I'd only been at them because Shay had a crush on a midfielder. I hated lacrosse. But of course I didn't say that. I just blushed. When he asked me for my number, I wrote it on a napkin.

He texted me later that afternoon.

That night we went to Kelly's Roast Beef, a local take-out place open late that was always crammed with rowdy kids stuffing their faces with shakes and sandwiches. I usually avoided it. Everything Kelly's served was fried, or came from a cow, or was slathered with mayonnaise. I hadn't eaten anything like that since before the whole Target bikini incident.

Normally, the idea of taking a bite of a roast beef sandwich or a sip of chocolate shake would send me into a massive panic. But that night, even though I'd already eaten my usual dinner—one banana, sliced in half lengthwise and cut again into twenty half slices, which I ate from a toothpick, one half moon at a time—something was different.

Here's what I ate:

1. One-third of a Junior Beef sandwich, no mayo or cheese
2. Five fries, two dipped in ketchup
3. Two small tastes of Charlie's coffee shake
4. Four sips of regular—not diet—Coke, because Charlie messed up when he ordered for me and I didn't want him to feel bad.

What was amazing was that when we were finished I didn't even feel full. In fact, I felt better than I had in months. I'd expected that I'd at least get a stomachache from all those calories, but it was magic, like my entire body was saying, *This is the guy for you*. And the night just kept getting better. After dinner, Charlie drove me to the beach in front of his house. He played Bob Marley, "No Woman, No Cry," a song that Katrina and I had decided made us want to hold hands with boys. And as the song was playing, like he'd read my mind, Charlie *held my hand*. When we got out of the car, the moon was bright and I could see his house stretching behind a thick wall of shrubs that bordered the beach. It looked even bigger in the moonlight. Houses like that cost millions.

We'd just stepped onto the sand when he pulled me toward him and kissed me. His touch was soft and his mouth tasted like french fries. I only worried for a second about potential calorie transfers. When he pulled his salty lips away from mine, my body buzzed. When he took off his shirt and ran, whooping and hollering, into the dark, rolling ocean, I realized that I really liked him. And when he came back a minute later, shivering and dripping and with goose bumps on his skin, I realized that, amazingly, he might like me, too. He kissed me again and everything in the world was perfect: the air, the night, the beach, even me.

# 10

**I HAD MY FIRST SESSION WITH MARY THAT SAME** morning. Mary's office was in the therapy wing. Her cinderblock walls were painted a soothing cream color. Everything at Wallingfield was painted soothing colors. It actually said that in the brochure Mom had slipped under my door the day they announced I was coming here. *Wallingfield's soothing decor,* it read, as if we were all a bunch of maniacs who might fall into hysterics if we came face-to-face with a rainbow pillow or hot-pink wall.

The brass ring hung on its satin ribbon beneath my clothes, swaying gently as I walked, a constant reminder that someone, somewhere, was thinking of me. I only wished I could be 100 percent sure it was Charlie.

Mary's hair was twisted into a bun, and she wore a black maxiskirt and matching tights, a bulky navy-blue cardigan, a long-sleeved matching navy blouse, and scuffed brown clogs. I could hear Mom's voice in my head: *Black and blue make a bruise!* Apparently Mary hadn't gotten the memo.

"Good morning, Elizabeth." Mary's voice was different from the other day. It sounded the way therapists' voices always sound on TV. Smooth, calming, and, just like the walls, soothing.

She leaned forward a little, gripping a notepad on her lap. "Since this is our first session, I thought maybe we could start off with you telling me a little bit about yourself."

"What do you want to know?"

"Well, anything that might help me understand what brought you to Wallingfield, and how I might help you while you are here."

"You mean like my life story?"

"If you think that would help."

"I don't know."

"Well, how about we start with your relationship with your parents. Why don't you tell me a little bit about them, and you."

"Well, my mom likes it when I'm thin. Dad is clueless. We have no pets, and I'm an only child. Mom wasn't able to have any more kids after me. I don't know why. Something about my birth, I think. And I'm here, obviously, so there's that. Although, for the record, I do think that I'd be fine at home." I paused.

"Anything else?"

"Nope. That's about it." I sat back. Her turn.

"Okay. Can you say a little more about your mom? You said she likes you thin. Why do you think that?"

"I don't think it. I know it."

She pushed harder. "Okay. Why?"

Why? Because she said so. But I couldn't tell Mary that. Not yet. Not until I knew how she'd take it. My mom wasn't a bad person. She just had expectations. Or, rather, hopes. That's it. She had hopes for me.

Hopes for my appearance, anyway. I realized just how high those hopes were last month, when Mom texted me and said she was leaving work early to pick me up from school to "hang with you and chill." Her words, not mine. Since I wasn't running cross-country anymore and my brain moved at the speed of sludge those days, I couldn't think of an excuse in time to get out of it.

I figured we'd have a quick coffee somewhere so Mom could check *mother-daughter time* off her weekly to-do list.

Instead, she surprised me. "We're going to Macy's!" she proclaimed. "I'm in the mood for some retail therapy."

"No, Mom, I don't feel like it. Can we just get a latte or something?" I hated Macy's. The clothes never looked good on me. Few if any of the outfits Mom had made me try on over the years "suited my figure," as Mom liked to say. Even so, she was relentless. She'd toss shirts and skirts and jeans and dresses over the top of the dressing room door, only to frown and look disappointed when I put them on. I'd taken to using Mom's credit card and shopping online, so I could have the clothes delivered to me and try them on alone, in my room.

"Come on, it'll be fun."

I'd never admit it, but a part of me was curious. I'd lost a lot of weight. Like, thirty pounds. Maybe things would be different now. "Fine. Let's go to Macy's."

"Yes!" Mom threw the car into drive and pulled out onto the street. "So, how was your day?"

"Fine."

"That's good," she said.

"How's work going?" I asked, to be polite.

"Great," she said. "Things are going really well."

After that we rode in silence. I pulled out my phone and texted Katrina.

Me: **Shopping with Mom. Pray for me.**

The typing indicator raced back and forth as she responded.

Katrina: **Yikes! Good luck!!!! Talk later?**

Me: **If I make it back alive.**

I put my phone in the front pocket of my backpack and squeezed the bag to my chest.

Macy's loomed, big and boxy. Mom parked right in front. "Isn't this fun?" she said, gathering up her Coach purse, the one she'd bought used on eBay. "You and me—shopping, hanging out. This is great!" We entered the store through the makeup department.

*You've never thought it was great before,* I thought, dragging my feet. Our shopping trips usually led to horrible fights where I begged her to leave me alone and she told me that if I let her dress me, I'd look great. *You just have to purchase the right clothes for your figure,* she'd say. *You don't have the right body for the juniors' department.* But the juniors' department was where all my friends shopped, and I wanted to shop there, too. And sometimes the things she hated on me, I didn't think looked that bad. Until she pointed out the flaws—my hips, my thighs, my chubby knees.

But today I kept my mouth shut. I didn't want a fight. I just wanted to get this trip over with.

In front of Clinique, Mom said, "I love Macy's!" and hugged me for no reason. Our collarbones clanked, bone on bone.

She took a deep, appreciative inhale. "Doesn't it smell good in here?"

I shrugged. I was starting to sweat. I think I had PTSD—post-traumatic shopping disorder. Over the last couple of years, stints in Macy's dressing rooms had taught me that, according to Mom, skinny jeans, low-rise jeans, high-rise jeans, boyfriend jeans, pencil skirts, long skirts, baggy sweaters, tight sweaters, yoga pants—basically anything made of semi-fashionable fabric—didn't "suit" me.

But I hadn't been this thin since, well, forever. I fingered my hip bones, which stuck out like handles. I liked how the skin was still bruised from lying stomach-down on our deck all summer.

Even so, I tiptoed through the juniors' department's racks of clothes, avoiding contact like they'd sting me if I touched them.

"Try these." Mom held up a pair of forest-green skinny jeans.

I loved them for anyone except me. My thighs would never fit in those. You needed a thigh gap for those. I didn't have a thigh gap. The tops of my thighs refused to separate. They were like two sausages stuffed tight in a package. "I don't think so."

"Oh, come on, Elizabeth. Try them on. I bet you'll look great." Mom grabbed my arm and looked straight at me. "You know you don't look the same anymore. I bet you'll be surprised."

"Fine." I grabbed them and without a word marched into the dressing room.

I'd always been a size 29. She'd picked a size 28. Too small for sure. But I was swimming in them. Mom went back out for a size 27, and then a 26. Then, a 25. She was giddy. "Oh, Elizabeth," she said. "Size twenty-five! That's like a size zero!"

Size 25. Even though I knew my body had tons of problems, I couldn't help but be proud. Size 25. Size 0. I'd never been a size 0. A few more pounds and who knew? Maybe I could have shopped in the kids' department.

Only later that day, alone in my room, did I wonder if Mom was at all worried about my weight loss. Did I want her to be? Losing 30 pounds in four months wasn't good for me, was it?

*Yes,* I scolded myself. It *was.* It was *very* good for me.

"Elizabeth?" Mary waved her hand gently in front of my face. "May I ask what you were just thinking about?"

I shook my head. "Nothing," I said. "I wasn't thinking about anything." I'd brought those jeans with me, but with the way the nurses were making me eat, I wondered how long they'd fit.

I wondered what Mom would say when they didn't.

73

# 11

AT NOON, I FOUND LEXI LEANING AGAINST THE wall in the lunch line, wearing gray sweatpants with holes in the knees and a faded black sweatshirt. She looked as beaten down as her outfit. Even her hair sagged.

She'd endured individual therapy that morning as well. Her therapist's name was Michael. A guy. I felt bad that she didn't get a girl, but she said she didn't care. "It's not like I'm going to tell him anything anyway," she'd said. When we'd parted ways at Michael's door, she'd winked at me, but now she was subdued and dark.

"Are you okay?" I asked.

She opened her mouth to respond but didn't get a chance.

"This is ridiculous!" A girl's voice came from the dining room, loud and stressed.

Everybody turned to look.

"I don't understand why I can't have it! I barely got any dinner last night, and barely any breakfast. Crackers and hummus aren't a meal. That's a snack! Aren't we *supposed* to eat in here?"

Willa's eyes widened.

"I mean, isn't this an eating disorder hospital? I'd think you'd be *glad* I'm hungry. God!"

"What the?" I mouthed to Willa, who made the universal sign for *crazy* with her finger near her ear. I looked away, uncomfortable. Who was I to judge crazy in this place?

Allie turned around. "It's Margot, the new girl who doesn't talk. My bet is bulimic with anger issues. You guys saw her. Not eating? Definitely *not* her problem."

That was mean. We were so hard on ourselves already. And of all people, why pick on Margot? It had to suck even more to be surrounded by people who lived in fear of looking like you.

"Seriously, WHY CAN'T I HAVE SOMETHING ELSE?" Margot shouted louder. She sounded desperate.

"Well," Lexi said, her voice still flat, "looks like she can definitely talk."

Coral tiptoed over to the double doors and cracked them open. This felt wrong. We were invading Margot's privacy. Even so, I couldn't stop watching. From where I stood I could see Margot's top half. Worry lines snaked across her pasty forehead. Her dull, unwashed brown ponytail was askew. Her arms looked pale and doughy. I wished I had the courage to run up and close the door. Instead, I just stood like a coward and watched with everybody else.

Kay had her back to us. "Margot, we serve healthy meals here. If you're hungry, you can take it up with your nutritionist when you have your first meeting. But until then—"

Margot snapped. "I AM JUST SO HUNGRY—" She stopped when she saw the open door. We ate her up with our stares. Her eyes widened and her face changed from flushed to white to reddish purple in all of five seconds.

"Why, Margot," Kay said, clearly stunned. "What's wron—" She turned and, upon seeing us, moved quickly toward the door.

Margot beat her to it. She pushed past everybody and ran down the hall to her room, slamming the door so hard the other doors on the hall shook. Two nurses followed her.

An electric current rippled through the rest of us. *Manic. Bipolar. Binger. Cutter.* It didn't take long—one minute maybe—for everyone to decide that Margot was the most screwed-up girl here.

Willa grinned, happy things were livening up around the place.

I stood there, unsure. A part of me wondered if I should

go after her. I'd known her once, after all. I imagined knocking on her door and reintroducing myself, maybe asking her to sit with me in the dining room. But I didn't. I just got in line for my tray like everybody else.

At the table, Willa could barely sit still. She crammed a cracker in her mouth. "Wow! Did you see that?" Willa's excitement took up too much room in her head; she was so keyed up that she was actually on track to eat all of her hummus and crackers.

When I said, "I feel bad. Maybe we should go and talk to her after lunch," no one answered me.

Lexi played with her hummus, spooning it up and dropping it back onto her plate, over and over.

"Lexi," I asked, "how are you doing?"

"Fine." Her voice was curt. She sniffed her hummus and grimaced.

"You sure? No offense, but you don't really seem fine."

"I am. Really."

"Okay, sorry. I didn't mean to pry."

She softened just a little. "I'm just tired." Her dark hair accented the half circles under her eyes. She looked like a member of the Addams Family. I guessed it was because of her evening workouts. That and all the Ensure.

I was having my own issues. I'd run out of crackers. "Willa, do they expect us to eat the hummus plain?"

"If you already ate your crackers they do," she said. "Do you think Margot will freak out at every meal?"

"I hope not." I stabbed at my plate. "I can't eat this hummus. I don't like hummus even *with* crackers." I never had. "I can't eat this plain. God, can you smell it? All I can smell is the garlic. I think I'm going to be sick."

Willa put down her fork. "No, you're not. You can do it," she said. "You totally can. Come on, just try."

I made figure eights in the hummus with my fork, turning it over onto itself as if I could somehow make it less.

Kay came over on her rounds. Lexi sat up a little, on guard. "Elizabeth, Lexi, finish your hummus, please."

"I can't, Kay," I said.

"Yes, you can, Elizabeth."

My jaw stiffened like it always did when I was being stubborn. "I'm sorry, but I can't. My brain won't let me." The day before I'd been able to overcome it, thanks to my cheering section. But now? Now my brain wasn't budging.

"Elizabeth," Kay said, "the only way to get better is to challenge those thoughts." I shook my head. No.

Kay sighed. It had been a long day for her already. "Lexi? How about you? I know you can do this." Kay pulled up a chair. To both of us she said, "To get better, you have to eat." Lexi didn't respond. For a second I forgot about myself. *What happened at her therapy session?*

"Last chance," Kay said. She paused a second and then, with one last pat on my shoulder, headed off to get an Ensure.

"Get her chocolate!" Willa called, her plate miraculously empty.

Kay brought one back for Lexi, too, then sat with us, checking the floor for Willa crumbs as she did. There weren't any. "Willa, you can go. Good job today," she said as she opened the plastic bottles of Ensure and stuck a straw into each.

"Thanks!" It was only after Willa had stepped off the linoleum and onto the hall carpet that I saw the cracker peeking out from the top of her jeans' cuff.

# *12*

AT MIDNIGHT, LEXI WAS AT IT AGAIN, DOING burpees on the floor next to her bed. *Boom-cha-boom-thump.* Her panting filled up the room, and even when I whispered, "Lexi, please stop," she didn't. It was like she was in a trance or something. I counted along in my head, the way other people might count sheep. I was up to seventy-five when the bedroom door flew open.

"WHAT are you doing?" The night nurse entered our room, a silhouette in the doorframe. I didn't recognize her.

"I—" Lexi, wet with sweat, struggled to her feet beside me. She panted and couldn't talk.

"Never mind. I saw what you were doing. Come with me, young lady."

Lexi stumbled. The nurse came over and roughly grabbed her arm.

"Where are you taking her?" I asked, afraid.

But I knew. So did Lexi.

The next morning on my way to weights and vitals I found her. She was in the fishbowl, a single bedroom in the middle of the unit with a wall of windows so nurses could keep an eye on her at all times. It was the closest thing Wallingfield had to a hospital room. Lexi was asleep, curled up in a sad little ball in her knitting-dog PJs. I got a lump in my throat just looking at her. I raised my hand to knock on the window and wake her up, like I always did, for weights and vitals, but I stopped myself. She needed her rest. And to be honest, I didn't know what to say.

A few minutes later, when the nurse weighed me, I swear I saw her write down a nine and a four. For a second I completely forgot about Lexi. Had I gained 4 POUNDS?

In four days?

Talk about making an already bad morning worse. I could practically feel the fat on my lower back increasing as I tugged on my robe. Miserable, I walked back and climbed under my duvet, which didn't smell like home at all anymore, and almost wished I'd done burpees with Lexi when I'd had the chance.

An hour later I stopped by the fishbowl on my way to breakfast. Lexi was sitting cross-legged on the bed, writing in her journal. Her arms looked like chicken wings with the meat chewed off. So did her legs. I shuddered. The curtains were wide open. She could close them only when she was changing, and even then, only for a minute at a time. I felt weird watching her, like I was invading her privacy.

I wanted to turn and leave, but Lexi saw me before I could. She didn't smile.

I stood in the doorway. "Hey."

"Hi." She kept writing, her journal filled with cramped cursive.

"How are you?"

"Fine." She spoke with no inflection.

"How long do you have to stay in here?"

She shrugged. "My therapist said I have to sign a contract or go home."

"Do you mean Michael?"

"Yeah. He said I needed to show more dedication to my recovery." Frowning, she scratched out the last sentence she'd written, pushing on her pen so hard it made a hole in the paper.

"Oh. Is Michael nice?"

"He's okay, I guess. Why?"

"Nothing really. I'd just wondered, because yesterday, after your meeting with him, you seemed upset."

She paused for so long I didn't think she'd answer. When she did, her voice was soft. "Michael showed me my medical records."

"He did? Do they usually do that?" I'd assumed medical records were off-limits, like our weight.

"I don't know. I asked him."

"What did they say?"

"I have something called mitral valve prolapse. My heart valve doesn't close right anymore. Blood can go backward in my heart instead of forward."

"Were you born with it?"

"No. They think anorexia caused it. It'll probably never go away. They say I'm lucky, that MPS isn't fatal, but it makes me feel sick sometimes. I get migraines. Sometimes, I'm so dizzy I can't even stand. And every once in a while my heart gets all fluttery, which freaks me out. I always think I'm dying when that happens."

"Oh." Panic bubbled up in me like acid reflux. Did I have MPS, too? My heart hammered away and felt loud in my ears. How could I never have listened to it before?

Lexi bent over her journal again. At the far end of the hall, the doors opened for breakfast. "Hey, Lexi, the dining room just opened," I said. "Come on." She had to eat. She had to protect her heart.

"You go on ahead. I'll be there in a minute."

I doubted that. "Lexi, please come with me. Maybe you could try to eat just a little?" She didn't answer. "Lexi, I'll eat with you. Please?"

"Okay, Elizabeth," she said. "Fine." With great effort she hauled her frail body up off the bed. "But do me a favor."

"Sure, what?"

"Don't waste your time worrying about me. Be scared for yourself. Really, really scared, because that's what's going to make you better."

She stared at me for a long second. Then, together, we walked down the hall to the dining room.

At breakfast Lexi sat with Willa and me, which I took as a good sign. When she looked at her eggs like they were a pile of poop and didn't even bother to pick up her fork, I took that as a bad one.

Willa cheered her on. "Come on, Lexi, you can do it!"

"Yeah! Go for it," I said. In solidarity I took a big bite of my eggs. They felt like plastic and tasted worse. If they wanted us to eat, you'd think they'd at least make the eggs taste good. I gagged a little. I tried not to let them fall back out of my mouth. I swallowed, somehow, eyes watering. "See?" I said. "Not too hard!"

"Oh my God, that was terrible," Willa said. I thought I saw the corner of Lexi's mouth tug upward.

Encouraged, I took another bite, this one smaller and easier to manage. "Yum!"

84

Even Willa got into it. "Look, I'm taking a sip of my milk now!"

Lexi pursed her lips together and started to cry. Willa took her hand. I rubbed her shoulder.

Lexi shook her head. If she didn't eat, she'd go home. Again. This was her second official attempt at treatment. What if she was one of those girls with eating disorders who never got better? Twenty percent never did. I'd learned that in my old support group. The number hadn't bothered me much before, but here? Holy crap. These were the kinds of girls they were talking about.

If you did the math, just fewer than five of the twenty-four girls in this dining room would never, ever get over their eating disorders. And if you wanted to get really morbid, one girl here might even die, since twenty percent of those who never get better do, either from health complications or by suicide.

I didn't want to die. Or for Lexi to die, or Willa, or anybody else here.

"Come on, Lexi," I said. "You can do this."

She took a tiny bite. She swallowed.

Our response was to holler like fifth graders at a Taylor Swift concert. Even Kay gave a whoop. And that's how breakfast went. Lexi taking a taste, us cheering. When time was up, Lexi looked like she might puke all over the table, but her plate was empty. And, focused on Lexi, I ended up with an empty plate of my own. And nobody in that entire room had to have an Ensure.

They let Lexi out of the fishbowl the next morning, and I had a roommate again.

# *13*

I DIDN'T WANT TO ADMIT IT, BUT I WAS EXCITED for mail call that afternoon. But when we arrived, only one package lay at Nurse Jill's feet. You could feel the disappointment ripple through the room. Everybody lived for mail call. It really was the highlight of our day.

The package was a brown cardboard tube covered with Janis Joplin stamps, just like last time. My heart blipped, but I didn't dare hope. The first package was probably a fluke. A second? Impossible. But then Nurse Jill held it up at boob level and called my name. I had the weird urge to turn to everybody else and apologize for being the lucky one, but I managed to rein it in as I took the tube, clutching the smooth, cool surface against my body. Twenty-four pairs of eyes stared at me.

"What *is* that?" Allie asked.

I shrugged, mumbled something about heading to the nurses' station, and got out of there as fast as I could. I didn't like the pressure of everybody's eyes on me, hoping I'd be their excitement for the day.

Willa followed me, ignoring the jealous glances. "What do you think it is, Elizabeth?" she asked, walking so close behind me that she almost clipped my heels. "Is it from your sec—"

I cut her off fast. "I don't know, Willa!" The last thing I needed was for the other girls to hear about Willa's secret-admirer theory.

"God, way to be all clique-y," Coral muttered as I walked by. She said it low, so only I could hear. Typical. If Coral had had an aura, it would have been a big black ring that darkened anything it touched, she was so sour. I didn't know how the girls in her cohort could stand her, pro-ana celebrity or not.

"Another package?" Ray asked when I arrived. "Some girls have all the luck!"

I leaned the tube up against the wall next to his station. That's when I noticed it didn't have a return address. Again. I smiled a little.

He craned his neck out of the nurses' station to check out my tube. "Looks like I better come around for this one," he said, walking to my side of the counter. "You want to know what it is?"

And, like last time, I shook my head.

He winked. "I get that. Surprises make life better."

I turned as he slid something out of the tube, unrolled it, rolled it back up, then slid it back in.

"All set," he said. "You're good. Carry on!"

When I got to my room, Willa was still on my heels. I closed the door and sat on my bed. Without asking, Willa jumped on, too. I tried not to be annoyed.

I popped off the end cap and slid out a poster. Against a black background, a terrified-looking kitten clung to a branch. Above the photo were the words *HANG IN THERE*.

"It's so cute!" Willa said.

"I guess," I said. "But doesn't it look like something you'd find on the cover of a third grader's notebook? And the kitten looks petrified." I felt sorry for the poor thing. It really did look like it was holding on for dear life.

"No! Definitely not. I love it."

I rolled it back up.

"Aren't you going to hang it?" Willa bounced next to me.

I took a deep breath and summoned my patience. Willa was driving me bonkers. Secretly I thanked the universe for making me an only child. Then I forced myself to smile at her. "Maybe a little later. Hey, pass me the tube, will you?"

When she lifted it, something rattled. Our eyes met and Willa's lit up. "Something else is inside!" she said. She dumped out a little plastic capsule, the kind you get from twenty-five-cent gum ball machines. It spun across the carpet and landed at my feet. My stomach dropped. No. It couldn't be.

"Ooh, what's that?" Willa said.

I knew exactly what it was. A plastic ring with a giant blue plastic gem glued on it fell into my hand. I knew these rings. I had three just like them, two reds and one green. They were all from the twenty-five-cent toy machine at Esterfall House of Pizza. Every time we went there, Charlie would get me one. It was a running joke between us. His friends loved to give him crap for it. They called him the plastic romantic.

It had to be him. But what did this mean? Did he want to get back together with me?

If so, that made no sense. He was with Heather now. Or should I say *back* with Heather, who'd been obsessed with Charlie since middle school. For a while they were together. Then they broke up. Then they were back together. And so on. Even when they weren't going out, Heather made it clear that Charlie was *hers* and hers alone, and that she'd do whatever it took to keep it that way. Back in ninth grade, when a new girl named Edith said she liked him, "somebody" (Heather, of course) started a rumor that

Edith had breast implants and had gotten a nose job to look more like Katy Perry. It was stupid and obviously not true, but people spread it anyway.

And last year, when Charlie and Heather were "on a break," he asked a freshman to the winter formal. "Somebody" spread a rumor that Erin had lice she'd caught in rehab.

Heather didn't mess around.

And then I came along. Charlie told me he'd called Heather after our first date and that she was fine with everything. And she did leave me alone—until the second we broke up. Then she'd gotten me good. But I couldn't think about that now. I wanted to think about happy things, like the plastic ring on my finger.

Still, I wondered what she'd do to me. Visions of insults on Instagram and Snapchat ran through my mind. But Charlie was worth it. Even if I pissed off the most vindictive girl in school.

*Hang in there.*

*Okay, Charlie,* I thought. *If you want me to, I'll try.*

# 14

THE NEXT MORNING, RIGHT AFTER BREAKFAST, reality hit. So, say Charlie sent the presents. That would be awesome. But it didn't answer the question: What the hell was I supposed to do about it? Call him? What if I ruined it by reaching out too early? What if he wanted to call *me*? My fingers itched to pick up the phone, but my gut said to wait. *Be sure,* it said. *See if he sends something else. Wait until you've got good news for him. That's what he'll want to hear.* So I listened to it. I didn't call.

Instead, I did something I'd been meaning to do since Margot's meltdown in the dining room. I knocked on her door. I wasn't sure why, exactly, I felt the need to reach out to her. Maybe I wanted to distract myself. Maybe I wanted see if she remembered me. Maybe it was because she felt familiar, even if we'd only been six in that ballet class.

Whatever it was, I felt bad for her. It wasn't like we were friends, but we'd known each other once. And I kept thinking about her walking alone into Wallingfield, how awful that must have been.

The door opened. Or, more precisely, I heard footsteps, saw the handle turn, and watched the door swing open a crack. Margot was already back on her bed. She hadn't brought sheets from home, so she slept on the same generic white-and-brown bedding there was in the fishbowl. The rest of the room looked just like mine except that her enormous suitcase had seemingly exploded on the second bed. Clothes—mostly black—were everywhere, mixed with toiletries, pens, hairbrushes, and her toothbrush, which was partially hidden on the floor by a running shoe.

"Thanks for letting me in," I said.

She didn't respond.

"HELLO?" I said again, louder.

She took off her headphones. "You're welcome."

"I don't think we ever officially met. I'm Elizabeth." This was ridiculous. Why had I thought she'd want to talk to me? Girls like Margot never wanted to talk to me. I was never bad enough, or angry enough, or rebel enough. I studied hard. I didn't get into trouble. I wasn't super popular. I did sports, but wasn't really an athlete. I was, despite my best efforts, a Goody Two-Shoes.

"I know who you are," she said. Was it because of ballet? Or because of here? I felt stupid asking, so I didn't.

Margot shifted her weight on the bed. The frame squeaked.

I tried again. "You're from Esterfall, right?"

She nodded.

"Me too." I hoped this would be when she said, *Oh yeah, from ballet, right?*

She said nothing.

"So, um . . ." Margot watched me fumble and did nothing to help. Coming here was a mistake. "Did you know we took ballet together when we were six?"

She squinted at me and said, "Oh, right. I thought you looked familiar." I didn't believe her.

"Yeah. So. I guess I'll go." I backed toward the door. "Bye," I said.

"Bye." She put her headphones back on and turned away from me.

I showed myself out. That's what I got for trying to be nice.

Back in my room, I stewed. I had to stop trying to rescue people. It obviously wasn't working. At least not here.

At home, though, I had a pretty good track record. If people had a superpower, I guess you could say mine would be helping the wounded birds. In fourth grade, when Katrina and I met Priya, she was the new kid, super shy, and had just moved to Esterfall from New Jersey. She was the

94

only Indian girl at our school. For the first two days, no one talked to her. She was invisible. So one day at lunch, when she was sitting alone, I'd invited her to sit with us. Within a week we were best friends.

When Shay arrived the next year, she befriended us, even though she was loud and flashy and not really our type. But she came up at recess, said, "I'm new. I need to play with you guys, okay?" Totally shocked, we said yes on reflex. In sixth grade her parents got a divorce. Her dad moved out of state and her mom went off the rails, and I talked my parents into letting Shay stay with us until things settled down. "Settling down" in Shay's world meant that her mom hired an Italian au pair. Which we were sworn to secrecy about, because who in sixth grade still had a nanny?

And now? When I'd told them I was coming here, Priya had said, "Oh my God. I promise I will call you every day."

Shay had nodded along with her. "Me too," she'd said.

Well, I'd been here for five days and I hadn't heard from Shay or Priya once except for that one package, the one Katrina had obviously sent by herself. *Junior year is busy,* I told myself. *If I were home, I wouldn't have time to call someone at a place like this either.* But deep inside, I knew they had time. Of course they did.

I was still sulking when someone knocked. I opened the door and there was Margot, taking up my whole doorway in her Carhartt overalls and Docs, headphones around her neck.

"Do you like the Smiths?" she said instead of hello.

"Sorry?" I had no idea who she was talking about.

"The band. The Smiths? 'Please, Please, Please Let Me Get What I Want'?"

I'd never heard of them. "Uh, yeah. They're cool," I lied. "Do you want to come in?"

She sat on my bed. I sat on the floor.

"What's your favorite of theirs? This is mine." Margot plugged a speaker the size of a playing card into her iPod. The room filled with a guy droning on about his girlfriend being in a coma. I didn't get it.

At the end Margot smiled. "Pretty awesome, right?"

*Or terrible.* "Yeah," I lied. "They are so great."

She put another one on. The guy begged to get what he wanted, and Margot studied me. "You have no idea who the Smiths are, do you?"

"No," I admitted. "I don't." Katrina made fun of me all the time for my lack of music knowledge.

Margot snorted. "I knew it. You are a terrible liar. Want to listen with me? They're really good."

"I guess. I mean, sure. I'd like to. But can I ask you a question?"

"Okay."

"Why are you here?"

"At Wallingfield?" Her face closed.

"No!" I said, trying to open it again. "I mean, why did you come to see me?"

"Oh," she said, tucking her dull hair behind her un-pierced ears. "I came because I was rude when you came to see me. Sorry about that. And I remembered you."

"You did?"

"Yeah. You were nice to me. Not all the girls were."

"Oh." I remembered. No one had wanted to stand next to Margot at the barre. Everybody wanted to stand next to this girl Jessica, who had a fancy glitter leotard and rhinestone clips in her shiny brown bun. Margot—Merry back then—was probably the only girl not trying to get a place next to her. Jessica didn't like that. "Merry has cooties," she announced. After that, no one would go near her. I wanted to stand next to Jessica, too, but I got shoved out of the way by a girl in a baby-blue leotard and matching tights. I ended up next to Margot, who smiled at me. I'd smiled back and asked her if she knew how to do a cartwheel. We'd stood next to each other for every class after that. "Yeah, so thanks for being nice."

"You're welcome?"

She nodded, smiled, hit replay, and the guy started singing again. "Okay, so, the Smiths. Let me tell you about the Smiths."

And that's how I made friend number three.

# 15

THAT AFTERNOON I MET SALLY TO PLAN MY MENU
for the next week. I couldn't wait to be able to finally have
some control over my meals, but at the same time, making so many food choices at once seemed impossible. It
was food overload.

We met in the therapy wing, in a room barely large
enough for two chairs and a desk. The walls were painted
light blue. Soothing, of course. I felt better the minute I
met her. Something about her gray bob and silver-rimmed
glasses and general grandma vibe made me feel safe. When
she said it was the end of veggie burgers, hummus, and
pita unless I asked for them, I could have hugged her.

"When you start to refeed, there's a risk of getting sick
from too much food too fast," she explained. "We call it

refeeding syndrome. So with new patients, we gradually increase as the week progresses."

The good feelings from a moment before vaporized. I shook my head, not quite understanding. "You mean the last five days were just a warm-up?"

"Well," she said carefully, "not exactly a warm-up."

"But what you're saying is that I have to eat even more next week?"

"Yes. But, Elizabeth, before you—"

No. The panic started in my jaw. I clenched my teeth so hard they shifted in my gums. "I can't do it. I can't eat more."

I don't know why I was surprised. I knew that's how these places worked, but even so. It's like I'd thought that if I was in control of my meals, I'd all of a sudden be able to cure myself while limiting my food to 800 calories a day.

Sally nodded, her smile full of sympathy. "I'm sorry, hon, but you don't really have a choice."

I knew she was right. I forced my jaw to loosen. "Okay, then, let's get it over with."

For my three meals and three snacks each day, I needed a certain number of what they called exchanges, which were basically premeasured portions of different types of food: vegetables, fruit, protein, milk, fat, and starch (carbs). Simple enough.

Then I saw how many exchanges I had to fill each day:

**Protein:** 6
**Starch:** 10
**Fruit:** 11
**Dairy:** 3
**Fat:** 10

That was a total of forty. Effing forty. And no veggies. Yes, that's right. Zero vegetables besides lettuce for salad. "They take up too much space in your stomach," Sally said. "During refeeding we focus on denser foods. We'll introduce veggies at a later date, I promise."

Here's how it all broke down on paper:

**Breakfast:** 1 Protein, 3 Starches, 2 Fruits, 1 Dairy, 2 Fats
**A.M. Snack:** 2 Starches, 2 Fruits, 1 Fat
**Lunch:** 2 Proteins, 2 Starches, 2 Fruits, 1 Dairy, 2 Fats
**P.M. Snack:** 1 Starch, 2 Fruits, 1 Fat
**Dinner:** 3 Proteins, 1 Starch, 2 Fruits, 1 Dairy, 3 Fats
**Evening Snack:** 1 Starch, 1 Fruit, 1 Fat

Torture. Pure torture. But Sally and I did it, and for the first time since arriving, even though I was totally freaking out about what would be on my plate, I felt a little thankful that I could at least prepare for it in advance. Like, I knew that on Saturday night I would have one chicken thigh with skin, one small baked potato with 2 tablespoons of sour cream, one slice of wheat toast with 1 teaspoon of butter and 1 teaspoon of jelly, 1½ cups of strawberries, half a banana, and one carton of low-fat milk.

That was a lot of food.

It was too much.

Too much.

Too. Much.

"So!" Sally beamed. "You did great!"

I nodded.

"Now, provided your bone density test comes back fine and we don't need to tweak anything, we won't meet again until a week from now."

"Bone density?"

"Yes, you're scheduled for Monday."

Bone density. To see if I'd basically starved my bones and made them weak like an old lady's. Mary had mentioned that on my first day. I'd forgotten.

"Oh," I said.

Sally saw the fear on my face. "Hon, I'm sure it will be fine. The test itself is a piece of cake. Really." She took my face in her hands. "Just keep telling yourself, 'Food is medicine. I have a disease and food is what will cure it.' Okay?" She patted my shoulder. "Everything is going to be fine."

I really hoped so.

Later that night, I wrapped my fingers around my wrist. It felt foreign, like a tree branch. I twisted as hard as I could. Pain shot up my forearm, but the bone held strong. I was okay, right?

I focused on my heartbeat. It careened along, too fast, then, a moment later, skipped a beat. Mitral valve prolapse, just like Lexi. It had to be. It was hard to breathe. My heart blipped again and sped up. I put a hand on the wall to steady myself. Was I dying?

*Breathe,* I told myself. *Breathe. You are getting better every day. You KNOW this.*

But I didn't know it, did I? Not really.

Allie came up behind me. "You okay? You look like you've seen a ghost."

Yes, I wanted to tell her, I had.

Mine.

# 16

**I WOKE UP ON SATURDAY TO A HARD RAIN, THE** kind that lashes at the windows and makes you want to burrow deeper into your blankets. Under there, I could almost pretend I was somewhere else. A cabin in the woods maybe, with furniture made of logs, a crackling fire, and a cute boy.

Instead, I trudged to the cold, dim breakfast room. When I saw my tray, my heart sank. Clearly, I was horrible at meal planning. Instead of yogurt and eggs I'd tried to mix it up with French toast, a cup of strawberries, a carton of milk, and a packet of instant decaf. I'd made a crucial miscalculation, though. By not including syrup on my menu, I'd assumed I wouldn't get any. But Sally thought otherwise. So there it was, at least a quarter cup of brown sludge so sugary it hurt my teeth. Straight calories. No nutritional value at all. And I had to eat all of it. All. Of. It. It took Kay threatening an Ensure for me to choke it all down.

But I finished.

After brushing my teeth three times, I headed to the nurses' station, but my mind remained on the syrup and where on my body it would end up—my arms or thighs or stomach or back. The possibilities were endless.

The dark rain matched my mood. Grim and gray. I guess if you want to get all deep, I was mourning the body I was losing each day a little, too. When I saw Ray, I barely remembered what I'd come for. "Everything okay?" he asked.

"Yeah. Just a bad breakfast. It's so hard sometimes."

Ray leaned forward. "Well, Elizabeth, you've been doing so well. You should be proud of yourself."

I bet he said that to all the girls. "Thanks, Ray. Do you guys have any extra journals, by chance?" The nurses kept stuff that girls might need—extra toothpaste, toothbrushes, shampoo—at their station. I'd brought my favorite journal from home, a purple Moleskine, but had run out of space. Doodling, mainly, and lists. Lists like books I wanted to reread now that I was sixteen (Harry Potter—all seven, *The Golden Compass,* and *The Giver*), cities I wanted to visit (Paris, Bangkok, Rome, San Francisco, New York), and college majors I thought were cool (psychology, nutrition, literature, philosophy). But most of the lists were of foods I'd eat if I weren't anorexic. Exhibit A of insanity: *Kinds of Dunkin' Donuts: French Cruller, Boston Kreme, Jelly Sticks, Chocolate Munchkins, Maple Frosted, Chocolate Frosted with Sprinkles, Glazed Munchkins, Old Fashioned, Powdered, Coconut.* Or Exhibit B, written in first-period AP Chem in hour twelve of a twenty-four-hour fast: *Breakfast: French toast, Belgian waffles, blueberry pancakes, coffee crumb cake, bacon, doughnuts, lemon ricotta pancakes, chocolate chip waffles, eggs Benedict, melted butter, whipped cream, strawberries.*

Anyone reading it would have thought I was nuts, and I wouldn't exactly have disagreed. When I got home, I'd burn the stupid thing in our living room fireplace. But until then, I'd settle for stuffing it under my bed in my room.

Ray grinned. It was hard to feel bad when he smiled at you. "You writing the great American novel?"

"Ha. Right." I couldn't help but smile back.

"Hey, you never know!"

A minute later, he handed me a speckled, wide-ruled composition book. I hated wide-ruled notebooks. They made me feel like a first grader.

"Don't fill it all in one day," he said.

I heard the front door open at the same time as Ray. He looked over my shoulder and his smile disappeared. When I saw who was standing there, mine did too.

Tristan. Charlie's best friend. And standing next to him in the doorway, his twin sister, Simone, also a junior, brushing the rain off her clothes.

When Simone saw me, she scowled like I'd offended her. She'd combed her hair over half her face. The one eye I could see was buried under a thick crust of eyeliner. She was in black from head to toe, the only color a bit of her knee peeking out from a rip in her black jeans. She towered over her brother, who was barely taller than me, and I was five foot six.

Their mom walked in after them, clutching a purse. She looked exactly like Simone, but better dressed. She ran a lot of the fund-raising events at Esterfall High.

"Well, look who's here," Ray said.

"Hey, Ray," Simone mumbled. Her eye flitted over me. "Hey, Elizabeth," she said. I wasn't sure what was weirder—that she knew my name, or that she knew Ray's.

"Hey, Simone," I muttered. I recognized the expression on her face. It was how I'd felt when I arrived: a combo of I've-screwed-up-my-entire-life depression plus fear plus anger.

But then again, she always looked pissed. It seemed to be a McCann family trait. Tristan was a curmudgeon, but he got away with being sour most of the time because of his friendship with Charlie, which gave him social cred.

But Simone didn't have any friends as far as I could

tell. The other kids called her Angry Girl. She'd missed a lot of school last year. Rumor was that it was mono and that she'd gotten it from a twenty-eight-year-old guy she'd met on Tinder, but no one knew for sure. Sometimes, when she was sitting alone in the cafeteria at lunch, I'd wonder how awful that felt, and I'd have an urge to invite her to join us. I never had, though.

So I was feeling pretty judgy in the foyer until I remembered what I was wearing. My stupid yoga pants desperately needed a wash, and my hair was lanky. I hadn't brushed it since I'd gotten up. Not to mention my horrible fatness. So who was I to judge Simone?

"I was just getting a notebook," I blurted out. "Except it's wide-ruled and I hate wide-ruled, but, you know, it's not like I can go to CVS and pick up something different. You know, because I am here and all. Beggars can't be choosers! Ha, ha."

Tristan stared at me like I'd been plopped down just to ruin his day. He opened his mouth as if to say something, but shook his head instead and ran his fingers through his hair. He had good hair. Dark and thick and curly at the edges. My stomach blipped. He'd looked at me like that, like I was ridiculous, the entire time I'd dated Charlie. When I'd complain, Charlie would say, *Trust me, he likes you. Look, everybody bugs Tristan. I bug Tristan. He's a little judgmental, but he'll come around. He's super loyal. And I know he likes you. He'll show it—someday.* Charlie said that last part—*someday*—like it was a big joke, but it wasn't one to me. Deep down, I couldn't help but wonder if maybe Tristan saw me for who I really was. A loser.

And now he was here. I hoped the universe was having a good, long laugh.

Nurse Jill arrived then and, oblivious to my world blowing up, said, "Simone, Kathy, let's get started on your registration," and ushered them out of the room, leaving Tristan and I standing a few feet apart from each other. He studied the floor. I searched my brain for something— anything—to say, but I came up blank, so I hugged myself and turned to Ray for help, hoping he'd tell Tristan to leave, or me that I had some appointment I'd forgotten about. Anything. But he'd disappeared, too.

So. Awkward.

I grabbed the brass ring on its satin ribbon around my neck and rubbed it with my thumb, letting it calm me. Tristan watched, his eyes intense, like he was studying my insides. I had the distinct feeling that what he saw horrified him.

"So . . . ," I said, hoping he'd say something to fill the silence.

"Simone is a day patient," he said, startling me.

"Day patient?" I didn't know Wallingfield took day patients.

"Yeah. She'll be here every day from four to eight. After school."

Then I blurted out, "Why are you here?"

"I'm not here by choice."

*No shit,* I thought. *Who would be?*

"I'll be driving Simone most of the time, per my parents' orders. She doesn't have her license because driving scares her." He used air quotes around the word *scares.* "And, since my parents bought me my car, they pretty much own me." He rubbed his face. He had a minor zit collection on the back of a cheek, near his ear, but his eyes were like his sister's—green, with dark-lined rims and long lashes. Pretty.

Neither of us could think of anything else to say, so we looked everywhere except at each other. I tugged at my sleeves with my fingers and wiggled my toes in my shoes. I couldn't bear to spend another second next to him in my horrible outfit.

"Sorry, but I've got to go," I said.

"No problem." He stared at me for a second.

"Okay. Well, bye."

For a second I thought he was going to say something else, but he snapped his jaws shut, gave me an almost wave, put in earbuds, whipped out his phone, and started scrolling, essentially dismissing me.

# 17

TRISTAN, SIMONE, AND THEIR MOM LEFT A HALF hour later. Through the big picture window in the hall I saw the three of them run, hunched over in the rain, and climb into a black Range Rover. Lightning, rare for that time of year, flashed in the distance.

My first family group session was at eleven, and I harbored an irrational hope that maybe Mom and Dad would use the weather as an excuse to cancel. Based on all the glummer-than-usual faces around me, I wasn't the only one.

No luck. Right before the group was to start, I saw our Honda pull into the parking lot. Dad stepped out first and came around to Mom's side of the car, holding an umbrella over the door. When Mom got out, she looked chic in her fancy raincoat that belted at the waist and the pair of high heels she always wore with a particular blue-and-white wrap dress.

I met them in the foyer. Sure enough, when Mom took off her coat, there was the outfit. She was totally over-dressed, but she still looked great. Her heels made her calf muscles look awesome, and her stomach was flat as a wall.

"Hi," I said.

"Hey," Dad said back. He hesitated for a second and then pulled me in close. At first I tried to stay stiff in his arms, but it felt too good, so I let myself squeeze him back for a second, like I had when I was little. When he let go, Mom, to my surprise, wrapped her arms around me, too. She let go only when Marcia arrived. I was shocked that I hadn't really wanted her to.

Thanks to the dismal weather, the group therapy room felt especially grim. Marcia led us inside, turning on the lights as she went. Someone had drawn a smiley face in-side the second *O* of *YOLO* on the whiteboard, and it looked like it was laughing at us. We took our seats, my parents making sure I was between them.

The circle was small. Allie's parents' flight had been canceled from New York. Lexi's parents had bailed, too, claiming the traffic from Long Island would be a night-mare. I don't know why Margot's parents didn't show, but she hadn't really expected them to anyway. Jean's came, though. They'd flown in from Toronto a couple of days early to visit and kept staring at her with watery, grateful grins. Beth's parents were there, too. I'd assumed Beth looked pale and ghostly because of her eating disorder, but her parents were practically translucent, too. They probably needed to use sunscreen in a rainstorm.

Willa's mom sat directly across the circle from me. I'd pictured her as an older Willa, wiry and short—maybe a cigarette smoker. But in real life she looked like Mrs. Claus. I bet if you stood close to her she smelled like fresh-baked bread. Even though she wasn't wearing one, I pictured her in a frilly apron, holding a wooden spoon. Willa sat next to her, rubbing up against her like a cat. I couldn't stop staring. They just didn't match.

After we'd gone around the circle introducing ourselves and saying a word or two about how we were doing— a lot of "fines," and a "nervous"—Marcia said, "Today we are going to do an exercise concerning food. Here's how it's going to work. I'm going to hand out a piece of paper with a list of different foods on it. What I'd like you all to do is to write down the first thing that comes to mind when you see each one. Then, afterward, we will share. Does anybody have questions?"

We didn't. Maria passed around the handouts and a bunch of clipboards. When Mom started to read hers, her brow furrowed. I almost whispered, *Wrinkles!* but managed to hold my tongue.

"There's no need to rush. Take your time," Marcia said. But of course the parents dug in right away. I snuck a peek at Mom, who held her pen a millimeter from the page as if she wanted to write but couldn't.

I looked down at the list. No wonder Mom was having trouble. There was almost nothing on there she'd have been willing to eat. Here were the foods:

Ritz Crackers
Carrots
Cucumber
Strawberry ice cream
Chips Ahoy! cookies
Cheese pizza
Diet Coke
Spaghetti

I had a choice. I could be honest and write down *NEVER* next to everything except Diet Coke and cucumber. But as mad as I was at Mom and Dad for sending me here, I didn't want to embarrass them. On the other hand, if I lied and answered like a normal person, the other girls would know I wasn't telling the truth, that I was weaker than they were. I hated that I cared. I looked around to see if any of the other girls were as perplexed as I was, but they were all busy writing.

I went with the truth. Call it peer pressure, or maybe survival. I had to live with these girls. I clicked the pen open and got to work.

Here's how I filled out my form:

Ritz Crackers—*16 calories and 1 gram of fat per cracker. Nasty, fake butter taste and TOTALLY terrible for you. Processed grossness!!!*

Carrots—*SO MUCH SUGAR!!!! More calories than you think. I will eat a few sometimes, but you have to watch out. They add up.*

Cucumber—*Almost all water. Eat away!*

Strawberry ice cream—*Frozen fat. Scares me. Makes me feel out of control.*

Chips Ahoy! cookies—*Stress me out. SO FATTEN-ING!*

Cheese pizza—*Disgusting fatty carby greasy fat thighs.*

Diet Coke—*A LIFE SAVER!!!!!!!!!! Breakfast, lunch, and dinner.*

Spaghetti—*Sickening. Gross. Carbs. Never.*

I put my pen down. I'd lied. The truth was, I *liked* pizza. Especially with spinach and sausage. And Ritz Crackers? I loved those, too. Not that I'd touch one now, but I used to beg Mom to buy them at the store the way other kids begged for Count Chocula. She always made me get the organic, boring wheat ones instead. And Chips Ahoy!? Katrina and I used to microwave them for a few seconds and, let me tell you, they were delicious. Soft, with melty chocolate chips. Yum.

But I didn't eat that way anymore. I doubted I ever would again, even if I got better. My body would probably self-combust. Or I'd stuff myself to death.

I looked over at Beth, who was sitting next to us. Her blond parents had worry lines etched deep into their faces. I'd heard there was a good chance Beth would be getting another NG tube soon. She wasn't eating enough at meals and was practically living on Ensure. She was also orthostatic, which meant that her blood pressure dropped whenever she stood up, so for the last two days she'd had a Gatorade in her hand all the time. She was so quiet and shy, but she seemed driven by this silent strength that kept her from eating, even when she wanted to. A part of me would have killed for her willpower. At an activity the other day, Marcia had asked us to write a list of things we liked about ourselves. Beth left hers blank. Now, on her form, next to every single one of the foods, with the exceptions of cucumbers and carrots, about which she'd written, *OKAY IF PLAIN*, she'd written one word—*NO*.

A few seats over, Jean wrote slowly. Sandwiched between her parents, she looked just as uncomfortable as I was. Her mom kept one hand on her arm, as if she was scared that if she let go Jean might fly away.

I looked over my form and added an extra *Gross!* next to spaghetti.

When everybody had finished, Marcia said, looking around with an encouraging smile on her face, "Would anyone like to start us off?"

None of the girls would even look at her.

And then good old Dad raised his hand. "I'd be happy to," he said, clearing his throat. "Okay, so forgive me if my answers are off. I've never done something like this before. So, when I thought of Ritz Crackers I thought of Cheez Whiz."

Most people in the room laughed a little. I smiled. Dad was a little obsessed with Cheez Whiz. Much to Mom's horror, he ate it on Ritz Crackers and made nachos with it all the time. He kept a jar of it on a special shelf in the kitchen. Mom made him keep all of his food there, separate from hers, as if his snacks might pollute her lifetime supply of brown rice and the probiotics she took every day for what she called her "digestive health."

When I was little, I loved Dad's shelf. He kept tomato sauce and mac 'n' cheese on there for the nights Mom wasn't home and he had to cook, plus his other favorite things too: chunky peanut butter, which he loved eating with Wheat Thins for lunch, dill pickles, and his junk food—Double Stuf Oreos, Cheez Whiz (of course), tortilla chips, jars of salsa, canned baked beans, and yogurt-covered raisins, which he argued were healthy because they were raisins. And he always, always kept Twizzlers, my favorite candy, right in the front, never saying a word when a few would go missing every couple of days.

Now Dad was running through his list pretty quick, and people were smiling. "So, for carrots I thought, hmm, tasty, and that I could use a good carrot or two right now. Um, for cucumber, I said no thank you—I've never liked them. Strawberry ice cream is my favorite flavor, preferably served in a sugar cone with chocolate jimmies. Chips Ahoy! cookies: I like them but think Pepperidge Farm is better. Ah, well, for cheese pizza I thought, with sausage? Yes, please! And, for Diet Coke, I thought of Elizabeth, which made me think of Twizzlers, because she used to use them as a straw when she drank Coke." Here he paused and looked right at me and smiled warmly. I saw a couple of the other parents and Jean smile too.

Dad was the best. I'd forgotten he'd kept Coke—I'd liked regular Coke back then—on the shelf. Each year on my birthday, I had a slumber party with Katrina, Shay, and Priya. Dad always put a box of brownie mix in his cabinet just so we could "sneak" it after he and Mom went to bed. We'd tiptoe into the kitchen, stir it up, and bring it back down to the basement playroom, where we'd eat the entire bowl of batter, giggling the whole time.

I wondered if the shelf was still filled with goodies, if there was a brownie mix in there from when I turned sixteen. I hadn't gone near it in over a year.

Dad was almost done now. "Okay, last but not least, I wrote that spaghetti also made me think of Elizabeth because it's her favorite meal."

I flushed again and fought the urge to turn to the other girls and say, *WAS my favorite meal. I don't eat that anymore, I swear.*

The counselor smiled. "That's great, Brian. Thank you so much for sharing."

Jean's dad thought of carrot cake, his favorite dessert, when he thought about carrots. Cucumbers made Jean's mom think of the spa. Willa's mom didn't care for Ritz Crackers, but she loved strawberry ice cream. Beth's dad said spaghetti made him think of Swedish meatballs, which he loved. Every parent found something they liked besides the vegetables. And then it was Mom's turn.

She cleared her throat and lifted her chin like a ballerina. "Okay," she said, tucking a nonexistent hair behind her ear, something she only did when she was nervous. "So . . . I don't know if I did this right . . . but . . . here goes. Ritz Crackers make me think of chemicals and

118

whatnot. Carrots are great. Cucumbers are refreshing. Strawberry ice cream . . . well, I hope it's okay, but I thought of a date—July Fourth." She paused and looked around, laughing nervously. We spent every July Fourth in Maine. The town we stayed in put on this totally old-fashioned parade, and every year we bought ice cream cones while we watched. This past summer I'd gotten mad when Dad ordered one for me. I'd refused to touch it. He'd begged me to take a taste but I hadn't given in, letting it melt down my hand until he angrily gave me permission to toss it. Mom didn't even order one. When Dad made her taste his, she acted like he fed her an ant.

"Okay, so, um, Chips Ahoy! cookies—funny how they always use that exclamation mark. Well, I wrote that they are delicious, but not for me. I avoid gluten for health reasons."

She did? That was new. And a total farce. I knew Mom didn't have celiac disease. She wasn't even gluten intolerant. She was just anti-calorie and obsessed with trends, and this was the latest one. She'd gone fat-free once. And then she'd avoided sugar. Once, she'd read this book on eating a special diet based on your blood type and tried that. More recently, she'd juiced, fasted, and drunk nothing but lemon water mixed with maple syrup and cayenne pepper for a week.

Mom continued. "Cheese pizza: grease and, again,

gluten. Not to mention the dairy. I try hard to limit my dairy. There are all these studies that question whether or not it's really good for you. Really, it's no better than junk food. Am I right?"

I'd forgotten about her dairy hang-up.

She laughed a little then, but it was high-pitched and fast. I wanted her to stop. We got the idea.

"Diet Coke: necessary. Very, very necessary." I'd written practically the same thing. My eyes started to sting a little and I worried that I might start to cry. Mom looked around as if she expected the other parents to agree, but no one did.

"For spaghetti I thought of spaghetti squash, which I eat instead of pasta since it is lower in calories and has few carbs and, of course, no gluten. Surprisingly good, I think." She put her paper down and flushed. "That's it."

She'd basically said that everything except carrots and cucumbers was gross. She could have been a resident. "Thank you, Karen," Marcia said.

It was one thing for a teenager to starve herself. It was another thing entirely for a mom to do the same thing.

"So, girls, how did it make you feel to hear your parents' reactions to food?" Marcia asked.

Allie spoke first. "Fine. I mean, they're parents. They're supposed to like that sort of stuff."

*What about my mom?* I almost asked, but didn't. I

couldn't get the words out. People already felt sorry for me. I could tell.

No one would ever have guessed my mom was anything besides a naturally thin woman who'd won the genetic lottery unless they ate with her. I remembered when we were at a doctor's appointment last June, the first time Dr. Brach told her that my weight was starting to get too low. Her response? "Okay, but how can we ensure that if she gains, she doesn't gain too much?"

When the family therapy session ended and we filed out of the room to say goodbye to our parents, Mom pulled me aside. "You okay?"

I slipped out of her grasp. "What? Yes. Why?"

"I don't know, honey. You just don't look good. I'm worried."

*Took you long enough,* I almost said, but I bit my tongue just in time. I didn't want a fight. Not now, anyway. "I'm fine."

She watched me for a long second. "I'm going to catch up to your dad."

"Okay." Right then, there was so much I wanted to say, so much I wanted *her* to say. But I'd say the wrong thing. She would, too. Instead, I watched her expertly dodge the other participants. Her waist was narrow in her dress. I hated that I noticed.

# 18

TWO DAYS LATER, ON MONDAY AFTERNOON, Nurse Jill shepherded Lexi and me out to a white van with the Wallingfield logo on the door in big blue letters. So much for being discreet. Might as well have suction-cupped a yellow diamond-shaped sign to the back window that read, *FREAKS ON BOARD*.

Ray was behind the wheel. The bone scan clinic was half an hour away, and on the highway we passed two shopping malls, both bustling with people. From the van windows, the action in the parking lots—the bright-colored cars circling for spots, the people in their rainbow of winter coats walking to and from Target and Best Buy and Nordstrom Rack with shopping bags in hand—looked like a movie set. It felt like forever since I'd done something as normal as go to Target.

After we parked, Ray escorted us into the drab office building and up to the fourth-floor waiting room. Three women, all about my grandma's age, sat in chairs. One frowned when she saw us. The second looked confused. The third's back was so hunched she could only look at her shoes. I kept my eyes on the floor. A nurse called Lexi and me in at the same time. "Good luck, guys," said Ray. "I'll be right here."

Lexi made a face at him. "Good luck? I've already ruined my heart. I'm sure I've completely destroyed my bones, too."

Her pessimism infected me. I pictured myself bent over like that old lady, leaning on a metal walker, staring at brown vinyl therapeutic shoes. My breath came in bursts.

But then I got inside and the bone density test was fast and painless. I didn't even have to take off my clothes. I lay on a big, padded platform as an X-ray machine whirred above me. The whole thing was over in less than fifteen minutes. Not so bad.

On our way back, the mood in the van was different. Relaxed, or maybe relieved. Ray turned on the radio and started singing along under his breath. At first, we refused to join in, but Ray is an infectious guy. He smiles, you smile. So, when "Thriller" came on and Ray belted it out, we couldn't help but sing along. Ray rolled down the front windows and drove us beside the bright blue Atlantic. The sun glinted off the water and the cool air rushed by our cheeks and the van flew over the windy roads and for a second I forgot where we were headed.

"When I was in sixth grade," Lexi shouted over the music, "I dressed up like Michael Jackson and sang this at our school talent show."

"Seriously?" I said, snorting with laughter.

"Yes! I wore a red leather jacket like the one he used to have and a white glove and everything."

Ray chuckled. "It's hard for me to imagine you moon-walking, Lexi."

She made a face. "Don't try too hard. It wasn't exactly my finest moment. But just so you know, the crowd loved me."

We cruised into downtown Grantham, the town before Esterfall. "Ooh, look! Starbucks!" Lexi cried. "Can we stop? Please, Ray? Please? I brought money." She turned to me. "I'll treat you."

Ray went serious. "Lexi, I'm sorry, but they're expecting us back."

"Please?" she begged. "We'll be fast. I'd die for a real coffee, not that instant stuff we get." We were allowed one packet of instant decaf a day. "I'll even get it with milk— no, cream!—if that makes you happy. You know, extra calories?"

Ray glanced at his watch. "All right, don't tell," he said, putting on his blinker. "You've got five minutes."

We took longer. It felt so good to be out, and free, and doing something normal people did. If I ignored Ray idling outside, I could almost trick myself into thinking I was just here with a friend. Just like I could almost trick myself into thinking that maybe everything wasn't that bad after all. That maybe this moment was an omen. That our bone density tests would come out fine.

I felt the lightest touch on my arm.

I looked over, startled. A little girl, probably ten. "You're from Wallingfield," she said.

"How do you know that?" I asked.

She pointed out the window, at the van. *Duh.*

Her arms were long and pale. Her face was all angles. Her eyes were older than the rest of her. "I wish I looked like you," she said.

When I looked at her, I saw myself.

Her mom appeared out of nowhere. "Come on, Lauren." She pulled her away. Then, when she thought she was out of earshot, I heard her mom say in a worried voice, "What did that girl say to you?"

Back in the van, with Lexi up front with Ray, I sat quietly. The coffee was bitter. I didn't want it anymore. "A fast-moving storm will drench the North Shore this afternoon," the man on the radio said, "making for a treacherous commute." Already, the sky was beginning to darken.

As we drove into downtown Esterfall, I worried I'd see someone I knew. I scrunched down just in case.

A few plops of rain hit the windshield. Ray turned the music down and rolled up his window.

Then, abruptly, he shouted, "What are you doing, Lexi?"

Lexi was standing, her entire upper body hanging out the front passenger window. "Can you feel the air, Ray?" she yelled, throwing her arms out. "It feels like freedom!" She turned her face to the rain, which was steady now. She didn't smile.

Our bone density tests were going to be bad. This was the real omen. The rain. That little girl.

*I wish I looked like you.*

People on the sidewalk stared.

Ray cursed and slammed on the brakes. Lexi fell back into the front seat, whacking her head on the doorframe. "Jesus, Ray!" she said, rubbing her head. "You could have killed me!"

"You could have killed yourself. Never stick your head out a car window. What the hell were you thinking?"

"Oh, come on, Ray." She climbed in back with me. "He needs to learn how to have fun."

Ray's knuckles whitened on the steering wheel.

"Shh!" I whispered, glaring.

Ray muttered something under his breath and eased the van back onto the street. I'd never seen him mad before.

When we got near Wallingfield, the hedges got higher and the road narrowed and it felt like the world was closing in.

The van pulled into the driveway. Thanks to the clouds, we'd lost the benefit of a late-afternoon sun. It would be night soon, earlier than usual. The rain came down harder.

*I wish I looked like you.*

*No,* I wished I'd said. *You don't.*

When we parked, Lexi thrust her empty coffee cup at Ray and flounced inside, still pissed, although I wasn't sure whether it was at Ray or herself.

I emptied my almost full coffee in the gravel. I bet Ray regretted the Starbucks stop, the music, everything.

"Thanks, Ray," I said, passing him my cup, too. "Today was nice."

His face softened a little. "No problem. Just don't tell anybody, okay?"

Nurse Jill greeted us at the door. Lexi was gone. "Elizabeth," she said, "Mary just got off the phone with the doctor who read your scans. She has your results. She's waiting for you in her office."

The walk down the dark hallway took forever. Mary's office door was open, the light like a beacon.

"Good news!" she said the minute I walked in. "You're clear."

"Clear?"

"Your bone density is within the normal range."

I needed to sit. She said other things then, but I'd already tuned out.

I was lucky. My brain flashed back to the older women in the waiting room, and the sign on the wall that read: *Are you a woman? Are you over 65? Then the National Osteoporosis Foundation recommends you get your bone density checked today.*

I was forty-nine years ahead of schedule.

I didn't want the bones of a sixty-five-year-old. I wanted to be sixteen. *Normal* sixteen. "Mary, you told me at one of our first meetings that most of the girls who diet don't end up like me. What makes me different? What makes me want to do this to myself?"

"Plenty of scientists are trying to figure that out, Elizabeth," she said. "One thing we now know is that there most likely is a genetic link."

"You mean this is in my family's DNA, like heart disease?" Shay's grandma suffered from heart disease, and Shay's mom, a total neurotic, was constantly checking her own pulse. *These diseases get passed on,* her mom would say whenever Shay told her not to stress so much.

Mary saw my concern. "Well, they're still trying to

figure that out. Eating disorders are very messy things. There's not one single factor we can point to. It's not one gene. Scientists believe there are probably a number of genetic markers that could make someone more likely to have an eating disorder, but we are still learning what—and where—they are."

I wanted it to be simple. I wanted to say, *I got anorexia because of this,* or *because of that,* or *because of the other thing.* I wanted to be able to blame something—or someone.

"It's a really complex and, frankly, confusing mix of genetics, society, parenting, and about a million other factors," Mary continued. "But research shows that people with eating disorders in their family are five to six times more likely to develop one themselves."

"So do you think I got sick because of my mom?"

Mary paused before answering. "From what you've told me, your mom does suffer from disordered eating—maybe more. But then there are people who grow up with a relative with an eating disorder and don't develop anything. And there are people who get one with no family history at all."

All the women in my family seemed to have a touch of anorexia. My grandmother, too. Some families pass down musical talent. We passed down starving ourselves.

"Mary, if I have a daughter someday, is she doomed, too?"

Mary's face was so sad it almost made *me* cry. "I don't think so. Elizabeth, if it's any consolation, there's a big study going on right now to try to find the exact genes that are affected and how. When they can figure it out, there's a chance it could lead to better treatment or even prevention someday."

I thought about the girl in Starbucks.

*I wish I looked like you.*

"I hope they hurry," I said.

Mary sighed. "Me too, Elizabeth. Me too."

When I left a few minutes later, I went straight to Michael's office to find out about Lexi. His door was closed. Muted voices snuck out from time to time, but no words. I heard Lexi's voice mixed in with others, so I sat on the carpet in the hall and waited. When the door finally opened, I saw Michael and Sally. Both looked grim. Then Lexi walked out, her face weirdly blank.

"Are you okay?" I asked.

"You go first," she said. "What were your results?"

I felt guilty telling her mine. "I'm fine," I said. "My bones are okay. What about you?"

Then, to my total surprise, Lexi's face lit up. "All I have is osteopenia in my spine and hip," she said.

I didn't get how she could be smiling. Osteopenia meant your bones were already weaker than they should be. It was the precursor to osteoporosis, where your bones were so fragile they could fracture anytime.

"I am so sorry," I said, reaching for her.

She pulled away. "No, don't be. Can't you see? This is something I might be able to fix. I may not ever get rid of my heart stuff, but this? The doctors say it might be reversible. I didn't ruin myself forever."

She took my hands then. "I have a chance, Elizabeth. Before, I thought it was too late. But now? I have a chance." She paused. "We both do."

# *19*

**I WENT TO BED EARLY, EXHAUSTED FROM THE DAY** and stuffed from dinner. Salad *with* dressing. But I ate it. I didn't want to get to a point where "just" osteopenia was good news.

Moments after retreating under my covers, Margot barged in, flopping down on my bed like she owned it, and tossed her iPod and headphones on my blankets. "Where's Lexi?" she asked, rolling onto her back and putting her feet up against the wall.

"Well, hello to you, too," I said, wishing my door had a lock. "She's watching a movie."

"Oh. How was your bone density test?"

"It's fine. My bones are good." I pointed at her headphones. "What are you listening to?"

"A book about how to find inner peace. It's by a monk. That's great news, about your bones."

"Thanks. Is the book working?"

"Not yet."

Margot constantly listened to audiobooks on her headphones. She said the voices relaxed her. Last week, she'd told me about a book she'd just finished on the Civil War, and as she spoke, recounting stories we'd never heard in AP History, I'd wanted her to keep talking. It was weird— I'd never felt that way about any history teacher.

Margot sat up and rummaged through the pockets of her overalls. "Hey, before I forget, I have a postcard for you. I picked it up at mail call."

On the front was a penguin wearing a scarf. *Stay Cool,* it read. On the back Katrina had written, *Miss you sooooo much! Get better! XOXO Katrina, Shay & Priya.* She'd signed all their names. Again.

Margot scratched her ear. "Good postcard?"

"Yeah. I guess." I must not have sounded grateful enough.

"Hey, at least you got something."

If she wanted to shut me up, it worked. We'd been here for eight days and she'd gotten nothing. "Margot, I'm—"

She cut me off. She didn't like talking about personal stuff. "Hey, can I ask you something?"

*No. I want to go to bed.* "Sure," I said to her.

"When did you first know you'd crossed over into the land of crazy?"

Now I definitely didn't want to talk.

I couldn't help but think about it, though. Was it when Katrina called me emo? Or in May, when I stopped going out with friends if food was involved? Or when I started not being able to go to sleep unless I'd run six miles that day? Or was it the night Charlie and I—I stopped myself from even thinking about it. *Don't go there.*

Besides, me coming here had nothing to do with Charlie. Not directly, anyway. When I went down, it was in flames. Public, painful flames. "Okay, fine. I'll tell you. The Harvest Concert, a week before I checked in to Wallingfield."

She raised one eyebrow. "Oh, how Americana of you. Do tell."

I shook my head. "Not something I want to talk about."

"Oh, come on. It's not like they won't make you discuss it in group sometime anyway."

She was right, and that, right there, was what sucked most about Wallingfield. They got everything out of you eventually. You had no secrets. Mary already knew what happened—she'd been briefed on it before I'd even arrived.

I sighed. "Fine."

When the choir director asked for a volunteer the day of our annual Harvest Concert, I'd shrunk down in my seat like everybody else in the room.

Ms. Parker wanted someone to dress up like a scarecrow, put on a harness, and fly above the crowd waving a cardboard moon as the choir sang Neil Young's song "Harvest Moon," which Ms. Parker had arranged for us herself. People weren't exactly falling over themselves to volunteer. Then Heather—who else?—called out, "Elizabeth will do it!" and people sat up straight again. A few snickered.

"Wonderful!" Ms. Parker said. "Now, altos, let's go over the chor—"

I raised my hand. "Ms. Parker, I don't think I'm a good candidate. I'm"—*what was I?*—"I'm afraid of heights."

She frowned. "Oh." Then she turned to everybody else. "Elizabeth is afraid of heights. Will anybody else volunteer? Raise a hand, please."

No one did.

Ms. Parker turned to me one more time and, in front of everybody, asked me to reconsider.

"I—I—don't think—"

"Great!" said Ms. Parker, who was a little desperate. "Thank you so much, Elizabeth!"

Heather smirked at me.

When Charlie and I broke up, and he "officially" started

seeing her again, I'd thought I was off the hook. But girls like Heather never forget. She was just waiting for Charlie to dump me, and when he did, she didn't waste any time. Almost right away the rumors started—that I was anorexic, that I'd become a druggie, that I had cancer. She wasn't exactly subtle. She glared at me during lunch. But a stunt like this was a new low.

"I think she does it because he still likes you," Katrina had said on our way out of Choir.

I didn't believe her. "*He* dumped *me*."

"Doesn't mean he doesn't still like you."

Not possible. Not after that night.

"Well, I heard that one of Charlie's friends called her 'sloppy seconds' behind her back the other day and it got back to her."

A flush of pleasure went through me even though this development would definitely make things worse for me. "How do you know?"

"I heard a rumor."

Crap. In addition to believing Charlie belonged to her, Heather considered herself the queen of everything at our school. And for the most part, she was: junior class president, "gifted" cheerleader, teacher suck-up. Possessor of both a great fake ID *and* a cousin who worked at 7-Eleven and let her buy beer with it.

"You're wrong," I said.

"I'm not. Besides, it's obvious that he still likes you."

"How?"

"The way he looks at you."

"He never looks at me," I said.

"You just don't see it. You never see anything good about yourself." She paused. "Anyway, when it comes to Charlie, I'm glad. You're better off without him."

"No, I'm not."

"Elizabeth, you are, and you know it. Look, I'm going to be late for class. I'll see you later, okay?"

I didn't answer her.

That night, I showed up for the concert a half hour early like Ms. Parker wanted and tried to make it all the way backstage without anybody seeing me. The black scarecrow vest she'd given me was full of patches and sprouts of glued-on hay that scratched me through my black T-shirt. I'd nixed the matching pants. Ditto the hat. No effing way was I wearing a spray-painted-brown witch's hat. I looked like a loser already.

To make matters worse, the room kept spinning like a carnival ride. I'd eaten four almonds for breakfast and was too stressed to eat lunch. The last things I'd eaten were my three bites of dinner, which I divided in half so they looked like six. I would've skipped the meal entirely except I didn't want Mom and Dad to get suspicious. I'd learned that as long as I ate *something* they were happy. Now, totally dizzy, I wondered if a few more bites would have been smart.

The air hung dark and heavy behind the navy-blue velvet curtain. Tuck, the pimply stage-crew guy, bustled around, carrying ropes, tying knots, and testing lines hanging from the ceiling. He was also a junior, but we'd never talked. He fastened the last carabiner and tested it with a shake. "You ready?"

I nodded.

He didn't look convinced. "Remember, hold on to the ropes so you stay upright. Got it?"

The harness was tight. Too tight. It hooked around the backs of my thighs, giving me a sweatpant bubble butt in the back and a penis-like bulge in the front.

Tuck ripped off a piece of duct tape. "I'm going to do the moon now, okay?"

My hairs stood up. "Why do you need duct tape? I'm just holding it, right?"

"Didn't Ms. Parker tell you? I'm taping the moon to you."

"What? You don't need to do that. I swear I'll hold it really tight." *Right in front of my face,* I almost added.

He shrugged. "Sorry. Ms. Parker's orders."

"Why do you guys even need a person at all? Couldn't you have just hung a paper moon up there?"

He started singing. "Only a paper moon . . ."

This was no time for singing. I glared at him.

"What? It's a famous Frank Sinatra song. Haven't you heard it?" He hummed a few more bars. "No?"

"No."

He sighed. "Personally I think it would have been easier to suspend a moon from the rafters with some rope, but Ms. Parker wanted a scarecrow to hold it. I think the whole thing is lame—no offense or anything."

"None taken. It wasn't like I volunteered or anything."

"Yeah, I heard you were voluntold."

"Voluntold?"

"Yeah, you know, someone asks for volunteers and then makes somebody who doesn't volunteer do it?"

"Oh, right." I wanted to ask him what else he'd heard, but the metallic rip of duct tape shut me up. Tuck wrapped a single piece across the moon, over my shoulder, and then around the other side.

"Are you okay?" he asked. "You don't look so good."

"I'm fine," I snapped. The room spun.

"If you say so." Tuck bit his bottom lip and gave the carabiners one last shake. "If you have any problems, just look for me down below, okay?"

"Okay," I said, wishing my voice wasn't shaking.

Ms. Parker blew in like a whirlwind, her heels clacking on the stage floor. "Is she ready?" Tuck nodded, and Ms. Parker looked me up and down. My feet were already asleep.

"Perfect." She peered at me. "Actually, you look a little peaked. Are you feeling all right?"

I shrug-nodded.

"All right, then," Ms. Parker announced, nodding to herself. "Showtime!" And with that, Tuck pulled the rope and I was jerked slowly up to the rafters.

The plan was for me to hang up high, where no one could see me, and then Tuck would lower me into position as the last of the three songs, "Harvest Moon," started. Then I'd swing around with the moon and be completely humiliated in front of the entire school. Good times.

As I dangled, I willed myself not to look down. The harness dug into my legs and cut off my circulation. I tried to wriggle my toes to get the blood moving, but they just hung there.

I glanced at my watch. Two songs, or about six minutes to go until my debut. I fought back the urge to vomit onto the floor. It would really splatter from so high up. The world went fuzzy. I shook myself back into focus. *Idiot. You should have eaten something. Anything.*

And then I heard it. The twang of a guitar. "On this har-vest mo-on," the choir sang. My ropes twitched, and when I looked down, I saw Tuck wrestling with them like a balloon handler at the Macy's Thanksgiving Day Parade. With every yank, I lurched violently down a foot or so, my dead legs swinging like a doll's. The audience tittered. The lights were hot. My head hurt.

The harness started to spin. I twisted backward, my bubble butt waggling at the audience. I tried to bicycle-kick my legs to turn around, but they stayed asleep. I waved my arms, frantic now, trying to gain momentum to reposition myself. Someone in the audience yelled, "It's a bird! It's a plane!"

Tuck yanked on something, and I spun around with so much centrifugal force it made me dizzy. I faced the audience now and immediately noticed a small group of senior boys, maybe on the lacrosse team, cheering and laughing at me. *This isn't happening,* I thought. *This can't be happening.*

In the crowd I saw Heather next to Charlie, gleefully clapping and yelling something I couldn't make out. At least Charlie wasn't cheering. He just stared at the stage like he was watching a car crash on YouTube.

And then Charlie's face and the rest of the audience started to pixelate. I gripped the ropes, but I felt the strength seeping out of my fingers. I tried to focus, but I could barely make out Ms. Parker nodding at me once, twice, and then continuously, frantically, while still trying desperately to conduct. Everybody was laughing now. The choir stopped singing and turned around to watch me. I fumbled with the moon, which had turned off-kilter, and accidentally detached the tape. The moon hit the floor with a *THWAP!*

And then I flipped over, my bubble butt waggling in the air. The audience gasped.

And that was the last thing I remembered.

". . . So I woke up in the hospital with a concussion and a gash over my eye. I guess Tuck screwed up and I fell. I heard later that he'd managed to slow me down with the ropes, so I didn't hit the ground super hard, but since I'd already passed out I didn't do anything to break my fall, so my head hit first.

"Later, at the ER, one of the doctors told my parents that my heart was way too slow, and that my weight was dangerously low for my height. Based on those two things, he thought I might need to go into residential treatment. So the next day, they brought me to Dr. Brach, the family doctor, who agreed. Two days after that, they brought me here."

Margot didn't say anything at first. She just looked at me, jaw open, as if she couldn't quite believe the words coming out of my mouth. "Holy shit," she said. "That's a crazy story." Then she giggled.

I crossed my arms. "I'm glad you find so much humor in my humiliation."

"I'm sorry," Margot said. "I know I shouldn't laugh, but—" And then she giggled again. "Come on. Picture yourself up there. Can't you see that it's at least a little bit funny?"

I wanted to say no, that I could still hear Heather's cackles in the audience. Or how Dad cried as he sat on that vinyl chair next to my hospital bed in the ER, saying over and over how much my anorexia scared him and made him think he'd lose me.

But I didn't tell her any of those things, because for the first time, I saw how the image of me in my harness, flailing around, might actually be sort of amusing. I smiled a little. And then I snickered, and before I knew it, we were both howling.

"And you know what was the worst?"

"What?" Margot said, snorting laughter.

"My sweatpant penis!" I shrieked.

"It's a bird! It's a plane! It's sweatpant-penis girl!" Margot yelled.

"Shut up!" I said, cracking up all over again. "I can't breathe!"

"Well," Margot said, panting, "I guess that explains the scar. I'd wondered."

I rubbed the pinkish crescent above my eyebrow. "Yeah," I said, the urge to laugh suddenly gone. "Okay . . . your turn. I told you my secret. Why are you here?"

"My story is pretty boring compared to yours, Elizabeth," Margot said. "Or should I call you . . . Wonderpenis?"

I threw a pillow at her, knocking off her glasses.

"Too soon?" she said innocently, taking her glasses back. "Sorry."

"Yeah. Well, thanks. So tell me, what's your story?" I tried not to act too eager, but to tell the truth I was *dying* to know. I barely knew anything about her. We lived less than a mile apart but existed in completely separate worlds. She'd been at a boarding school in New Hampshire since sixth grade. When she was home, she spent most of her time at the local country club, a huge, old brick mansion at the end of a long, tree-lined drive, taking tennis and golf lessons to make her parents happy.

Margot sighed and evaluated me over the edge of her glasses, like she was praying. "I ate food." Her words were clipped.

"Huh?" I was confused. That was what we were *supposed* to be doing.

"I started bingeing and purging about a year ago, the summer between my sophomore and junior years. I'd only do it every couple of weeks, and no one ever found out. But this past summer it got worse. I started purging every few days. I thought I'd stop when I got to school, you know, because people would be around all the time and so it would be hard to throw up. But instead it got worse. I started doing it every day. I'd steal food from the cafeteria and eat it at night after my roommate, Laurel, was asleep. Or I'd hide bagels and cookies and anything else I could fit in my backpack and wait until she was out. Then I'd stuff my face and throw up. If Laurel came back before I'd made it to the toilet—we had a private bathroom off our room—I'd just have to sit with it, which was hell."

I knew how she felt. Whenever I ate too much I'd go on a double-length run, minimum eight miles, and do a liquid fast the next day. Fasting was my punishment, but also a gift. The pounds just fell off when I did that.

"The last week in September, my great-aunt died, and I came home for the funeral."

"I'm sorry," I said.

"It's fine. I barely knew her. Anyway, my parents freaked out because I'd gained all this weight even with my purging. They contacted the school, and the counselors talked to my roommate, Laurel. Turns out she knew what I was doing all along. She told them everything."

"Oh, Margot. I am so sorry. What happened after that?"

"The school made me take a medical leave. And then my puke clogged the pipes at home and backed up the entire upstairs system. Our house is old—ancient plumbing. It started bubbling up in my parents' shower."

How do you respond to something like that? I nodded.

"They sent me here the next day. But it doesn't matter. Nobody can help me. Everybody talks here about loving ourselves for who we are, but I can't. I hate myself. I'm an idiot."

"Margot, that is the silliest thing you have ever said."

"No, Elizabeth, you don't understand. Compared to the rest of my family, I'm dumb. I've never done well in school. Everybody in my family goes to Pasker." Pasker was in Connecticut, one of the oldest and most prestigious boarding schools on the East Coast. "We're legacies there, but when I applied for sixth grade they wouldn't take me. I had to go to Lewiston in New Hampshire. Have you heard of it?"

"Yes," I said. Lewiston was known as the school where rich kids who'd messed up went. "I didn't know they had a middle school."

"Yeah. They do. Do you know how dumb you have to be to not get into a school where your family name is on a *building*? Pasker said my test scores were too low. The thing is, my parents have always known I can't take tests. Even when I know the material, I can't get it from my head to the paper. My brain just can't do it. Reading gives me headaches. That's why I listen to books. Teachers told my parents for years that I might have a learning difference, but Mom and Dad never listened. Dad always told them that I'd grow out of it, that he'd been a late bloomer, too. He doesn't believe that, though. He thinks I'm stupid. I heard him tell my mom once that I was lacking in 'intellectual capital'—he actually used those words."

"I'm so sorry, Margot. That's so not true." How could

146

her parents not know she was smart? Then again, they'd sent her to boarding school when she was eleven. And when she was home, Margot said, they barely spoke. They probably didn't know her at all.

Margot shrugged. "After the whole plumbing incident, my shrink told my parents I should come here. Dad was horrified. He said he couldn't believe I was his daughter, that a Camby doesn't fall apart like this. It was bad enough I was seeing a therapist. But to go into residential treatment? That just isn't done."

I didn't know what else to say. "So, it must be interesting being a Camby." The auditorium in our school was called the Camby Center for the Performing Arts. They were next to royalty in Esterfall.

"Definitely not the word I'd choose." She grabbed a tissue from the bedside table and blew her nose.

"Right. Sorry," I said, to fill the silence. "Did you know the Harvest Concert was held at the Camby Center?"

"That figures," she said, wiping her eyes and chuckling a little. "Of course it was."

I took her hand, and she didn't pull away.

# 20

ON WEDNESDAY, CLOUDS ROLLED IN AFTER LUNCH
and the blues came right along with them. Reliving the
Harvest Concert had made me remember just how much
everything would suck when I eventually went back to
school, and for the past two days I'd spent a lot of time
trying to come up with a way to get my parents to let me
homeschool. Aside from breaking a leg, I had nothing.

I wasn't the only one feeling down. At mail call, even
Allie shrugged when she received a fluorescent-pink teddy
bear with giant glitter-green eyes from Hugh. "I have the
same one at home," she sniffed, tossing it back in the box.

"What's up with that?" I asked Willa.

"You didn't hear?" she whispered. "Her boyfriend took
another girl to her school's fall formal and didn't tell her.
She found out from a friend." I'd missed group on Monday

thanks to my bone scan. "But she said she's not going to break up with him because she wants him to keep sending her presents."

Allie could say that she was in it for the gifts, but my bet was that she wanted to pretend everything was fine, that her friends and boyfriend were waiting for her, that they weren't moving on. I knew I was doing that. I still hadn't heard from Priya and Shay, but if they called, I knew I'd act like we'd just talked yesterday. It was easier to pretend that everything was fine.

I didn't expect Nurse Jill to call my name, but she did, a shoe box–sized package covered with fireworks stamps in her hands. When I stood up, Coral said loud enough for all the other girls to hear, "Is that another one of your 'secret admirer' presents?" putting *secret admirer* in air quotes, like I was making the whole thing up. Girls turned in my direction. Allie perked up.

*How did she know?* I looked at Margot and Willa. Willa turned beet red. "Sorry," she mouthed.

At the nurses' station, I didn't recognize the lady checking packages. She didn't smile or talk to me; she just opened the package and looked inside with a frown. "We'll allow it," she said, like she was a judge on *The People's Court* or something.

When I got to my room, I opened the box and found a jar inside, a regular jelly one with a screw top, full of sand

and seashells. On the lid was a label in the same handwriting as the address—*CHORUS BEACH*. I thought I might cry. This was the sweetest, most romantic gift ever. Chorus Beach was our beach. It was where Charlie's house was, where we went to be alone when his parents were home, and where we had bonfires at night. It was also where I ran, back when I could run. It was where my mind felt most clear. I'd told Charlie that once.

It had to be him. But I still didn't get why. It made no sense. He was with Heather. And that's when it hit me. The one person who probably had all the answers was due to show up at four o'clock sharp, Simone in tow. Curmudgeon or not, I vowed to get Tristan to tell me what Charlie was thinking.

Tristan was right on time. At exactly four o'clock his Jeep rumbled up the gravel drive. I stepped into the foyer just as Tristan stopped in front of the white columns marking the entrance. He turned off the engine. From where I stood, I could hear that Simone and Tristan were arguing.

It was rude to eavesdrop, but I did it anyway. Simone was pissed. "You were, weren't you? You were listening to me in there. Who does that?"

Tristan's voice wasn't any cheerier. "Who does that? I'll

tell you who. Someone with a sister who has bulimia, that's who. Besides, I wasn't spying. I was checking to see if the bathroom was free."

A long silence followed. Had they heard me?

"Tristan," Simone finally said, "don't do this."

"Do what?"

"You can't fix me, you know." Simone didn't sound angry anymore. She sounded sad.

"Who said anything about fixing you? I just wanted to brush my teeth."

"Seriously. You need to lay off."

"Lay off brushing my teeth?"

"Don't make this into a joke."

"I'm not. You need to get over yourself."

Their voices were getting louder.

"I'll be fine. Just leave me alone, okay?"

"You aren't fine."

"Whatever."

I heard footsteps then. Before I could get out of sight, Simone hustled past me, barely noticing I was there. Then Tristan stormed inside, almost smashing into me.

"Ah, excuse me," I said, turning bright red. *Busted.*

"Jesus Christ," he muttered, and stormed off down the hall.

When I passed by the breezeway, there he was, sitting in a rocking chair. "Hey, are you okay?" I asked.

He glanced away and shrugged, and when he did that, he looked like a little boy.

I didn't speak. I'd learned from Mary that if you want people to talk, say nothing.

"She just pisses me off so much." His voice was angry, but sad, too.

I lowered myself into a rocking chair.

"She knows what she needs to do to get better, but she won't do it. And she won't let me help her." He put his head in his hands.

"I don't know if it works like that," I said. "Simone could want more than anything to get better, but maybe she isn't ready yet." I didn't know if I was talking about Simone or myself.

"Bullshit! She could get better if she tried, but she's not even trying."

"It's really hard, Tristan."

"Whatever. She should have figured it out the first time."

"She's been here more than once?" I knew it. That's how Ray had known her the day she'd arrived.

"Yeah. Last year. First she was in Philadelphia for her bulimia. Mom and Dad claimed that they chose the place there because it was good, but I think they sent her that far so they could be sure no one from Esterfall would see her. You know, the whole Yankee keep-it-in-the-family thing. But then, when she flunked out of that one, they didn't care as much anymore. They wanted her close by, so they sent her here. But apparently it didn't work, so here we are for round three."

I wanted to correct him, to say that you didn't really flunk out of a place like this. Usually, failure meant that you came back, that you flunked in.

The chairs made quiet creaking sounds as we rocked and looked out the windows. The view was beautiful, all trees, but I wished that when I looked out, I could see people walking by, or stores, or any sign of civilization. The woods were starting to feel like walls keeping us in. Like prison.

Apparently Tristan felt the same. Or something. "Can we get out of here?"

"Um, I'm not exactly allowed to leave."

"No, I mean, can we go outside or something? I need a cigarette."

"Um, yeah. Sure. If you want. We can go to the patio."

"Great." He stood up a little fast, sending his chair rocking wildly.

When we got to the patio, he knocked a cigarette out of the pack, brought it to his lips, and lit it. The smoke made me feel ill.

If he'd been anybody else, I'd have given him grief. But Tristan already thought I was a Goody Two-Shoes, so I kept my mouth shut. He could worry about his own lungs.

We sat down on two hard outdoor chairs. "I was the one who caught her this time." He spoke softly. "Things had been better. And then I heard her puking again. And I was so angry. She didn't even try to deny it. She just begged me not to tell, but I didn't have a choice. Do you know what it's like to make your dad cry? Do you know how awful that is?"

*Yeah,* I thought. *I do.* "I'm sure Simone didn't want that to happen."

"Simone doesn't care about anything but herself."

"You know, this whole thing sucks for her, too."

"Yeah? Well, why does she keep choosing it, then?"

Was he saying all this because he wanted to talk to somebody and I happened to be there? Or did he want to talk to *me*? "Well, I don't know if she's choosing it. At least, not now."

"Oh, she's choosing it."

"It's not like that." Did he think that about me, too? That I'd just "decided" one day to get all anorexic?

What he didn't understand was that we weren't choosing this. Not anymore, anyway. The first time Simone threw up, she made that choice. And no one else made me go on my bikini diet. But after a while our eating disorders messed with our brains. They became something we didn't have control over. Something we couldn't stop by ourselves even if we wanted to.

He scoffed at me. "But all you have to do is *eat* something. All she has to do is not puke. It's not like you guys have *cancer*."

The blood rushed to my cheeks. "I wish it were that easy, Tristan."

Tristan took a drag of his cigarette. "So were you happy to come here?"

"No! I didn't speak to my parents for three days before I came. I feel sort of bad about that now." I'd locked myself in my bedroom. Dad had knocked on my door over and over, begging me to come out and talk. Mom had texted me every couple of hours. I'd ignored them both.

Tristan looked at his watch. "I've got to go. I have soccer practice."

"Okay," I said, relieved.

Tristan smiled then. "I feel a little better." That made one of us. I hadn't even gotten a chance to ask about Charlie.

He fished in his pocket for his keys.

I was gone before he found them.

# 21

**I KEPT WALKING UNTIL I'D REACHED THE HALLWAY** with the phone. I leaned against the wall and tried to calm myself by taking deep breaths. I knew some people felt the way he did about eating disorders, that they were a choice, but no one had ever said it to my face before. Anorexia wasn't something I ever wanted. It was something that happened to me. Right?

The phone rang, and I ignored it. No one liked answering the phone. If it wasn't for you (and it never was), everyone expected you to find a pen that worked, and some paper, and take a good message, and find some tape to fasten the message to the bulletin board. If the person on the other end of the line said the message was private, then you had to actually find the person and deliver the message yourself, which was a huge pain in the ass, especially if they were in a different cohort.

I relaxed when the ringing stopped. But then it started again. This time I sighed and picked up the receiver.

"Hello?"

"Hi. May I please speak to Elizabeth Barnes?"

"Katrina?" I couldn't believe the phone was actually for me. That *never* happened. I felt guilty for not picking up the first time. "Hi! It is so good to hear your voice! What's going on? How are you?" Hearing her voice was like taking a happy pill. I smiled like an idiot in the empty hallway.

"Good! Guess what?" She sounded excited, too.

"What?"

"Are you free right now?"

"For about fifteen minutes. Why?"

"Perfect! That's all I've got too. You need to go outside to the driveway. Like, right now."

"Why?"

"Because somebody, and by somebody I mean me, is here . . . standing in front of . . . HER NEW CAR! Come outside so I can show it to you!"

I squealed so loudly it could've matched Allie's mail squeals, but I didn't care. "Oh my God! K, that's amazing! I'll be right out."

I hung up the phone and walked as fast as I could to

the foyer. Ray was in the nurses' window, filling out forms on the counter. "Ray, my friend got a new car and wants to show it to me. Is it okay if I go outside for just a second? Please? I promise I'll walk really, really slow."

Ray nodded without looking up from his paperwork. "Don't be gone long, though. Nurse Jill will read me the riot act if she finds out."

"I promise."

Katrina was right outside the door, leaning against the cutest cherry-red Honda Civic I'd ever seen.

"Oh my God! It's adorable!"

"I know!" We hugged and jumped up and down a couple of times.

"Why did your parents get it for you?" Had I missed her birthday? No. She was a July baby.

"Because I just took the SATs, and guess what my score was?"

The SATs. I'd forgotten that they were a couple of weeks ago. Katrina and I were supposed to take them together, for practice. I'd backed out, saying I had allergies. The truth was that I couldn't concentrate on anything for more than a few minutes at a time. The SATs were four hours long.

"I got a fifteen hundred! Can you believe it?"

I tried to ignore the simmer of unease in me and be

happy for my friend. But I couldn't help it. What was I going to do about the SATs? And my grades?

"Can you go for a drive? Please tell me you are allowed to go for a drive."

I totally wanted to. But leaving the property was about as against the rules as you could get. "I can't."

"Oh." Her whole body slumped. "Well, can you at least sit in it for a second?"

I glanced back toward the door. Ray was nowhere in sight. "Sure, I guess I could. For a second, anyway."

I climbed in. It smelled like a new car. "This is so nice," I said, settling back into the black cloth seat. I'd gotten my permit back in May, on my sixteenth birthday. I'd started driver's ed at the end of the summer, but I'd had to drop out to come here. I was supposed to get my license in November, but who knew when I'd get around to it now. I thought for a second about Katrina, Shay, and Priya driving around together. It gave me a stomach cramp. It seemed impossible that I'd only been here for ten days. It felt like a month.

Katrina turned toward me like she'd read my mind. "Things aren't the same without you, E."

"Thanks. You know what I was thinking about the other day?"

"No, what?"

"Remember when we went ugly hunting?"

Katrina beamed. "Totally. Oh my God. That was so funny."

Of all the things I missed doing out in the real world, ugly hunting was up toward the top of the list. The four of us used to do it every time we went to the mall. We'd go to a department store and try on the most hideous formal dresses we could possibly find and then Instagram the results. The best selection was always around prom, when the racks were overstuffed with taffeta, sequins, satin, and general tackiness.

Once, Priya tried to get us into the bridal department at Nordstrom; she'd pointed to Katrina's stomach and said with a wink at the saleslady, like she was letting her in on the secret, "The sooner the better." The lady didn't buy it, and we ran out of the store, three of us shrieking with laughter and Katrina swearing she was going to kill Priya, which somehow made the whole thing even funnier. It hurt to think about now.

"Katrina, are Priya and Shay mad at me for some reason? I don't get why I haven't heard from them."

Katrina stepped closer. "They miss you," she said. "Some people just don't know how to handle stuff like this. It's hard, E."

"What's hard about picking up the phone?"

"You know what I mean. It can be tough to know what

160

to say. Like, right now I don't want to tell you too much about what's going on at school because I don't want to make you feel like you're missing anything. That's all."

"Oh." I didn't believe her. I was sure that with Shay and Priya, it was out of sight, out of mind. Other girls brought this up in group, too. How they felt forgotten.

Katrina glanced at her watch. She wanted to leave now. I could tell. I racked my brain for something I could say to make her stay.

It came to me a second later. *Of course!* "Guess who checked in the other day?"

"Who?"

"Simone McCann."

Her eyes widened. "Wait, Simone, Tristan's sister? Whoa. Why?"

I opened my mouth to tell her, but something stopped me. Karma, perhaps? Maybe, if I didn't talk about Simone now, she wouldn't talk about me at school later. So I back-pedaled. "I don't know."

"Huh. Is it weird?"

"No, not really. I don't see her that much yet."

"Well, that's good."

She wanted more info, I could tell, but I didn't want to tell her about seeing Tristan. She'd make a big deal out of it.

"Tell me what's going on at school," I said instead.

She launched into a story about a freshman I didn't know or care about. I waited as long as I could before I asked what I was dying to ask. "So . . . seen Charlie lately?"

Katrina scowled a little. "Yes," she said, full of scorn. "He's the same. Still an ass." She paused. "He asked for your address." She obviously did not think this was good news.

My stomach flip-flopped. "Really? When? Why?"

"The same day you came here. I'm sorry I didn't tell you when it happened. It's just that, well, I didn't want to upset you. Has he sent you anything?"

"No. Nothing." Except for *perfect* things, I wanted to say. But I kept my mouth shut. She wouldn't understand.

"Elizabeth, you can't let this mess with your head, okay? I don't want you waiting for something that never arrives."

"Katrina, I am so much better now. Seriously, I'm not like that anymore." We both knew what she was talking about. After Charlie and I broke up, my anorexia got worse. I started existing on six cans of Diet Coke, four almonds, and two cucumbers a day, down from one yogurt, a few almonds, one banana, and three bites of dinner. By the time I got here, six weeks later, I weighed 90 pounds, 15 less than when we broke up.

Katrina wasn't buying it. "He's still toxic, Elizabeth."

"I know. But don't worry. He hasn't sent me anything and I bet he won't. I don't even want him to."

"Well," she said, "just don't get your hopes up. He probably asked me because he knew it would kill Heather. They were in a huge fight at the time."

I played with my seat belt and looked away, embarrassed by how excited her words made me. "How do you know?"

"Priya told me. It doesn't matter anyway, because I think they made up."

"What was the fight about?"

"I don't know. Why do you care?"

"No—no reason," I stammered. "I'm just bored here, that's all. I like to keep track of things."

"Um, okay. But, Elizabeth?"

"Yeah?"

"He's still a jerk."

"I know." I almost said something then, so she could see how great he actually was, how he had this little-boy smile he sometimes gave me. Or how, when he learned I had a total phobia of being in speeding cars, he slowed down and didn't drive as fast as he usually did. Or how, at night, he liked to have tea with his mom, which I thought was ridiculously cute. Or how he'd bring me nuts or a Clif Bar at work and encourage me to take bites. I knew she'd approve of that.

Katrina's phone chirped. She checked it and whacked the steering wheel. "Shoot. I have to go. We have an Amnesty meeting in an hour and Devin messed up the copies. I need to unjam her printer." Katrina was the social conscience of our school. She was president of the Amnesty International club and the community service club, and secretary of student government. Her college application was going to be amazing. Mine, on the other hand? Let's just say being here wasn't helping.

"I wish you could take me with you."

"Me too. Hold on." Her thumbs flew across her phone screen. "I just need to let her know I'm on my way."

"Okay." I opened the door and got out. I desperately wanted her to stay, but I couldn't think of the right words to keep her there. "Katrina?"

"Yeah?"

"Thanks for coming. I miss you."

She jumped out of the car and ran around it to give me a hug. I held on to her, not wanting to let go.

"Me too, E." She stepped back and I wiped my eyes, embarrassed that I needed her so much. But then I saw her eyes weren't exactly dry either. "The second you're out of here we will go for the most epic drive ever."

"Okay."

She walked back around to the driver's side. Looking at me over the roof of the car, she said, "I wish I could take you out of here. Or make you better."

I nodded. "Me too."

Then she climbed back into the driver's seat and was gone.

I hadn't noticed the chill before, but now it seeped into my bones.

On my way back inside, Tristan's Jeep came roaring into the driveway.

My stomach sank. *Be strong.*

He hopped out. The gravel crunched under his feet.

"My mom needed me to hand in some forms for Simone. I forgot before," he mumbled.

"Oh."

It was so cold. I shivered.

"What are you doing out here, anyway?" He looked at me like I was crazy.

"Katrina got a new car. She was just showing it to me."

"Oh yeah, I thought that was her. I saw it at school. Pretty sweet." We walked the last couple of feet to the door together. He reached around me to open it. His iPhone and a bunch of papers spilled onto the ground. I reached down to retrieve them. He did too. Our heads cracked together.

"Ouch," I said, rubbing my forehead.

"Sorry." His ears turned pink from embarrassment.

When he gathered up his stuff, he stood, and for a second we were only inches apart.

I held my breath and stepped away. I hadn't brushed

my teeth since lunch, and it couldn't be good. That was another lovely anorexia side effect—"hunger breath," aka breath that STINKS.

"Um, do you need me to get you ice or anything?"

"No thanks," I said. "I don't need it. A lot of us here bruise easily. It's a low-iron thing. You know, a side effect of the eating disorders we all choose to have."

"Look, I'm sorry about before. I just—I'm upset. I love my sister. And it kills me that she's doing this to her—that this is happening to her. Don't take what I said personally. Seriously."

How could I not? "Forget it," I said. "It's not a big deal."

He sucked in his cheeks and looked toward the door.

"Looks like you need to go," I said. Then, when he didn't move, "See you." *I hope never again.*

"Yeah. See you." He jammed his hands in his jeans' pockets and left. I saw him light up a cigarette the minute he was out the door. I didn't remember him smoking so much before.

And then I put him out of my mind. He was nothing but noise. Charlie had asked for my address. That was the sign I'd been waiting for. It was time to call.

# 22

AT 5:45 P.M. I WALKED TO THE PAY PHONE, TOOK A deep breath, and dialed the number Charlie had scrawled on the scrap of paper he'd slid across the counter to me at Scoops that first day. It was still in my wallet, folded up small.

I hung up as soon as his cell started to ring. What if he felt the same way Tristan did about eating disorders?

No. Charlie didn't feel that way. At school he might have come off as a pompous asshole—he was loud and a show-off and loved to drive his fancy BMW too fast in the parking lot. That's how Katrina saw him. That's how I'd seen him, too. But then we went out, and he was different with me. Sensitive, even. He'd always say, "Elizabeth, you are perfect just as you are." Those were dreamy words, even if they were untrue. "I'm worried about you," he'd tell me sometimes. "What can I do to help?" I always acted like I had no idea what he was talking about.

No, he wasn't like Tristan. He was kind. Besides, he'd sent me all this stuff, so obviously he *wanted* to talk.

My breath left a fog on the receiver as I redialed the first three numbers. 9-7-8 . . . My finger slipped and I hit a 5 by accident. *Crap.* I hung up. *Don't be a loser. Do it!* I told myself.

This time, with shaking fingers, I made it all the way through.

"Hello?" When Charlie answered, his voice sounded even better than I remembered—low and rumbly. I was quiet. "Hello?" he said again, and this time his voice was annoyed.

I cleared my throat. "Um, Charlie? It's me."

"Who?" I could hear "No Woman, No Cry" playing in the background. It was just like our first date all over again. It had to be fate. I spoke a little louder. "It's me, Elizabeth."

"Elizabeth?" There was a pause. A long pause. "Wow." In the background, the music shut off.

I pushed on. "How are you?"

"Good. Thanks." I wanted him to feel me missing him through the phone. I wanted him to reach out. I wanted him to say he missed me. I wanted him to say, *Let's get back together.* As it was, he sounded cool and a little distracted.

I took a deep breath. "I was calling to say thank you."

He didn't say anything at first. I heard him breathe into the phone. "Sorry," he finally said. "I can't really hear you. Hold on, okay?"

"Why is *she* calling?" said a girl in the background. A girl who sounded suspiciously like Heather.

"Babe," he said. He muffled the receiver then, but I could still hear. "I'm just going to see what she wants. I'll be back in a sec."

My grip on the receiver tightened. He'd called me *babe* too.

"Are you still there?" His voice was different away from Heather. Softer. "Sorry about that. How are you?"

I took a deep breath. "I'm . . . um . . . I'm good. Listen, Charlie, I wanted to thank—" My confidence totally evaporated. Suddenly, I doubted everything. "Charlie," I said, "I got some packages recently. They . . . I . . . Well, someone sent me a brass ring, a jar of sand, a House of Pizza ring, and a poster. Any of these sound familiar?"

He didn't answer right away. Instinct was telling me to shut up, but I couldn't stop. It was like I was possessed.

"Packages?"

*He has no idea what you are talking about. Stop!* I told myself. *Don't say another horrible word.* But it was too late. I blurted out, "Yeah. It's okay. You can tell me. I figured it out." My voice petered out at the end.

"Figured what out? Wait—do you think I sent you that stuff?"

"No, I—"

He interrupted me. "Elizabeth, I didn't send you anything. I mean, I should have. Mom said I should send flowers, and so I asked Katrina for your address, and I meant to do it this week, I swear. I've just been busy, but I'll send them now if you want. Wait—did these things have my name on them or something?" he said, confused.

Oh my God. I'd done it. I'd completely humiliated myself. "Oh, no. I mean, yes, but it must have been my cousin, Charlie. You guys have similar handwriting." I had to get off the phone.

"Oh. Well, did you need something? I mean, I'm sure my mom would—you know—send something if you needed it."

His *mom*? "God, no. I'm fine. Okay, well, I better go and give my cousin a call to thank him. He's so thoughtful, you know."

"Didn't you tell me once you didn't have any cousins?"

"What? No! I have lots of cousins. Tons." I didn't have a single cousin. Mom was an only child, too, and Dad's brother, Tom, wasn't married.

I could hear the confusion in his voice. He cleared his throat. "Um, Elizabeth?"

"What?" *Hang up! Hang up! Hang up!*

"I'm glad you're getting the help you need. And thanks for calling."

"No problem," I said, my voice barely audible.

After I hung up, I could still hear his voice in my ear. I slid off the stool and onto the floor, bringing my knees to my chest and wrapping my arms around myself.

I was so stupid.


At dinner I kept my eyes on my plate and didn't make eye contact with anybody. I was embarrassed just to exist, like all my weaknesses and shortcomings were listed on a flashing neon sign above my head: *Pathetic! Anorexic! Can't keep a boyfriend! Makes fool of self on regular basis! Loser!*

Charlie didn't care about me. He wasn't missing me, or thinking about me, or even worrying a tiny bit. He'd erased me. My heart hurt, but I didn't know if it was because it was broken or because I was dying.

I needed to move. I yearned for a trail in the woods where I could sprint until I collapsed. But no one here would let me go. No one would understand how the only way to fix this would be to run the shame right out of me.

And then all of a sudden everything inside me exploded, like a shaken-up soda. The rules didn't matter. I jolted out of my seat, overturning my water glass in the process. I made for the doors, head down, ignoring the nurses calling, "Elizabeth, sit down. The meal isn't over yet"; Lexi saying, "Wait!"; Willa saying, "Come back! You'll get an Ensure!"; and Margot saying, "Elizabeth, you are bold."

I got to a door and rattled the handle. It was locked. I'd walked straight to the utility closet. The door to the hall was one over. Face burning, I yanked it open and sprinted away, my strides long and fast. I was determined to get outside. Then I'd run and let fresh air fill my lungs and then I'd be okay.

I threw open the front doors. It was dark. No moon. No stars. The cold air made my nose burn. The frost-covered driveway beckoned, and I broke into a run, but my legs barely responded. I willed my breaths to energize me, but I only made it twenty feet before I bent over double, sucking wind. *My lungs have shrunk,* I thought hysterically. *My legs are concrete blocks. I've ruined myself.*

I remembered how, back in July, I'd woken up early one morning unable to sleep. The sun was rising and I could tell it was going to be hot, but at that hour it was still cool. I'd laced up my blue Nikes and set out toward the beach. It was deserted at that hour, just me and the seagulls, and as I ran toward the water, my feet barely

172

touched the ground. It had been a short run; I'd already started to tire faster, but for those few minutes, feeling the cool air in my lungs and the strength in my feet, I'd felt like I could fly. Now I wondered if I'd ever feel that way again.

I sank down on a rock and pressed my eyes into my kneecaps as I tried to catch my breath. Behind me I heard the door open and Ray's voice. "Elizabeth?"

I heard his feet crunching on the gravel.

I wasn't ready to go back. "Um, do you think you could give me a second?" I asked, trying to sound normal. "I just need a minute. Please? I'm not going to run anymore. I couldn't even if I wanted to."

Ray paused before answering. "Okay, kiddo. You got a minute. Not much longer, though, okay?"

"Thanks." I put my head in my hands.

And right then I knew. If I went home and started to restrict my eating again, I would shrivel up like a dry plant. If I ever wanted to run again—to *live* again—I'd have to get better. And I'd have to do it for me.

I sat on the hard rock for a few more minutes until the bump on my tailbone started to ache. Then I stood up and walked inside.

Margot and Lexi were waiting for me on the bench next to the nurses' station. They weren't supposed to be there. Evening group had just started, and activities were mandatory around here. I shot them a questioning look and they held up two cups of fluorescent-yellow Gatorade. Of course. If you said you felt dizzy or like you might pass out, the nurses gave you Gatorade and let you sit on the bench to drink it.

"I felt faint," Margot said, gesturing to the cup in her hand.

"You never feel faint." I sat down heavily next to her.

"True, but tonight I did," she said.

I looked at Lexi. "I felt faint too," she said.

Lexi took a tiny sip of her Gatorade. Lexi was drinking calories. By choice. Just so she could make sure I was okay. I should have felt a rush of gratitude or something, but all I felt was flat.

Margot leaned over and awkwardly patted me. I leaned against her, assuming she'd put her arm around my shoulders. Instead, she jerked away. "Sorry," she said. "Touchy-feely stuff isn't exactly my family's specialty."

"It's okay." I sat there, staring at my hands.

"You know," she said, bumping me with her shoulder, "when you want to run away, it helps to actually run. For more than, like, ten paces."

I sighed. "Yeah. I heard that works. I'll try it next time."

"Actually, don't," Lexi said. "We sort of like having you

here." She put her arm around me and squeezed, hard. I closed my eyes and let my body relax.

After Lexi and Margot took their final swigs of Gatorade, we went through the foyer doors. Nurse Jill awaited, arms crossed, holding an Ensure. I sighed and took it without complaint.

# 23

AT BREAKFAST THE NEXT MORNING, DAY 11 AT
Wallingfield, I was sure all the girls would stare at me
after my great dinner escape. But aside from a couple of
quick glances, everybody seemed to have their own issues
to worry about. Like their breakfasts.

I found a big bowl of cottage cheese on my tray. I *hated*
cottage cheese. When I asked Kay why it was on my tray,
she said I'd assigned it to myself. Sure enough, when I looked
at my check sheet, there it was: *½ cup cottage cheese—2
proteins*—in my very own handwriting. How could I have
done that? The stuff was vile, all watery and chunky like
vomit.

I hadn't cried last night, but the tears were there, just
waiting for the right opportunity to spill. I could picture
them inside, each little blob of salt water fighting in its

hurry to be number one in line to get out. When that first spoonful of cottage cheese passed under my nose, the tears burst out of me. I bawled like a kid getting a shot while, around me, everyone tried to eat and pretend my sobbing wasn't happening. I cried so hard that when I asked Kay if I could take my tray to Mary's office, she walked me there herself.

After I arrived, sniveling and all snotty, Mary took one look at me and passed the tissue box. She waited until my sobs slowed and turned into hiccups before saying, "So, what happened last night?"

"I called Charlie."

She nodded. I'd told her our basic story already. We'd gone out and he'd dumped me and I was sad. Now, on that couch, I thought I'd just tell her about the phone call. But then I kept going and recounted the entire conversation word for excruciating word. Then it was like I couldn't stop, like I had diarrhea of the mouth, and I told her about the jar of sand, which I'd dumped into the trash in a fit of anger before I went to sleep, along with the House of Pizza plastic ring and the poster. I'd meant to toss the brass ring in the trash too, but when I'd reached for it, I couldn't get myself to take it off. I showed it to Mary now, rubbing it with my thumb like I always did. And, like it always did, it calmed me down a little.

When I said, "It's my fault we broke up in the first

place," Mary put her notepad aside and gave me a look that said, *I was listening before, but now I'm REALLY listening.*

I'd worn a dark blue sundress that night. I'd bought it just for our date. I'd borrowed Mom's gold necklace that dangled almost to my belly button, and painted my toenails a matching blue so they'd look good in my favorite pair of brown strappy wedge sandals.

Charlie had dressed up, too, in a navy-blue blazer and green Vineyard Vines tie with little swordfish on it. He'd texted earlier in the day, told me to be ready at seven, and to wear something nice. No occasion, he'd said when I asked. Just because. It was all very romantic. And then, when he picked me up, he looked so hot that I decided right then and there. It was time.

We'd come close to having sex a couple of times, but I'd never felt ready. Two weeks earlier, when we were messing around in his room, I'd stopped him at the last minute. "I'm sorry," I'd said.

"It's okay," he'd responded, whispering into my hair. "It has to be right."

But a few days later he'd tried again when we were fooling around on the giant sectional couch in his basement. I'd moved his hand just as he reached for the zipper on my jeans. This time, when I said no, he'd groaned and said, just a little annoyed, "It's okay if you're not ready. I get it."

I'd said I was sorry, and he'd sighed. "No, I'm sorry," he said. "I shouldn't push you."

Now, as we walked to his car, I imagined how excited he'd be when I told him I was ready. Then I pictured myself naked next to him and shuddered.

*I can't.*

*You can. You have to.*

"Where are we going?" I asked in the car, raising my voice over the radio.

"You'll see!" he said, smiling. Music blaring, he threw the car into drive and off we went. Summer air rushed in through the sunroof and rippled my hair, and I felt like I was flying.

And then we rolled up to the Navigator Room. It was the fanciest restaurant in town. Dad took Mom there for her birthday dinner every year. This had to be a punishment from the universe. My stomach cramped. *Breathe, Elizabeth. You can get a salad.* But I knew that wasn't true. You didn't get just a salad at a place like the Navigator Room.

"Are you okay?" Charlie put his hot hand on my bare knee and squeezed.

*No. Not there. I have lots of fat there.*

I tried to smile. "Oh yeah, I'm fine. I just got some dust in my eye, that's all."

Charlie let out a short, tight breath and shook his head a little. He'd been doing that a lot lately.

He'd made a reservation, and the hostess led us to a

big table with a white tablecloth, a vase with a single white rose, and wineglasses. I immediately pictured the table loaded down with food and couldn't sit still. I started jiggling my foot, a preemptive strike against the calories I knew I was about to consume.

Charlie pretended not to notice, but I know he did. "It's my treat, okay?" He was trying hard.

"Wow. Thanks." Him paying made everything worse. I didn't want to waste his money, but I couldn't eat the food on this menu. *Salmon en croûte.* What the heck was that? *Chicken with browned butter. Breaded pork chops. Veal.* Everything came smothered in sauce, or was fried, or was fattening.

"Elizabeth?"

"Huh?"

"Elizabeth, you're so pale. Are you all right?"

I spoke faster than I should have. "Totally. Sorry. It's just that everything looks so good I can't decide what to order." I scanned the options again. *Manhattan clam chowder. Tomato-based broth. No cream. Yes!* "I think I'm going to have a cup of the Manhattan clam chowder and maybe a house salad."

His face fell.

I panicked. I could feel his disappointment from across the table. I'd been feeling it more often lately. I tried again. "You know, actually, the salmon sounds good. I'll have the salmon." I didn't want the salmon. But I didn't want to upset Charlie more.

He exhaled. "Cool. I'm getting steak. Oh, and fried calamari. Do you like calamari?"

I had, once. "I love it!" I said.

We ordered, and when the menus were gone, I relaxed. Charlie told me funny stories about sailing and his summers on the Vineyard, and before I knew it I was having a good time.

And then the waiter brought the calamari, and the night came to a shuddering halt. Charlie didn't notice. "Awesome," he said, practically drooling over the plate of golden tentacles and rings in the waiter's hands. "Thank you so much."

Charlie offered the plate to me first. "Take some," he said. "This stuff is so good."

I plucked one ring off the overwhelming pile. "Oh, come on, take more than that," he said, and shoveled a greasy heap onto my plate. Then he bulldozed an even bigger pile onto his plate and dug in, swishing each piece in the tartar sauce it came with.

After eating almost his whole plate, he looked at mine and frowned. "Aren't you going to eat yours?"

*No.* "Of course! I love calamari. Seriously." I picked up a ring and held it to my lips. My fingers already felt greasy. I nipped at it with my front teeth. "Mmmm," I said, "so good!" I took a second nibble. Then I scraped the crust off the remaining bit, making sure to get even the tiniest crumbs off the inside of the ring. Next I dabbed at it with my napkin to get the remaining oil off, and finally put the rest of the slimy piece in my mouth. I chewed. I swallowed. I exhaled.

One down. Only about twenty more to go.

"Elizabeth." Charlie's voice caught me by surprise. I'd almost forgotten he was there. "Please eat."

"I am, silly! I just ate one." I touched his hand. He yanked it away.

"Barely. Have you been eating at all?"

"Yes! Of course," I snapped, but a part of me wanted to tell the truth, to say, *All I ate was one apple and four Diet Cokes today. And I'm scared.* But I couldn't. "I'm fine," I said instead.

Our entrées came. Charlie ate his steak in silence, stabbing each piece with a fork. I ate two peas and ignored the fact that Charlie wasn't speaking. He'd been less patient about food in general with me lately, and I'd started trying to make plans with him that didn't include eating.

The salmon in front of me was wrapped in pastry dough. What did he want me to do? Eat *that*? The whole thing was drowning in hollandaise sauce. I couldn't touch it even though I really did want to make Charlie happy.

But I couldn't let that grossness enter my body. So I sat there, miserable, and watched his steak disappear, the only noise the occasional scrape of his knife on his porcelain plate.

He asked for the check while our plates were still on the table.

Back in the car Charlie drove fast, and it scared me. When we got to my house, the windows were dark.

"Want to come in? My parents are out for at least two more hours."

He hesitated, so I leaned over and pushed my lips hard against his. I placed my hand on his thigh, rubbing it with my thumb. "Please?" I whispered, biting his lip just a little.

He paused before nodding.

When we got to my room, I locked my door and kicked off my sandals, heart pounding. I removed Mom's necklace and placed it carefully on my bedside table. From his one-word answers in the car, I could tell he was frustrated. What happened next needed to be perfect. I slid under my cold covers. Goose bumps popped up on my arms and legs, and I prayed that they'd disappear before Charlie felt them. I wriggled out of my sundress and tossed it on the floor.

"Will you come in with me?"

He didn't answer right away.

"Please?"

"Okay." He sat down and took off his clothes piece by piece, laying each one over the back of my desk chair, until he was wearing nothing but light-blue boxer shorts.

He slipped under the covers next to me. I leaned over and kissed him. I was never this forward. But my gut said if I wanted to keep him, this was what I'd have to do. He curled his fingers around my waist. I tried not to flinch. I'd lost 2 more pounds, was down to 105, but I still wished there was a way to do this without him having to touch me at all.

He kissed me again and our teeth hit. "Sorry," he whispered, smoothing back my hair. "Did that hurt?"

I shook my head.

He ran his hand up my spine, his fingers lingering on my vertebrae, each one a little hill. In the dark he couldn't see the bruises that crested each one like bluish snow.

I shivered even though Charlie's skin was warm.

"Are you sure you're all right?" he whispered, pulling away.

"Yes. I want to do this. Now. I want to do this with you." I meant to sound strong and sure, but my voice shook.

"Okay," he murmured in my ear. Then he leaned over and fiddled with what I guessed was a condom. I couldn't get myself to look.

When he ripped it open, I heard the flutter of the wrapper

on the floor and I made a mental note to make sure I hid it so Mom wouldn't see it later. After he'd put it on, his hands explored me and his lips were on my shoulder and I couldn't breathe and suddenly all I wanted to do was put on my comfy clothes and cry.

But I stuck with it. His skin pulsed hot and smooth, and once he was on top of me I felt small and hidden and I relaxed a little.

"Is this okay?" he whispered.

I nodded.

"Tell me if it hurts. I can stop whenever."

I nodded again and wrapped my arms around him. He was warmer than a blanket and I loved him for being so sweet and for touching me with such gentle hands.

*I'm about to not be a virgin anymore.*

And then, right that very second, he rolled off me, taking the covers with him.

I snatched them back, wondering what part of me he didn't like. "Is everything okay?"

He didn't answer. He was breathing hard and I thought I heard him curse under his breath.

"What's wrong? What is it? What did I do?"

He stayed quiet for a few seconds before answering. "I can't do this. I thought I wanted to, but I keep worrying that you'll break. All I see are your bones and it scares me. I thought that if we got, you know, all into it, I wouldn't

185

notice. But you feel like a skeleton." He scooted to the far side of the bed and balled up my purple sheet in his hands.

"Charlie, I'm sorry. I can be softer. I'm just nervous. Let's try agai—"

His jaw muscles tensed. "Elizabeth, your bones *hurt* me. Your hips dug into mine so much that I couldn't even concentrate on what I was doing."

"I'm sorry," I said, my voice thick. "Let's try again. I was just nervous. That's all." I knew I sounded desperate, but I didn't care. I *was* desperate.

"I can't, Elizabeth. You didn't even move. You barely kissed me. I want to be with a girl who wants me, too."

The hurt in his voice surprised me. Wasn't he supposed to be happy just *having* sex?

"I do want you. I'm sorry. Please."

He sat on the edge of the bed.

"Charlie, wait."

He stood up, shirt and blazer in hand. He looked so tall and his brown hair was messed up in the cutest way and I desperately wanted to run my fingers through it and pull him back to me, but I couldn't get out of bed because then he'd see me.

But if I didn't get up, he'd leave.

In desperation I pulled my duvet around me like a robe and stood. Except that I stepped on a corner and stumbled and the duvet fell to the ground and then I was standing, naked, behind him.

Charlie turned around and when he saw me he went still. Even though I wanted more than anything to dive back under the safety of my covers, I forced myself not to move, to let him look. To show him I was his.

His eyes traveled over me for a long second. Then he reached past me, picked up the duvet on the floor, and carefully wrapped it around my shoulders.

"I'm sorry," he said. I heard his voice catch. "I can't do this. I can't handle it. I—" And then he was gone.

I heard his car rumble to life and the scatter of gravel on the driveway, and for a second I wondered what Dad would say when he saw the tire marks tomorrow. Then I got into bed and tried to keep from coming completely apart.

The next morning, I lay there, hollowed out. My stomach growled. *Let it complain,* I thought. *I don't deserve to eat.*

At ten a.m. I got a text.

**I think we should just be friends. Sorry.**

When I finished talking, Mary didn't say anything at first. Her brows were scrunched and her lips were pursed, like she was deciding what to say.

I squirmed in my seat like a little kid and bit my thumbnail down to the painful part. I waited for her to ask me how I could possibly think he'd sent all those packages after we'd broken up like we did. Because, now that I thought about it, I didn't know myself.

When she finally spoke, all she said was, "That sounds like an incredibly painful experience, Elizabeth. Thank you for sharing it with me." She paused. "I'm curious to know how you are feeling now that you've spoken about it."

I didn't answer. Wasn't it obvious? I fought the urge to say, *How do you think I'm feeling?*

"Mary," I asked instead, tears in my eyes. "When does the pain go away?"

"I don't know," she said, her voice soft. She felt sorry for me. I could see it in her eyes. I'd been getting that look a lot before I left for Wallingfield. From teachers, random strangers, even the checkout guy at the grocery store. But after I said the story out loud, I was a little sorry for me, too. For both me and, I realized, for Charlie.

Mary leaned over like she wanted to touch me, but she didn't. "I don't know when the pain will go away, Elizabeth. But I, for one, think that you are so brave. You took a chance and put yourself in a situation where you weren't in control. That must have been incredibly scary, but you did it. Maybe it didn't go your way, but you survived. You are strong, Elizabeth, and I think that the more you face these feelings, the more you talk about them, the less power they'll have over you."

I wanted to believe her. I just didn't know if I could.

"Elizabeth, from what I am hearing, it sounds like Charlie was worried about you, that he stopped so that he *wouldn't* hurt you, not because he wanted to."

I nodded. Someone knocked on the door. Mary glanced at her watch. "Elizabeth—"

"I know," I said. "Your appointment is here." Then I stood up and left, leaving the door ajar behind me.

# 24

SIX DAYS POST-CHARLIE, ON A TUESDAY, FLOWERS arrived. They were the 1-800 kind, all daisies and carnations with a red teddy bear and a sagging helium balloon inscribed with *Get Well Soon* in rainbow bubble letters, the exact type of gift Katrina and I had laughed at. The card read, *Get better, Elizabeth. —Charlie.* My heart blipped once, but that was it.

"Aren't those nice?" Nurse Jill said, handing them to me before lunch.

"Yes," I said. "Very nice."

I waited for the Charlie jolt, the pain that came when I thought about him. But I got nothing. So I gave the flowers to Willa. She loved them.

And then, on Friday, another package arrived. It was wrapped in brown paper, and the script was familiar. I caught my breath.

No. It couldn't be.

After my phone call with Charlie, I'd just assumed the packages would stop. But why would they? *They weren't from him, remember?*

When Ray cut open the top of the box, I peered into it with him. Snuggled down beneath crumpled-up pages of the *Boston Globe* lay a black travel umbrella, the kind you can buy at CVS for five dollars. Tied to the handle was a note in the same handwriting: *For the next big storm.*

What was that supposed to mean?

Ray slid the box back to me. "Worried about rain?" he said.

"Not really. I have no idea why someone would send this." I tried to think of someone, anyone, who might want to send me an umbrella. My mind came up blank.

Ray seemed impressed. "Looks like you have a mystery to figure out."

"I guess." I hustled back to my room, where I hung the little travel umbrella on a hook in my closet with the rest of the gifts, which were in a sorry state. I'd taped the poster back together. I'd collected as much sand as I could out of the trash and poured it back in the jar. I'd rescued the plastic ring and set it on my dresser.

I'd think about this later, I told myself. With Mary.

\* \* \*

". . . Elizabeth? Hello? How are you feeling about today?"

"Huh?"

Mary shot me a questioning look. I'd arrived early for therapy and, while waiting for my session to start, had let my mind wander to my mystery. Could it be Katrina? *No.* Shay? Priya? One of Charlie's friends? No, no, and no. Shay and Priya would never send me stuff like this. And Charlie's friends cared about Charlie. When he broke up with me, they did, too. When we'd gone back to school in August, it was like I'd never existed. They ignored me again, just like they had before Charlie and I went out.

Could it be Wyatt, the kid in Algebra II who sometimes helped me with my homework? Could it be Tuck, feeling guilty after practically killing me at the Harvest Concert? Dad?

"Elizabeth?" I snapped back into focus. Mary was speaking to me. "Where were you right then?"

I forced my attention back to her. "Nowhere. Here. Just thinking."

A week ago, I was so sure that it was Charlie. All my ideas and theories about the presents led back to him. But now that he was out of the picture and the presents were still coming, my thoughts flew around with no home base.

"Well, if you felt nervous, I would understand."

Mary's words jarred me back to her little office. "Nervous? About what?"

"I'm just thinking back to the other day, when I told you about the family therapy session. You'd expressed some anxiety then."

Oh. My. God.

Family therapy.

Today.

No. Not today.

"You seem a bit caught off guard," Mary said.

"Yeah, well, I sort of forgot." Every patient at Wallingfield sat through at least one individual family therapy session in addition to the group. Since my parents were at work, ours was over the phone. Mom had scheduled it; I don't think it was an accident it was on a day they couldn't be here in person.

"Okay. Let's talk for a minute about what will happen when your parents pick up the phone."

"They'll tell me I just won a million dollars?" I bit a nail too far down and blood appeared. The sting focused me.

"It's okay to be nervous."

I just shrugged. "I'm not nervous. So what are we going to talk about?"

"Well, my main goal is to help you through the conversation. I'm going to start us off by focusing on how everybody can best support you, both here and, eventually, at home. Do you have anything you want to focus on?"

Not having the call? "No, I don't think so."

"Well, if anything comes up that you want to discuss in private, you just write it down on this paper and I can put your parents on hold, okay?"

"Okay." *Can we put them on hold for the whole conversation?*

"Here we go." Mary hit dial.

I hadn't seen Mom since family group. Both she and Dad had called a few times over the week, but the conversations always went something like this:

Mom/Dad: *Hi, honey. How is treatment going?*

Me: *Fine.*

Mom/Dad: *Good to hear.*

Me: *It's been nineteen days. When can I come home?*

If Dad was calling, he'd say, *Don't rush things, Elizabeth. Take all the time you need. There's no reason to cut and run before the treatment works,* like I'd get some magic drug that would just all of a sudden kick in and cure me. When it was Mom, she'd just get irritated and say, *Elizabeth, we don't know, okay? We just don't know.*

Now Dad picked up fast. "Hi there," he said. His voice sounded unsure, nervous. It bothered me to hear him like that. I liked my dad sounding strong. Always.

"Hi, Brian. It's Mary and Elizabeth here."

"Hi, Dad," I said.

"Hi, sweetie."

Mary spoke next. "I'm going to click Karen in. Just a moment, please."

Two clicks later and Mom was there, clearing her throat. "Hello," she added, her voice small and far away. She sounded nervous. Like me. I pictured her at her desk, her big computer in front of her, and suddenly I was glad that we were doing this by phone.

"Okay so far?" Mary mouthed. I nodded. Mary gave me a thumbs-up. I wasn't so sure that would be the gesture I'd choose.

"How are you doing?" Dad asked, his voice overly cheerful.

"Good, Dad. I'm good." The least I could do was lie about that, I thought.

Then Mary dug in. When she leaned over, her shirt bloused out and her body looked barrel shaped. "Hi, Brian. So today I wanted to focus on addressing some of the issues and concerns Elizabeth has been talking about over these last couple of weeks."

"Okay," he said. He sounded guarded, defensive.

"I'd like to start by talking about family support both while Elizabeth is here and when she goes home." Mary spoke like she was telling someone where to find the bathroom. I admired her cool demeanor.

"Sure," Dad said hurriedly. "We'll do anything we can."

195

"As you know, Elizabeth has been working very hard."

"I know she has. We are very proud," said Dad.

I chewed my fingernail.

Mary cleared her throat. "Karen?"

Mom hesitated, and then, with surprising power, "Yes?"

"Elizabeth and I have been talking a bit about how meals go at your house. I'd be curious to hear your impression of them."

Mom didn't even pause. "Well, I'm the one who cooks for all of us. We eat together every night," she said. "I like to think that Brian and I model healthy eating habits for Elizabeth."

I shook my head and wrote on the pad: *Mom doesn't eat anything!!!!!*

"Karen? Elizabeth has something to say." She smiled encouragingly at me.

"I . . . I don't know if I agree, Mom." We were in uncharted territory now. In our house, Mom's next-to-nothing eating was normal.

"Karen?" Mary sounded so encouraging, like she was trying to get Mom to tell her a secret recipe or something.

Dad jumped in, talking fast. "Karen has always been a mindful eater."

"Karen?" Mary asked again.

I gripped the arms of the chair and counted the ceiling

tiles. *One . . . two . . . three . . . Stay calm, Elizabeth. Stay calm.*

"Well, Brian is right. I am cautious about what I choose to put in my body. You can't not be these days."

Mary nodded. "I see. Can you describe what you mean by cautious?"

Mom's tone turned defensive. "Well, you know, I eat a lot of vegetables, low-fat meats, watch my carb intake—I basically don't eat white foods."

I raised my eyebrows.

"And why is that?"

"White foods are processed foods, you know?"

I looked at Mary as if to say, *See!*

"Got it. Do you count calories in front of your daughter?"

Mom paused. The silence stretched a few too many seconds. "Only to be healthy."

Mary switched tactics. "What will be most helpful for Elizabeth when she does eventually come home is to have parents who eat well-balanced, fulfilling dinners without worry. Ones where everybody eats the same thing. Do you feel that you can do this for her?"

"Of course!" Mom's confidence was back. "We do healthy already. We don't overindulge, but we eat. We go to restaurants, enjoy our meals, et cetera. I think we're fine in that regard."

But she'd never been fine. A memory of a dinner out popped into my head. I was ten. I'd ordered a cheeseburger. Mom had ordered a grilled chicken sandwich. It came with mayonnaise. By the time she'd carefully sliced off the surface of the chicken—simply scraping wouldn't remove all the mayo, she claimed—and cut off the polluted parts of the bun, she'd had about four bites left. "Now it's perfect!" I remember her saying. Except that then, she didn't touch it at all. Watching her had made me self-conscious, and I'd refused to touch my burger, ashamed that I was such a pig.

I scribbled furiously on the pad. *SHE IS LYING!!!!!!*

Mary gestured for me to speak. I shook my head *no*. I didn't trust myself. My heart hammered hard against my chest.

So she spoke instead. "Elizabeth just reacted very strongly to what you said, Karen. Why do you think that is?"

Mom paused, and then said, "Well, I have no idea. I mean, I am happy with my diet, and like I said, I've always encouraged Elizabeth to eat when—"

I shook my head. *No.* She was lying. And Dad, by supporting her, was lying, too. When I opened my mouth I had to force the words out, and they came out softer than I wanted. "Mom," I said, my voice catching, "you don't encourage me. It feels like you do the opposite sometimes. When I'm with you, I get so stressed about food."

"Elizabeth! Why would you say such a—"

"Mom, other kids' moms, they don't seem to care if their kids have ice cream sometimes. Like, I've never seen a mom tell their kid they could only get the frozen yogurt." I paused, took a deep breath, and then I said it. I went where no Barnes had ever gone before. "Um . . . I could be wrong or projecting or something, but I sort of think that maybe you think about food a little too much."

In sixth grade, Mom had plucked a bowl of ice cream out of my hands. "Your metabolism can't handle so many sweets," she'd said apologetically as she jammed the scoops of melting mint chocolate chip down the roaring disposal with my spoon. At the time I didn't get it. Ashamed of my appetite, I burst into tears. Mom thought I was crying because I wanted more ice cream. All the other girls in my class ate ice cream. Was my metabolism different from theirs?

Mom sniffed in the background. Great. I'd made her cry.

"Elizabeth, let's be kind. Your mom sounds pretty upset!" Dad's voice sliced through me as he took her side, like always.

"Dad, do you think I'm wrong?" My breath quivered.

Mary popped in, unruffled, like we were discussing the weather. "So, Brian, Elizabeth has brought a lot of emotion into the conversation. What do you—"

Suddenly I felt left out. Mom and Dad always took each other's side. But who was taking mine? I didn't want to talk to anybody. What was the point, really? "I need to go," I whispered.

"Brian, Karen, one minute please," Mary said quickly, hitting the hold button.

"I'm sorry, but I have to get out of here. I can't do this right now. I just can't—"

"Elizabeth, we are just getting into—"

I stood up. The office felt tiny, almost nauseatingly small. "I can't talk to them anymore." The pillow in my lap fell to the floor. I left it there.

Mary hit the hold button again. "Karen, Brian," she said. "Elizabeth would like a break. What do you say we continue this at another time?"

"Oh? Oh, okay. I guess so," Dad said.

"I'll e-mail you some dates for follow-up, or we can touch base next Saturday." Saturday was Family Day, which was different from all the other weekly family group sessions because everybody ate lunch together, too. I wanted to throw up.

"Sure." He cleared his throat. "Elizabeth, honey, we love you." His voice caught on the word *love*.

On Mom's end, all I heard was crying. And then, nothing. The receiver clicked.

Mary looked over at me. "Elizabeth, I—"

I interrupted her. "It's time for lunch." And I walked out.

# 25

LUNCH WAS STIR-FRY. OILY STIR-FRY. THE GOOD
news? It had broccoli, the first vegetable besides lettuce to
appear on my plate since Sally told me fourteen days ago
that veggies weren't allowed. The bad news? I couldn't get
my parents out of my head.

When I was little, Mom used to never let me have three-
person playdates. "Someone always ends up feeling left
out," she'd say. I never thought it would be the same way
with families, too.

"Elizabeth!" Lexi said, holding up her fork. "Look! Broccoli!" She seemed to be in a great mood—I had no idea
why—and hell-bent on cheering me up.

Not wanting to be a downer, I held up my fork. "Broccoli!" I said. Her being all happy made me feel good, and
all of a sudden, right there at the table, I decided I wanted

to be happy for once, too. So I put my parents in a box and pushed it to the back corner of my mind.

And besides, getting broccoli really was a thing to celebrate.

"Cheers!" I said, only faking my smile a little.

"Cheers!" Willa raised hers, too.

"You guys are all nuts," Margot said.

"Wait! I have a toast," Lexi said. We all held our broccoli up in the air. Even Margot. "Ahem . . . Okay. Here's to the men we love. Here's to the men who love us. If the men we love aren't the men who love us, then screw the men! Here's to us!"

"Hear, hear!" I said, and we clinked our broccolis together.

The chicken was too fatty and the sauce was salty and my parents were a whole separate problem, but we had broccoli and I cherished every single limp and floppy piece.

And, when I thought about it, I did have things to be happy about. I'd finished my lunch. In fact, I was proud to report that I'd finished every meal and snack in the past week. Because of that, I felt better both in my body and my brain. I wasn't psyched to be gaining weight, but my thoughts were clearer and they moved through my head faster.

Even so, when I went back to my room, I couldn't help walking in jittery circles, the greasy chicken haunting me.

Lexi watched. "The stir-fry was bad," she said. "But you'll be okay."

I stopped walking. "How can you be so calm?" Lexi was like a little island of Zen on her bed, calmly writing in her journal like lunch had never happened. "Didn't you see all the *oil*?"

She shrugged. "Yes, but I'm trying not to think about it." In the eleven days since our bone density tests, Lexi had become a star patient. I guess getting her test results really had changed her. She made it look easy.

"Oh." I shut up.

To calm down, I lay on my bed and tried to take long, slow breaths. Breathing like that was supposed to calm you down, right?

I was at ten when Lexi interrupted me. "Hey, Elizabeth? I know this probably isn't the best time, but I have something to tell you."

"What?" I asked, only half listening.

I felt a slight weight on my bed as Lexi sat next to me. "I had a meeting with Michael last night."

"Oh?"

"I'm leaving."

"What?" I sat up. She couldn't leave. I must have heard wrong. "When?"

She paused. "Tomorrow."

"So soon? That's impossible!" Usually, when people left,

there was a protocol Wallingfield followed. The staff would always take you out to eat to "practice" in the real world, schedule extra therapy sessions, and plan out your home meals. No one left with only a day's notice.

"I know it's soon, but my insurance will only pay for four more days, and since Dad has business in Boston tomorrow, it's most convenient for him to come then. Mom wanted me to stay for the four days and then fly home, but of course, once Dad heard Mom's plan, he insisted that they pick me up in person, so tomorrow it is." Lexi's parents were divorced.

"But there's all that stuff you need to do before you can go. What about eating out?" Lexi and I were supposed to leave on the same day, together. That's what I'd always pictured. Wallingfield wouldn't be Wallingfield without her.

"I don't need it." She turned to me and took my hands. "Elizabeth, I feel ready. I know I can do this."

"How do you know?" She'd only been doing better for ten days. Ten. Barely enough to warrant a departure, in my opinion.

"I just know. I can feel my body wanting to eat. I don't want this life. From the minute I saw my health records, I realized what I was doing was crazy. I want to *live,* Elizabeth."

I could already feel her pulling away. "Will you write to me?" I felt stupid as soon as I asked the question.

Lexi whacked me gently on the shoulder. "What? Of course I'll write you! Do you think I'd just leave here and never think about you guys again?"

That's *exactly* what I thought. I'd never seen a girl here get a letter or a package from somebody who'd left. Ever.

"Elizabeth, everything is going to be fine. I'm going to be fine. And I think you are going to be, too. I just know it in my gut." She stood up. "You'll see," she said.

I wished I felt as confident.

The next morning after weights and vitals, Margot and I sat on my bed and watched Lexi pack up her suitcase. She'd breezed through her meal, looking like she actually *enjoyed* her eggs.

Girls came in our room for the next half hour to say goodbye. With everybody there, it felt like a party, or rather the first few minutes of a party, before it gets fun, when people are all quiet and awkward and super polite. Beth told Lexi she was a role model. Jean said she was a wonderful person. Margot told her to "do good things out there." Willa cried a little and said she'd miss her. Allie told her to call us, "like, every day, okay?"

And then it was time for our first meetings of the day. "Elizabeth," Margot whispered as everybody around us procrastinated. No one wanted to leave Lexi. Or go to their appointments, for that matter.

"Yeah?"

"You didn't say anything!"

"I don't know what to say," I whispered back.

Margot gave me a stern look, the space between her brows crinkling. "You have to say something! You're her roommate!"

I sighed. "Hey, Lexi," I said from my bed. She and Jean were giggling together. She looked over, caught in mid-laugh. Her eyes shone. She looked beautiful. *Please stay,* I wanted to say. *Wait for me. Don't leave me in our room alone.* But all that came out was, "Good luck." It sounded lame, even to me. Her smile evaporated. She opened her mouth like she was about to say something, but right then Jean stood up and announced, "We are going to be so late!" and Willa and Beth and even Margot got up and rushed Lexi like she was a Kardashian, literally waiting in line to give her a hug. I hung back, watching the circus, hoping that if I didn't participate, she wouldn't actually leave.

My first activity of the day was art therapy. The girls were cheery and the sun was out, but the room still felt dark. Our task was to decorate wooden picture frames with stick-on jewels, paint, feathers, buttons, and the other dribs and drabs left over from past art projects. In between the tacky decorations, we were supposed to write positive affirmations, like *STRONG! BRAVE! WORTH IT!*

I glued one hot-pink feather to mine and then put it down. I couldn't let Lexi leave without a better goodbye.

She deserved that from me. When the art therapist wasn't looking, I stashed my picture frame under a rainbow-colored pile of feathers and snuck out. No one noticed.

Back in our room, I found her perched on her bed, back to me, filling out forms. Even after all this treatment she still looked like a Disney princess—impossibly tiny waist, minuscule wrists, huge head. I tapped her on the shoulder and she turned around.

Holy crap. It wasn't Lexi. It was her mom. Lexi often complained about her mom's weight, but I never imagined her looking so small and emaciated. Sick, like Lexi when she'd first arrived. She peered at me over the top of a pair of reading glasses. Her hair, the same color as Lexi's, was thin, and her skin was caked with makeup.

"Oh, hello," she said, in a hoarse, tinny Long Island accent. "Were you Lexi's roommate?" She looked me up and down. I wondered what she saw.

"I'm Elizabeth." I stuck my hand out. Hers was limp and cold, like shaking hands with a vampire. I thought of my mom's own firm grip. I felt a pang. I hadn't talked to her since phone therapy.

"Lexi has talked about you a lot. Where are you from?" Her mom smiled at me. Her teeth were nearly translucent.

"Esterfall."

"You're lucky you're close by." She sounded overwhelmed. "We have a drive of six hours ahead of us."

Lexi walked out of the bathroom. She was wearing jeans, which I'd never seen her in, and a short leather jacket, also new. She looked like a different person. Older. Pretty. I remembered her that first day, how colorless she'd been. Now she actually had a tinge of pink in her cheeks.

"Where's Dad?"

"He's in the car on a call. God forbid he clears his schedule for his daughter."

Lexi ignored her and turned to me. "You're supposed to be in art!" she said, hugging me hard.

I returned the squeeze, whispering, "I couldn't let you leave without a proper goodbye. I'm sorry I didn't say something better before. I should have."

"Don't worry about it."

She held me at arm's length, like a mom would. "You're going to leave soon too. I just know it."

My brain flashed back to the conversation with my parents. I wasn't sure if I wanted that or not. "Can I ask you something?"

She nodded. I pulled her into the bathroom.

"Lexi, don't take too long," her mom called after us.

She turned to me, her face open. "What's wrong?"

At first I thought I wouldn't be able to get the words out, but then they poured out in a rush, tumbling over each other. "Do you think there will be a day when we don't think about food at all? That we'll just eat it, enjoy it, and move on with our day?"

She looked me right in the eyes. "Yes. I do. I believe we will have a day when we eat lunch and never think about it again." Then she smiled.

"Lexi, honey, come on!" Her mom's nasal voice needled its way into the bathroom with us.

We hugged. "Well, you better go. Smith is waiting." I followed her out of the bathroom.

Her mom smiled at me. "Thank you for being such a good friend to Lexi. I hope you two stay in touch. Lex, honey, you ready?"

Lexi nodded. They both turned toward the door, and that's when I saw that her mom was carrying an inflatable plastic ring, similar to a pool floatie. She was too thin to sit without one. Her bottom didn't have enough cushioning.

Lexi stared at the doughnut. She flushed. I pretended not to see it.

"Good luck, Elizabeth," Lexi said with a final squeeze of my hand. "I'll never forget you." Then she grabbed the handle of the suitcase, tipped it onto its wheels, and left, her mom trailing almost weightlessly behind her.

# 26

**THREE DAYS AFTER LEXI LEFT, WE GOT A POSTCARD,** just like she'd promised. On the front was a picture of a bakery in the Hamptons. I snickered. *Nice irony.* On the back it read:

> *Being home is great. Taking it meal by meal, but so far so good! Mom put in a call to Smith, so we'll see what happens! Thinking of you all, all the time. If I can do it, you can, too! Love you all!*
>
> *xoxo Lexi*

I brought it with me to group.
"That's so great," Jean said as we waited for Marcia.
"That's cool," Margot agreed.
Willa looked at it. "Can I have the card?"

I knew the nice thing to do would be to hand it over. But I shook my head. "Maybe later, Willa. I have to show it to a couple of other people first."

Willa sat back and pouted. I didn't look at Margot or Jean, but I could feel their disapproval. Still, I carefully tucked the postcard into the back of my journal.

I missed Lexi terribly. More than the other girls did. Without her, our room was quiet and cold. It made me homesick.

Parents aside, I couldn't stop thinking about home. I wanted to be able to watch TV whenever I felt like it. I wanted to be able to shave my legs and go to the mall and get coffee—real coffee. I didn't want to feel like a prisoner anymore. Oh, and I wanted my phone back. I was *dying* to have my phone back. And I wanted to sleep in my own bed, which definitely DID NOT have a plastic cover that crackled when I moved, and I wanted, more than anything, not to have an empty bed next to me that looked like a coffin in the dark.

Marcia arrived and produced a Magic 8 Ball, the black plastic toy where you ask a question about your future, shake the ball, and then turn it over to see a prediction appear on the bottom. I got one in my Christmas stocking when I was ten. I'd ask it questions like, *Will I be rich someday?* or *Will I be a famous movie star?* It always said stuff like, *My reply is no,* or *Don't count on it.* Once, I asked it if I would be pretty. I got, *Reply hazy, try again.* When I tried again, I got, *Does not look good.*

I promised myself that when Marcia asked for a volunteer, I'd raise my hand. If I wanted to go home, I needed to be an A student, just like Lexi.

"So." Marcia held out the ball like it was a diamond or something. "I want you to look ahead to the end of your time here at Wallingfield. What will you want to have accomplished? Where will you want to be? What would you like to be able to do that maybe wasn't possible before because of your illness?" She paused and looked around at the six of us, all dramatic-like. Across the circle, Allie picked at her fingernails. Jean, as always, listened and nodded. I, personally, was disappointed. This was basically regular group. The Magic 8 Ball was just a gimmick, a stand-in for the talking stick, a wooden baton covered with glitter glue and ribbon that we took turns holding during discussions.

Marcia continued. "I'd love for you to take a few moments to either draw or write down your thoughts, and then we'll share. If you have the 8 Ball," she said, shaking it for emphasis, "you have the floor. And, like always, if you aren't comfortable, you can pass, okay?" We nodded.

What did I want? I thought about what Lexi had said the other day as she was leaving. *I believe we will have a day . . . ,* she'd said. So I wrote about that.

212

*I want a day where I wake up and eat pancakes for breakfast with butter and hot maple syrup. And then I want to go to school and have a muffin during study hall. I want a day where I eat school lunch and a chocolate chip cookie and Jell-O for dessert like Priya. For dinner I want to have spaghetti and meatballs with tons of Parmesan cheese on top and cake—two fat slices. I want to eat all that and be happy with how I look. And I want to stay a size 0.*

I scratched out the last sentence. We weren't supposed to talk about sizes or weight. If I wanted to go home, I needed to stop saying stuff like that. But it *was* true. I did want to stay how I was *and* eat pancakes. There were healthy size 0 girls. Why couldn't I be one?

Marcia cleared her throat and said, "So, how's it going?" She looked around as Jean, the last to finish, put down her pencil.

"Okay," Marcia said, "who would like to share?"

I took a deep breath, sucked it up, and raised my hand like I'd promised myself I would. "I'll go."

"Great!" Marcia passed me the 8 Ball.

I opened my mouth to read what I'd written, but no noise came out. Suddenly, I couldn't read what I'd said about food. I was embarrassed by all my wanting.

"Well, I want to get better. I want to run again. I want to, um, feel like I have a lot of energy."

Marcia looked around, her eyes inviting other people to respond to what I'd said.

"Those all sound like good goals, Elizabeth," said Jean obediently. "I liked the one about you having energy. I feel like I have more energy, but it makes me feel uncomfortable, like there's this voice inside my head that says I'm a failure if I have more energy, or want to eat."

I nodded, passing her the 8 Ball. That voice talked to me constantly, too.

"Do you think that's Jean's voice, or her eating disorder's voice?" Marcia asked. "The eating disorder's voice can be very strong sometimes. It doesn't want to let you go. It's a terrible bully. But that other voice, the one that is glad to have more energy, that's *you* talking."

Jean nodded, brows furrowed, like Marcia had just announced that cronuts were good for you. She wasn't convinced, I could tell.

"Remember, everybody," Marcia said, "that your eating disorder is not a person. It isn't *you*. If you have measles or chicken pox, are *you* measles or chicken pox? Are *you* strep throat? Or pneumonia? Or the flu? No, right? You might fight those illnesses, but they don't define who you are. Eating disorders are the same. They do not make up your being."

I got that, sort of. But who was I without it? "What would I think about all day? What would I do with all my time?"

I didn't realize I'd said that stuff aloud until it was too late. Everybody was staring at me. I wanted to reach up in the air and grab back every word.

Beth answered, "When I was first in recovery, it took me a while to figure out what to do with myself." She pulled her long gray cardigan tight around her shoulders and tucked her chin-length blond hair behind her ears. This was her third stint at a treatment center. She'd made it a whole year before she'd relapsed. This time was the worst, she said. It was like her anorexia had settled in her bone marrow and she couldn't get it out.

"But then, as time went on, I started to realize that I'd liked to do lots of things, back before all this stuff happened." As she spoke, the room was so quiet that you could hear new age music playing in the dance studio down the hall.

"Like what?" Willa finally asked.

"I liked to cook dinner. I loved taking college classes. Swimming was pretty fun, too. And I played field hockey. I was a forward, and I was good." Her cheeks reddened when she said that, like she was embarrassed to give herself credit. "After a while, I started cooking again, and I signed up for a class on Jane Austen." I knew she'd dropped out of college when she came back here. "I thought I'd finish college, finally. I'm twenty-three. All my high school friends are done with school, but I only have one semester of credits." Beth stopped talking, and everyone was quiet for a moment, thinking of all the things we used to do, before we got sick.

And then Jean spoke. "I hope Jasper forgives me." Jasper was Jean's horse. In group therapy, she'd told us how she hadn't missed a day riding him in ten years until she went into treatment the first time, six months after her coach said she needed to lose weight if she wanted to make the Olympic trials. She called Jasper her best friend.

"I had my bone scan yesterday," she said now, voice flat. "It turns out that I have osteoporosis in my back and osteopenia in my hips. My bones could break if I fall, so I can't ride."

Everyone in the room sat up a little straighter. We leaned in, as if getting closer would comfort her somehow.

"How long until you can ride again?" Allie asked.

"I *can't* ride again. Ever." Jean's voice cracked on the last syllable. "They're going to sell Jasper as soon as I get home. They're waiting so I can say goodbye."

I stared at Jean, trying to send her sympathy via mental telepathy, but that's not what she needed. She needed a hug. I jumped out of my seat and threw my arms around her. She started bawling. I cried too. How could I not? It was just all so sad. And I wasn't the only one.

Marcia waited until most of us were in the sniffle stage, and then she tried to lead us in figuring out why we were all crying at once.

"Maybe the 8 Ball knows," Margot said, which made us giggle. When she added, "Why don't you ask it?" we started full-out laugh-crying.

And that's how our Magic 8 Ball session ended.

# 27

**THE NEXT MORNING, AS I WAS GETTING OUT OF** bed, I felt a wetness between my legs. Was I leaking pee? Sweating for some reason? *Ugh. I hope not. Disgusting.* I went to the bathroom, and when I pulled down my underpants I didn't know whether to laugh or cry when I saw the bright red splotch. My period.

I was eleven and in the sixth grade when I got my period for the first time. I was the first of all my friends. Mom cried, and even though I asked her not to, she told Dad, who pulled me aside that same day and said, "I heard you got your little friend." Beyond humiliating.

When I told Katrina, she refused to believe me until I showed her the extra pad Mom had stuffed into my backpack. At the time, I was horrified. It was bad enough that I was the first girl in sixth grade to need a bra. Rance

Potter, a horrible boy I am happy to say moved to New Jersey in eighth grade and was never heard from again, announced that fact to our entire science class, telling everyone that I had the biggest boobs in sixth grade. If I could have chopped them off right then, I would have.

And here I was. First again. As far as I knew, I was the only girl in my cohort at Wallingfield to get her period. I felt ashamed, just like I had in sixth grade.

I didn't tell anybody except Nurse Jill, and that was only because I needed tampons, but people found out anyway. At group, I saw Allie looking at me funny. I realized later that my tampon was sticking halfway out of my pocket. If she knew, that meant everybody else probably did, too. I imagined all the girls around me feeling superior, that they weren't losing control of their body as much as I was, even though anorexia was supposed to be our sworn enemy.

That night, right before eight p.m., Simone came into my room and said, "Hey, congrats on your period."

*Sigh.*

And then, in the same breath, like she was asking if I wanted my door open or closed, she added, "Oh, Tristan wants to see you."

Of all the people in the world I wanted to see right now, Tristan was at the bottom of the list. No, he was below the bottom. He wasn't on it *at all*. I'd avoided him since the whole Charlie disaster by making sure not to be anywhere near the front door when Simone got dropped off or picked up. Whatever Charlie had told him couldn't be good.

*Elizabeth,* my rational side said, *it was two weeks ago.* Besides, Tristan knew. How could he not? Was that why he was here? To rub it in? I couldn't think of any other reason.

I turned to the door. "I don't want to—" But Simone had already vanished.

I swallowed and turned toward the mirror. I wished I'd showered.

My yoga pants were dirty, and my faded green sweatshirt with *Morgan Middle School presents* MY FAIR LADY in big letters on the front wasn't doing me any favors. I traded it for my favorite cardigan—a red, fluffy angora Mom got me for Christmas last year—and brushed off the lint.

Mom. Just the thought of her made me catch my breath. We'd ended things so badly at phone therapy. I should call and apologize, even if I wasn't sure what for.

*No. She should call me. She's the grown-up.*

I found Tristan alone on the cold patio, his back to me in a wicker chair, a second empty one beside him. I hadn't been outside in three days and I'd forgotten how good fresh air, even chilly air, felt in my lungs. I ignored the bite of it on my bare, sockless ankles. "Hey," I said, in as unfriendly a voice as I could.

*Stupid.* I shouldn't have said that until I got closer,

because now he turned and watched me lumber over to him, every little movement awkward and ugly. I tried doing what Mary said to do when I panicked like this. I told myself I was just nervous, that my body hadn't changed that much in the last week. It didn't work.

I sat next to him, and the wicker wheezed with my weight. I winced.

"These chairs creak when anybody sits on them," he said.

I didn't respond.

The seats were closer together than I realized. He smelled like something, something I couldn't quite place. Doughnuts. I *loved* doughnuts. Not that I'd eat one. But they were so good, especially when they were fresh and hot.

"You smell like cinnamon," I blurted out.

"It's probably the cider doughnuts I ate."

"From Russell Orchards?"

"Yeah. They're pretty awesome. You had 'em?"

"Yes." And then, without thinking, I added, "I could go for one right now."

"You could, huh?" His green eyes widened in surprise and he swiveled around to look at me, reading my face.

"I mean, if I wasn't here."

"Huh." He sat back in his seat.

It felt like five minutes but was probably only a few seconds before he finally said, "I heard about the whole Charlie thing."

I felt a prick of fresh embarrassment. "Did he tell you?"

"Yeah, in private. Heather, though, she sort of brought it up at lunch today. I guess he'd asked her not to tell and at first she didn't, but then they got in a fight yesterday and so she told everybody just to piss him off."

"Oh." I imagined Heather and Charlie and Tristan and all their friends sitting at one of the round wood tables in the cafeteria, laughing hysterically as Heather, eyes sparkling and in total story mode, tore me apart.

"What did Charlie say?"

Tristan paused. He reached in his pocket and whipped out his pack of Marlboros. Then he seemed to think better of it and put them back just as fast without taking one. "Nothing. He just let her talk."

I pulled the brass ring out from under my shirt and rubbed it between my fingers. It calmed me, like always.

"Did *you* say anything?"

"No." He stared at me rubbing the ring. "It wasn't my business. It was Charlie's."

"Oh." I don't know why I was surprised by his answer. "Figures."

He stared at me for a second and then looked up at the sky as if asking the clouds how to possibly deal with annoying people like me.

"Yeah. I should have said something," he said instead.

"Forget about it. It's not like we're friends or anything."

He shot me a look I can only describe as surprised. And hurt.

He stood up and took out his car keys. "Just so you know," he said, voice sharp, "I don't like half the shit Charlie does."

"Could have fooled me." I couldn't tell if I was standing up for myself or just being mean. Either way, it felt good.

"Look, I'm my own person."

I raised my eyebrows. "There's no doubt about that."

"Great. Fine. I'm out of here," he said.

"Fine," I said.

He took another cigarette out of the package. It broke between his fingers. "Shit," he said.

"You're going to get cancer, you know," I said, fuming.

He turned around then. "I'm *trying* to quit." And then he stomped across the patio and was gone. A minute later I heard his Jeep peel out down the driveway.

I sat there in the cold for a minute, waiting to feel embarrassed or sorry for the way Tristan and I left things. But I didn't. It had felt good to tell him how I felt. A month ago, I wouldn't have said a word. Who was this feisty Elizabeth? I had no idea, but I sort of liked her. She felt strong. And healthy. The kind of girl who would eat food and like it.

# *28*

AT FOUR O'CLOCK THE NEXT DAY, WHEN SIMONE
arrived, she walked into the hallway where Margot, Willa,
and I were sitting on the floor playing a card game.
"Tristan is here," she said, clearly annoyed. "He wants to
see you again. Sorry in advance."

What was that supposed to mean? With a sigh I headed
out to the foyer. I couldn't think of why he'd want to see
me after yesterday. Or for that matter, why I'd want to
see him.

Tristan stood up from the bench when I walked in. His
brown hair had fallen in front of his eyes and looked a
little greasy. He smelled like cigarette smoke. Clearly,
quitting wasn't working.

I didn't say anything.

He took a small paper bag out of his pocket and

thrust it at me. "I'm sorry about yesterday," he mumbled. "Here."

I didn't reach for it. It had grease spots. "What is that?"

"A peace offering." His green eyes caught mine. I looked away.

And then I smelled it. Cinnamon sweetness. A hint of apple. He'd brought me a cider doughnut. *Shit.*

"Go on, take it. It's for you." He shook the bag a little and put it down on the bench.

I didn't budge.

He frowned and pulled a second bag out of his pocket. "I got one for me, too."

There was no way I could eat that doughnut, even though it smelled amazing. Like, stomach-rumbling good. I tried to do what I always had in the past—turn on the part of my brain that made saying no easy, that would never even entertain the idea of putting something as fattening as a doughnut into my mouth.

"Elizabeth? Are you okay?" He looked at me like I might spontaneously combust or something.

And then Simone spoke up behind me. I hadn't heard her come back. "Tristan, Elizabeth is here for anorexia. She doesn't want a doughnut."

He stiffened. "Yesterday she said she did, okay?"

"What did you think, that you'd feed her a doughnut and everything would be great?"

"No. I—"

She didn't let him finish. "You have to stop doing this, Tristan. You aren't her doctor, okay?" Simone said, her voice sharp. Then she turned on her heel and left, muttering words we couldn't quite hear as she stormed away down the hall. Tristan's shoulders slumped and he glanced at me, his eyes pleading with me to take the doughnut.

But I couldn't do it. I left the bag on the bench. "I'm sorry," I said. "I'm so, so sorry." And then I ran off too, leaving Tristan alone in the foyer.

Back in my room I cursed myself and felt twisty inside because all I could think about was that stupid doughnut. I could practically taste the warm golden crust and the tender, hot insides the same color as vanilla cake. And I wanted it bad. I had half a mind to go back out there and see if the greasy bag was still on the bench.

One bite. That's all I'd take.

*No. No effing way.*

Fifteen minutes and my mind wouldn't budge. I told myself that Ray had probably found it and tossed it already.

Five more minutes of pacing and I told myself I'd just go check to make sure.

Tristan was gone, but the doughnut was still there.

I almost turned away, but the smell stopped me. It brought back memories—good ones—of when I was little: of the piles of fall leaves I liked to kick through on our front lawn, of how the crisp air felt on my cheeks, of having the freedom to run and skip and yell and not feel like an idiot doing it. It reminded me of everything I'd been before I even knew what a calorie was, like when I was ten and at Russell Orchards with Dad, eating hot doughnuts fresh out of the fryer without guilt or worry, and for a second I missed my old life so much that I ached.

Maybe that's why I didn't register the bag in my hand until I was back in my room. When I did, I threw it on my duvet like it was poison ivy and wiped my hands on my pants.

Then I opened it.

It looked like all the cider doughnuts I'd eaten as a kid. In other words, perfect.

I stood up and paced. I sat back down on the bed, plastic mattress pad crackling, and jiggled my foot. I jumped up again. I wanted it so, so bad. I wondered if this was what a heroin addict felt like right before he got his fix.

I pinched off a tiny piece of the crust with my thumb and pointer finger. Barely a taste. I put it on my tongue, swallowed, and then waited for something terrible to happen. I didn't know what that would be, but I knew it would come. I'd convinced myself that my body couldn't handle food like that anymore. I waited for my throat to close, my stomach to heave, or cramps to start. Anything.

But nothing happened. The bite was small, but the flavor was pure and delicious. I took another pinch, this time from the inside of the doughnut, and it, too, was as I remembered. And you know what? I was glad for that taste, that memory. But I was sad, too, because that time in my life was gone. I was ruined.

But . . . but what if I wasn't? There were people who'd survived anorexia all over the Internet. The day before I'd come here I'd seen a girl's blog where the title was one big run-on sentence: "I had anorexia and now I don't anymore and I love ice cream and I love who I am so suck it Ana!" Maybe I could be like that girl.

I'd love to eat ice cream again.

And then, just like I predicted, that bag was like a magnet and all I wanted was to vacuum up every single crumb with my big, fat mouth. Except that I didn't. I took another tiny taste, let it dissolve on my tongue, and then quietly, almost calmly, took the bag out into the hall and shoved it in the trash can.

I made it back to my room before I started shaking.

I sat on the bed and pulled my knees into my chest and yearned for the cookbooks I kept under my bed at home. They always distracted me. I don't know why looking at photos of food made me feel better, but it did. Mostly I just flipped through the pages, but once, the week before I came to Wallingfield, I'd baked something: a coconut cake with raspberry filling and cream-cheese frosting. My mouth watered just thinking about it.

I don't know why I'd entered cake-making mode that afternoon. I'd lost 5 pounds in eight days. I was a little delirious. My vision often spun, and sometimes I saw double. I'd been staying home sick a lot; I was just too tired to do anything. But then, on that day, I took out my favorite cookbook, *Cakes for All Occasions*, and it was like one minute I was reading a recipe and the next I was wrestling my old bike out of the garage and riding to the store to buy cake flour, cream cheese, coconut, and butter.

Three hours later, I'd baked a four-layer cake. My first. And I'd made it all without ingesting a single calorie. Not a lick of a mixing spoon or a finger-swipe of frosting. Nothing. I was so proud. I put it on a cut-glass cake stand I'd bought Mom at a vintage store a few years before for her birthday, back when I still thought that maybe she'd use it and bake something for me, back when I would have welcomed it.

When Mom walked in the door an hour later and dropped her keys on the table, she froze, her nose in the air like a dog sniffing for birds.

"What's that smell?" she said, almost dreamily.

I'd just finished cleaning the kitchen. "I baked."

She whipped around to face me. "Sorry, what?"

"I baked a cake."

"You baked a cake." She repeated the words back to me like I was a toddler.

"Yes. It's in the dining room."

Mom looked at me, alarmed, and rushed down the hall. I went upstairs.

A few minutes later I heard her on her phone. She sounded upset. And I got it. It was totally weird. Honestly, I didn't understand why I'd done it either. I barely even made myself a cup of coffee these days. "She baked a cake . . . No, really. I'm not kidding . . . I'm looking at it right now . . . It has coconut all over it . . . I don't know where she got the ingredients . . . She probably went to the store . . . Honey, she's sixteen and very capable of going to the grocery store by herself . . . What? . . . No! I will not have a piece to calm down . . . Just hurry up and get here."

She snapped her phone shut; I bolted to my room before she saw me and did sit-ups until my stomach burned.

When Dad came home, he whistled downstairs. I heard him say to Mom, "I think it's a good thing," and offer to cook dinner.

I came down at six o'clock to find that someone had put the cake in the middle of the dinner table. The top layer looked uneven; it had slid ever so slightly off to the left.

I fought the urge to fix it.

I sat down and Dad set a plate completely covered with a mountain of pasta, two meatballs perched on top like eyeballs. I hadn't eaten anything like that in months.

"To our wonderful chef," Dad said then, smiling at me.

"May you find your happiness here at our table." And then we clinked glasses and I realized that Dad was celebrating because he thought the "phase," as he liked to call my anorexia, had passed.

After a few minutes, Dad put down his fork. "Elizabeth, aren't you going to try it? I made your favorite." On the word *favorite* his voice turned to flat-out pleading. "Please, honey, take a few bites. I made it just the way you like."

I shook my head. I didn't have a favorite meal anymore.

On a regular night, Dad would have sighed and escaped as soon as possible. But now he refused to play his part. He slammed his fork on the table. Mom and I jumped. "Damn it! Elizabeth Barnes, take a bite of your dinner."

I shook my head, tears dripping off the end of my nose and onto my Parmesan. I so wanted to please him, to make him smile, to keep from breaking his heart. But I didn't have a choice.

"I can't," I cried, leaping up so fast I knocked over my chair. Then I bolted, leaving Mom and Dad sitting there in silence.

Later that night, after my parents went to bed, I snuck downstairs. The cake sat on its pedestal in the kitchen. One slice was gone—Dad, of course—and the whole thing was covered in plastic wrap. I unwrapped it slowly, one clear piece at a time. The delicious, sweet-and-slightly-sour smell of coconut and cream cheese drifted into my nose. I admired the moistness of the cake itself, the perfect pale yellow color of the layers, just like the cakes Martha Stewart made on her TV show. A lip of pale, rich frosting, perfect for a one-finger taste, clung to a cut edge. I scooped it up with my finger.

It smelled divine.

I brought it to my mouth, so close I could taste it. I knew how the frosting would feel silky on my tongue, how the cream cheese would cut the sweetness and make it delicious. I salivated. It would be so good.

I went to the sink and turned the hot water on high. And then, after one last sweet inhale, I put my finger under the hot water and watched the frosting melt away. I scrubbed until my skin was red.

After I shut off the water, I turned back to the cake, so pretty it could have been in a magazine. I fixed the crooked layer, pushing it back into place with a fingertip. When I picked it up, it was heavier than I'd thought it would be. "Sorry, cake," I whispered. Then, with all my strength, I hurled it into the garbage can and watched all four layers sag down its metal insides, leaving a thick trail of frosting behind.

Now, though, as I pulled on my PJs in my room that still smelled faintly of cider doughnut, I wished I'd at least tasted the frosting. I bet it was delicious.

# 29

SATURDAY CAME BEFORE I WAS READY FOR IT. AT home, I loved Saturdays. I'd go for a long run, then sit around and drink coffee, and then Katrina and I would hang out or go to the mall or something. But at Wallingfield? Not so much. It was Family Day, which meant a group session and lunch with our parents. Everyone pretty much hated it.

I still hadn't talked to Mom since our phone therapy appointment. We were at a standoff, and I was determined not to be the one to give in first.

At 10:30, people started to filter in. From my spot on the couch in the common room, I watched the reunions taking place. There were tears (sometimes), happy squeals, awkward silences, and one angry tirade when Coral yelled at her parents about being late, which they weren't. They just stood there looking exhausted.

Beth's parents sat on either side of her on a couch. They talked quietly. Allie gave her parents a tour. I wondered whether she'd take them to the fishbowl—*And here, Mom, is the room where we go when we're super screwed up. See how windows surround it? That's so that the nurses can watch us all the time to be sure we don't kill ourselves or run in place for six hours straight. I love the dull brown decor, don't you?*

By 11:15 I began to wonder if my parents weren't coming. To be honest, I was a teeny-tiny bit hurt. Despite all my mixed-up feelings, I wanted *them* to *want* to come. And then, at 11:27, when I'd just about given up waiting for them, there they were, walking down the hall toward my room. A little blip of glad went through me, but only for a second. "Hey," I said super casually, like I didn't care. "I thought you weren't coming."

They didn't take my bait. "Well, hello to you, too," Mom said.

She wore an expensive-looking blouse I hadn't seen before, pearls, a black skirt that went to her knees, and black boots. I bet she'd bought her outfit just for today.

Her eyes traveled my body, and when she got to my legs, she pursed her lips before forcing an I-love-my-daughter-and-am-so-happy-to-see-her smile. That's when I remembered why I hadn't wanted them to come.

But then Mom opened her arms, and for a second I forgot I was mad at her. She smelled familiar and all Mom-like and I squeezed her hard, not wanting to let her go.

We were mid-hug when it all came back: the phone conversation, the way she hadn't called all week, and I pulled away. She pretended not to notice, saying in this fake perky voice instead, "When is lunch? I can't wait to eat!" Her voice kicked up a notch at the end, like she'd rehearsed in the car or something.

Dad winced.

And just like that, my warm feelings for her turned to ice. "Mom, when have you ever been excited for lunch?"

"I don't know what you mean. I love lunch!"

I didn't know this person, this TV-ad mom, chipper and sunny and incredibly annoying.

Maybe that's why I imitated her tone when I said, "There is cheese and yogurt and salad with TONS of dressing— full-fat ranch! And muffins, and bread, and all sorts of stuff we never have at home. Everybody has to eat everything." I watched her face. She just stared at me, her face blank. "And they told us to watch you guys today, because you'd show us what normal people eat like."

That last line was a lie. Nobody had said that to us. But finally, my mother would have to eat everything on her plate. Everything.

Mom watched me for a moment and then said softly, "Look, Elizabeth, I am trying, okay? I'm really trying." I didn't acknowledge her or the little tug of remorse inside me.

As we walked into the dining room we passed Margot, tray in hand. She'd told me her parents weren't coming, acting like it was no big deal.

"Margot," I said, a little too quickly. "Meet my parents. You guys, this is Margot." Mom looked her up and down. For a minute I was ashamed of my friend and her black-dyed hair with its mouse-brown roots, her faded black T-shirt, jeans worn through at the knees, and holey black Converse high-tops. She looked like a slob. "So, um, where are you eating?"

She replied drily, "The orphans get to eat in the guest dining room."

Through the doors in the back of the room I could see a lonely table where two girls were already sitting, hunched over their trays.

I reached out to touch Margot's shoulder in sympathy, but I wasn't fast enough. She turned to my parents, said, "Nice to meet you," and left.

Mom looked after her, eyes narrow. "Where do we know her from?"

"We don't."

"Yes, I'm sure of it. Who is she?" I knew Margot hated

being defined by her last name, but before I could control myself, I blurted out, "She's Margot *Camby*, Mom."

"Oh!" She looked toward the doors where Margot had disappeared. "That's how I knew her. You two took ballet when you were six. I think she went by Merry then." Mom leaned in close and, in a whisper, said, "She was such a darling-looking little girl. What a shame."

"Mom! That's not nice!" Only five minutes in and she was already judging. "We aren't supposed to talk like that about people."

We picked our way through the room, looking for seats. "Well, this isn't so bad," Mom said. They'd put pots of bright red, yellow, and orange Gerbera daisies on the tables. It looked like a nursing home.

"They never have flowers on the tables," I said. "It's for you guys."

"Oh." Her smile flickered like a dying lightbulb.

Then Nurse Jill stood up. "Hello and welcome! We are so happy to have you here. I have enjoyed getting to know each and every one of your beautiful girls. They are wonderful, strong, resilient spirits who bring light and life to our facility." Apparently everybody was going to lie today. She stood with her hands clasped as if she were a happy nun about to sing "Climb Every Mountain."

Then she announced, like we were at a wedding or something, "The buffet is now open. Enjoy!"

The buffet was for the families only. I grabbed my loaded green tray like usual and went back to the table. Mom and Dad ambled over to the food line with the rest of the parents, all silently sizing each other up, reassuring themselves that they were better parents than, say, Allie's mom, who waited in line with big rocks on her fingers, a Botoxed face, and probably half a bottle of foundation caked onto her skin.

Willa's mom waited behind my parents. When she came out of the kitchen with her tray, Willa sat up straight and smiled. She suddenly looked different, sparkly almost. She looked twelve. Like, normal twelve, like a kid who would be hanging out at the mall food court on Fridays with her friends while a mom sat off to the side, trying not to look. Willa's mother sat down beside her and they leaned into each other, both looking really happy.

My parents, on the other hand, were like a before photo for an anti-anxiety drug.

"Well, doesn't this look delicious!" Mom said, perching on the edge of her chair after they'd found me. Dad handed her a bowl of lettuce and a yogurt. Then he passed over a turkey-and-cheese sandwich. "This isn't mine," she said.

I guess trying wasn't so high on her list after all.

Dad shot her a look. "Yes, it is. Remember how much you were craving a sandwich in the car?" This was interesting. Dad never made Mom eat. Ever.

"Right," she said, paling under her foundation and blush. She poked the bread with a finger. "Looks delicious."

"The selection!" Dad said. "You can eat like a king here!"

Mom didn't take a bite. I didn't either. Finally Dad picked up his own sandwich. "Mmm . . . I'm starved," he said, taking a monster bite, tearing through the tomato, the lettuce, the whole wheat bread, and the smoked turkey. It was so easy for him.

"Honey, do they have mayonnaise?" he said, still chewing.

"I . . . um . . . I don't know. I could ask, I guess."

Dad suddenly looked ashamed. "No worries. Never mind. The sandwich is delicious, and my waistline doesn't need any mayonnaise anyway." He looked stricken. "I mean, sorry, I . . ."

I shrugged. "I'll ask."

Nurse Jill got a little cup of it from the kitchen and brought it to Dad. "Thanks," he said, smiling at her. "Bet you don't get many requests for that around here!" He looked stricken again. Nurse Jill smiled and walked away. "Sorry, honey," he said. "This is all a little strange for me."

I shrugged again.

I still hadn't touched my meal. Mom hadn't either.

Dad said, "Karen, the salad looks delicious," which was obviously code for *Eat, Karen*.

"Um, yes, it does," she said nervously.

I watched her stab a bit of lettuce with her fork and delicately dip the tip of it into her plastic container of dressing. She put it to her mouth, touched it with her tongue, and placed it in between her teeth. She caught me staring and started to chew.

I knew how she felt, but I didn't say anything. I just watched, chewing my peanut butter and jelly sandwich. I still had a granola bar, a banana, and a yogurt in front of me.

I looked around. All the other moms were eating like it was no big deal, like they did this all the time. And here was mine, taking bird-size bites she could barely handle. Why couldn't she just be *normal*?

"Mom, aren't you going to eat?"

My parents stared at me. My mother turned red.

"Mom! It is so hard to eat when you're acting like that. You're supposed to model normal behavior for me!" Before Wallingfield I'd watch Mom eat and feel guilty if I ate more than she did. Now, though, I saw her eating for what it was. Screwed up. I opened my granola bar and broke off a piece. I forced it in my mouth.

Mom put her fork down and stared silently at her plate.

Dad hissed, "Elizabeth, that's enough!" loud enough that a couple of parents glanced in our direction.

"Sure, Dad, take her side, like always." I took a miserable bite of banana.

Nurse Jill stood up. "Excuse me, everybody," she said. "We have ten minutes left for lunch, and then we'll begin the family program. Ten minutes, everybody. Enjoy!" The word *enjoy* seemed especially cruel.

For the rest of lunch we sat in silence, Mom and me struggling, Dad having no idea what to do about it. With every bite I took I was convinced Mom was watching me, worried about the food making me fat. I knew what Mary would say—*Elizabeth, most likely your mom is worried about her own meal and not paying attention to yours*—but I couldn't process her words. I finished, but barely.

When Nurse Jill finally announced that lunch was over, I didn't know who was more relieved: Mom, Dad, or me. Without a word, Mom walked out of the room, leaving Dad, her untouched lunch, and me behind.

I followed her. When I glanced back, Dad was still sitting there, staring at Mom's full plate like the saddest man in the world. Considering the people in the room, that was saying a lot.

# 30

ALWAYS ONE TO KEEP UP APPEARANCES, MOM saved two seats next to her in the group therapy room. Reluctantly I took one, careful to leave a seat between us. I crossed my legs and folded my arms across myself.

Simone and her parents sat in the front row. I thanked the universe Tristan wasn't with them.

Margot was in the last row with the other "orphans." She'd wrapped a huge knitted scarf around her neck and I could see an earbud peeking out of one side. Smart girl.

Behind us, Willa was negotiating with her mom. "I want to go home," she pleaded. "Please don't make me stay here. What do I need to do to get you to take me with you today?" Her mom seemed so great. Just watching them at lunch—the way she leaned in when Willa talked, and laughed when she spoke, and hugged her when she finished her lunch made me jealous. And annoyed at Willa. I wanted to turn around and say, *If you want to go home so bad, Willa, eat something! Stop hiding your food!*

"Um . . . hello?" Mary tapped the microphone. The chatter in the room died down. "Thank you all for coming. The point of this meeting is to give parents and patients a chance to share experiences. So often, when I speak to people dealing with an eating disorder in their family, they speak of feeling like no one else can understand what they are going through." A few people around the room nodded in agreement. "Well, here at Wallingfield, you are not alone. We are in this battle together."

She talked about Wallingfield and what it wanted (us to get better) and who needed support (everybody). Then she said, "I'd like to open the floor up to you. No need to raise hands."

No one spoke. Only the shuffling of feet and an occasional cough broke the silence. And then, in the row in front of us, Jean's father stood up. He was tall and narrow like his daughter. Awkwardly, he walked to the front and took the mic.

"My name is Frank Parsons. I'm here to support my daughter, Jean. I guess what I want to say today is that it is really hard as a dad to know that your baby girl is hurting and that the situation is completely out of your control. But I want to thank everybody here at Wallingfield for taking such good care of our Jean and, to some extent, taking care of her parents, too. This has been the darkest year of our lives, but we are comforted to know she is so well cared for here. She looks wonderful. Healthy. Happy. So thank you." Nurse Jill and others nodded. He sat down and gave Jean's shoulder a squeeze. Jean leaned into him.

Willa's mom got up next. She cleared her throat before speaking. "As some of you know, I am not Willa's biological mother."

I felt my eyes widen and I resisted the urge to turn around and say to Willa, *What?*

"I adopted her out of foster care when she was five. Since then, she has been my beacon of light. But the last couple of years have been hard. Terribly hard for both of us. I want to thank Wallingfield for caring for my baby so well. I wonder sometimes why the good Lord would pile so much on one little girl's shoulders. But I have faith Willa will persevere. Thank you."

Willa was adopted? Why hadn't she ever said anything?

And then I heard Mom's folding chair creak. She stood almost defiantly, picking her way through the crowd of about thirty parents and patients until she reached the microphone. I forgot all about Willa. I prayed Mom was just going to do the same thing as the other parents. Thank Wallingfield, profess her undying love for me, and then sit down.

"Hello?" The microphone whined. Mom's head snapped back. Mary darted out of her seat and fiddled with the knobs on the amplifier. The whining cut out. Mom leaned in again. "Hello . . . So, I am Elizabeth's mom." I looked over to see Dad gripping the metal edge of his chair.

"I came here today relieved, because I knew Elizabeth was safe. I didn't have to worry about her." Willa's mom nodded along with a few other parents. "So thank you, for your care and concern for our daughter." Then Mom leaned closer to the mic like it was an ear and she had a secret. I sat up straighter. "This has been a tough experience for all of us. Right before Elizabeth was admitted, the doctor told me I needed to model good eating habits for my daughter. I always thought I had—we live a healthy life, at least in my opinion. We did everything we were supposed to—no sweets, no carbs, low fat or fat free whenever possible. A healthy weight is a part of that. That's why, when the scale snuck up, I would monitor my food more carefully. And I did the same for Elizabeth because I didn't want her to ever feel ashamed of her appearance. We would talk about it together, the importance of staying fit and trim." The room was quiet—so quiet that it felt like everybody else was holding their breath.

"I just meant for her to stay healthy. But apparently, I was supposed to just let her eat whatever she liked and never comment, even when she hit puberty and started to gain. Apparently saying something made me a bad parent." She looked around, but this time people didn't nod. They just sat there, staring at their laps. Dad's face was as white as a dinner plate.

I elbowed him. "Make her stop," I whispered.

He didn't say anything. Mom kept going. I sank down in my seat until I could barely see her over the heads of the people in front of me. "And what about the moms I see in the grocery store? You know, the ones with the carts loaded up with frozen pizzas and ice cream and Kool-Aid and candy and . . . Well, you get the point. What about them? Aren't they bad parents too? Aren't they?"

She looked suddenly surprised, like she couldn't believe she'd just said all that out loud, here, in front of me. In front of everyone. Dad stood up and shimmied his way out of our row. Mom didn't seem to notice. When he got up to where she was, he took her arm, but she shook him off, cleared her throat, smoothed her skirt again, and leaned into the microphone one last time. "But now I'm thinking that maybe I am. A bad parent. And I feel terrible. But what does that help?" She paused. She let Dad put his hand on her elbow this time. "Thank you," she said, and stepped away from the microphone. Except, instead of coming back to her seat, she walked straight out of the room. Dad left too. Abandoned, I sat in my seat for a moment, too stunned to know what to do. After a moment or two, I stood up and

246

followed them out the door, every eye in the room watching me go.

When I turned the corner, Mom was crumpled on a chair in the hall. Dad was on one knee next to her, kneading her hand and speaking quietly. I hadn't even reached them when I heard footsteps behind me. It was Mary.

"Is there anything I can get you?" she asked them softly, like she was a funeral director or something.

"No, thank you," Mom said, laughing humorlessly. "I'm sorry about what happened in there. I don't know what came over me. It's just a difficult time. That's all."

Mary shook her head. "Don't worry, Karen. Why don't we go into my office where we can speak privately?"

"No, thank you," Mom said, clearing her throat and standing up. "Brian and I actually have to be going."

Dad looked startled. "Karen, I—"

"Brian," Mom said. "Elizabeth—I'm sorry. I can't stay. I need to collect my thoughts. Maybe in a couple of days . . ." She didn't look at me.

"What? You guys are leaving?" I said, my voice wavering. "How can you just leave? We haven't met with Mary yet, and . . ."

"I know all that," Mom said, "but I can't do this right now. I am so sorry. Brian, I'll be in the car." She looked pale and like she might pass out.

"Mom, did you have breakfast?" I said this softly. I didn't want to make her feel worse, but I had to know.

"Of course, Elizabeth. I had what I always had." She'd had nonfat Greek yogurt, exactly one measured half cup, half of the recommended serving size. A total of 65 calories. She ate it every day at exactly 6:45 a.m., no matter what her schedule. It was 1:30 now and she'd barely touched her lunch. She needed to eat something. For a second, I felt like the mother. "Mom, you haven't eaten enough today. Why don't we ask Mary for a sna—"

"Elizabeth, I'm fine." She turned to Dad. "I'll be in the car." Her high heels clicked down the hall.

Dad turned toward me. "Elizabeth, I . . ."

"Dad, stop." He couldn't make this better. Nobody could.

"But, honey, you need to . . ."

"Dad, Mom has a problem. Do you hear me? She needs help."

"What? I don't think so."

"Oh my God! How can you guys be so in denial? Mom. Doesn't. Eat. She doesn't. How can you not see that?"

"Elizabeth, I don't think it's fair—"

"Fair? You want to talk to me about fair? I'll tell you what's not fair. That I'm in here taking one for the team while you and Mom just turn your heads and pretend she's normal. You know what? Go," I cried. "Now. Go, okay?"

"Honey, I think that your mom, she's ju—"

The look I gave him shut him up.

He cleared his throat and tried again, speaking fast. "She's upset. It isn't that she doesn't love you or support you. She's hurting, that's all."

"What? She's hurting? SHE'S hurting? When are you going to wake up? Look at me! Look where I am!" The family meeting had ended and people were coming out of the community room.

Somewhere in my anger I heard Mary. "Elizabeth, let's take this into my office, where . . ."

"No," I said. "I'm done." I left my dad in the hallway and ran to my room. That short sprint, a total of maybe fifty feet, set adrenaline coursing through my body and all I wanted to do was keep running, but I was already at my door, stuck in this stupid hospital. Stuck with my crappy mother. Stuck with my own crazy thoughts.

Ten minutes passed. I rolled over on my back and looked at the ceiling. It had those tiles where, if you threw a newly sharpened pencil hard enough, straight up, it would stick. We had those in Mr. Roberts's US History classroom. Whenever he turned his back, people would chuck their pencils at the ceiling. A few would stick, but most wouldn't and they'd end up clattering onto the linoleum floor. He never admitted that he knew what we were doing; he'd just ask in his most cynical voice why so many people were always dropping their pencils. *I have duct tape if your fingers can't hold a writing implement,* he'd say crankily.

When the knock came I didn't get off my bed. I wondered who'd drawn the short straw to come talk to me—Mom or Dad.

"Go away," I said, even as I realized that I didn't really want them to leave.

"Elizabeth," Willa said through the door, "can I come in?"

I didn't answer right away. I didn't want Willa to see me cry. Willa at my door meant that my parents had left. They'd gotten in their car, put on their seat belts, started up the engine, and left me without even saying goodbye. When I'd told Dad to go, I'd wanted him to refuse. I wanted Mom to come back inside, for them to still be waiting for me outside my door, unwilling to leave until they knew I was all right.

Willa knocked again. "Elizabeth? Are you okay?"

I wiped my eyes, opened the door a crack, and lay back down, this time on the carpet. The hard floor felt good. I don't know why. Willa and Margot stood over me, looking down.

"Hey," Willa said. "You're on the floor." Her tiny mass

was a shadow; the light from the bedside lamp seemed to shine through her.

"Yup," I said.

"Want to go to your bed?" Margot asked.

"Nope. I'll stay down here, thanks."

They sat next to me on the floor. My parents might have left, but Margot and Willa were here. And that was something. Willa squeezed my hand.

"You're adopted?" I asked.

She nodded. "My mom is actually my aunt. My birth mother left me when I was four. Mom didn't even know I existed. It took a year for them to find her. She took me in when I was five and adopted me a year later, when my birth mom gave up all rights. I don't know for sure if my real mom is even still alive."

"I'm sorry, Willa." And then I touched her scars. I'd never asked about them before. "What happened here?" I asked softly.

"I used to cut myself. That's what got me in here. Well, that and my eating. The doctor, who I saw after I did this," she said, pointing to a thin red line across her wrist, "said I was the youngest self-harmer he'd ever seen, that it usually starts around fourteen."

"How old were you when you started?"

"Ten." Willa caressed her arm for a moment before pulling down her sleeves.

What are you supposed to say to something like that? If there was a correct response, I didn't know it. So instead of saying anything, I squeezed her hand. She squeezed back and put her head on my shoulder. Margot patted both of us a couple of times, and then it was time for snack.

# *31*

WEDNESDAY WAS HALLOWEEN, WHICH MEANT THAT
I'd been at Wallingfield for an entire month. Not that
you'd know it. The only thing that made October 31 different from all the other days was the rumor flying around
that we'd all have mini candy bars on our lunch trays.
And of course there was the joke Margot made at lunch.
"Funny how so many girls decided to dress up as skeletons
this year," she'd said, totally straight-faced.

By now, the sting from Saturday had mostly worn off.
When Mom's tirade came to mind, I no longer felt an im-
mediate stab of mortification. It had mellowed to a dull
throb. Mom and Dad had called, but I'd made Jean take
a message, and I'd never called back.

And then, after lunch, Nurse Jill found me, a white

padded envelope in her hand. "This came for you yesterday, but we missed it somehow. I am very sorry."

I wasn't. For once I wouldn't have the entire Wallingfield population staring at me. "Thanks," I said, ripping open the top flap and handing it to her to check. Again, there was no return address and a lot of American flag stamps. Another mystery. She looked inside, nodded curtly, and handed it back. Reaching in, I pulled out a spiral-bound journal with a picture of the sinking *Titanic* on the front. *What the hell?* Was I supposed to be like a sinking ship? A disaster? Or was it that I was *titanic*, as in *massive*? If this was supposed to be a joke, I wasn't laughing.

"Can I see?" Margot grabbed the book. She opened it and snort-laughed. Willa, right behind her, peeked over Margot's shoulder, her face like a little heart.

Inside, printed at the bottom of each page, was a quote in cursive:

*Seize the moment; remember all those women on the Titanic who waved off the dessert cart.*
—*Erma Bombeck*

I frowned. "Who's Erma Bombeck?"

Of course Margot knew. "She's a writer. My mom likes her. She's actually pretty funny, which is shocking, because usually Mom has terrible taste."

"Oh," I said. How her parents didn't recognize her intelligence was beyond me. Sometimes when I was with her, I felt small, but not like size 0 small. Stupid small.

She looked thoughtful. "That quote is sort of inspiring, in a twisted way."

I didn't find it inspiring at all. If I started to think of all the things I'd missed out on because of my stupid eating disorder—all the times that, Erma Bombeck would say, I'd skipped "dessert"—I was going to wish I *had* been on the *Titanic*.

But still. I flipped it over. Someone had highlighted the description on the back that read, *250 college-ruled pages*. Weird, the highlighting. Why highlight that? A picture of me stammering like an idiot on the day Simone arrived flashed through my head. Besides Simone, there was only one person who knew I'd needed a new journal. And that I hated wide-ruled.

Tristan.

# 32

**WHY?**

Why would Tristan, if it even was Tristan, send me anything? Charlie would hate him for it. He was big on loyalty—bro code, he called it. And number one was that friends' girlfriends—and ex-girlfriends—were off-limits. When Charlie told me that one night while hanging out in his basement, the feminist in me said, "I get the girl-friend part. But exes, too? Girls aren't property."

"It's not about the girl," he'd replied. "It's about friend-ship."

Carefully, I spread what he'd sent me out on the bed. Every single present screamed Charlie. What was Tristan thinking? It was creepy. Stalker-esque even. Wrong on so many levels.

If Lexi were here, she'd help me figure this whole thing

out. Instead, all I had was another postcard. It had come yesterday, in the mail. This one had a picture of a golden retriever with three tennis balls in its mouth.

*Hi, ladies! Things are still good. I miss you all, though. Visiting Smith this weekend! Hoping they let me come back and finish the semester!! Fingers crossed! Miss you guys. xoxo Lexi*

I tucked the postcard into the back of the journal, parked myself on a couch in the common room, and used the first page to try to figure out my feelings. So far all I'd written was, *WTF?????????*

Nurse Jill tapped me on the shoulder. "Elizabeth?"

I turned around.

"Your mom is here to see you."

A couple of girls looked up. They all remembered my mom. Who could forget her?

At first I didn't move. But I knew she wouldn't go away, not without a face-to-face. "Thanks." I sighed and walked into the foyer, smoothing my hair and already regretting not changing into something a little nicer.

Mom was sitting on a bench, beige trench coat still on, looking tired and smaller than I remembered. She wasn't wearing any makeup. With a jolt I realized her jeans were an old pair of mine she usually wore for painting or other messy chores. I looked at her fingernails. No manicure. No perfect hair. Something was wrong.

"Hi." Her voice was soft.

Had something happened to Dad? To Grandma? "What's wrong?" I said, voice shaking.

She read my face in a heartbeat. "Oh, no, honey. Everybody is fine. I just wanted to talk. Is that okay?"

If this were a phone call, I could have said I had group or something. But now she was sitting here, looking like she might burst into tears, and it wasn't so easy to put her off. It scared me, seeing her like that. But I couldn't say no. "I guess so."

She surveyed my black pants covered in lint, my long-sleeved purple T-shirt, and my messy ponytail. I waited for the frown of disapproval. It never came. She just looked sad.

"I hated how we left things the other day. I came here to say I'm sorry."

"Oh." Sorry wasn't enough.

She walked to the window, arms crossed over her chest. "I understand why you're angry. I don't blame you."

I didn't look at her.

"You know, when you came here, I was convinced that they'd keep you a few days and then send you home a few days later."

*So was I.*

Out the window the tree branches, newly bare, scraped

against one another in the wind. "But then they said you needed to stay longer, and even though I argued with them, a part of me knew they were right."

She bit her lip. "And I realized that maybe this—where we are right now—that maybe it's all my fault, that I pushed you too hard to look a certain way. And I'm sorry about that."

I knew it wasn't all her fault. Even so, I would have thought hearing her say that would make me feel better. But it didn't. Mom's fragility scared me. My mom was diamond hard. She seemed unbreakable, and her I-know-better-than-you attitude always brought out the worst in me. When we'd fight I'd get meaner and meaner, just to try to wipe that look off her face. It never worked. Now that it was gone, though, I didn't know how to handle the person sitting in front of me, and I almost wanted her to put her hard shell back on.

She sighed. "You know, I've never liked the person I saw in the mirror."

Just like me.

She twisted her green Kate Spade bracelet, the one Dad got her for Christmas last year. I coveted that bracelet. "In high school, I felt like I didn't have a personality worth sharing. I always thought of myself as this mousy girl no one noticed. It was a terrible feeling. I didn't want you to feel that way."

What? Grandma was full of stories about Mom from high school, about how she'd throw parties and get caught, or how she'd sneak out at night. "Mom, you were really popular in high school."

"It might have seemed that way, but I always felt like an imposter, like no one knew me. It was a terrible loneliness, Elizabeth. Terrible. I hated who I was. I constantly compared myself to other girls in my classes, and I always came up short. For me, dieting helped. Looking better on the outside helped me feel more like I was a match for my friends. And as you got older, I worried that you'd feel the same way."

I wanted to dismiss her, but the scariest thing was that I knew exactly what she was talking about. I wasn't about to admit that, though.

"You thought I'd hate myself?"

"Oh, honey, no."

"But you just said that you saw in me what you hated in yourself."

"I'm sorry. That's not what I meant. I could never think that. My problems and my realities were never yours. I was projecting. That's what I meant." Mom reached into her bag. She grabbed a tissue and held it in one white-knuckled fist.

"How?"

"How what?"

"How did you figure all this out?" Mom wasn't about the feels. Ever.

"Well, to tell you the truth, I've started seeing a counselor."

"What?" Mom? Seeing a shrink?

"Yes, well, your father and I both have. At first, it was to understand what was happening with you. But as it turns out, the counselor thinks I have a few issues to work on, too."

She put her hand on mine. I let it stay there. Her skin was soft.

"Do you agree?" I asked.

"Agree with what?"

"That you have issues?"

"Sure. Who doesn't have issues?"

"But what about issues with eating? And your weight? Does your counselor think you have those?"

She brushed a piece of imaginary lint off her sleeve and didn't look at me. "Oh, I don't know, Elizabeth."

"Well, does she?"

"Yes, but I'm not convinced. I—"

"Mom, you eat, but barely. You're so picky; it isn't normal."

"It's normal for me, Elizabeth. And I'm fine."

She was in such denial, and there was nothing I could say to change her mind. I knew that, because there would have been nothing anybody could have said to change my mind. Until I got bad enough, that is. And Mom had never crossed that line. She'd straddled it, sure, but she'd never gone full anorexic. Lucky her.

"But one thing I know for sure, Elizabeth, is this. We need to focus on your recovery. Your dad and I want you to get well so much. You are our everything. And you shine, Elizabeth. So much. I'm so sorry that I didn't help you to see that."

I nodded. It was weird to hear Mom apologize. She didn't usually do that.

"And I should never have said it would be great for you to lose a few pounds. Moms aren't supposed to say that stuff."

"But you said it because it was true, Mom. You thought I was fat."

She wiped her eyes, but she didn't deny it. "I'd take it all back in a second if I could."

She couldn't, though. The words were a part of me. But still. She was trying. "I know," I said.

Then I reached over and hugged her. She felt like bones. Her clammy skin chilled me. She wasn't comforting—or comfortable.

And that's when I wondered if that's what Charlie felt when he hugged me.

# *33*

**AFTER MOM LEFT, ALL I WANTED TO DO WAS RUN.**
Or walk, at least. Through the window I could see a path
that led into the woods, blanketed with pine needles. I
hungered for it. But we weren't allowed off the patio, so all
I could do was head for the nearest chair in the sun. I lifted
my eyes to the clear blue sky and felt my soul stretch. It
was so, so cold, but I didn't care. I'd barely settled in when
Simone's voice cut through the quiet. "Elizabeth! Hey."

*Please, not now.*

Her voice turned bossy. "Say hi."

"Hi, Elizabeth."

Tristan. I froze, then slowly turned around.

His face matched the crimson color of Simone's Boston
College sweatshirt. He glared at his sister, who had a tight
grip on his arm. "Get off me. Now."

She raised her eyebrows at him. "Say sorry."

"Sorry," he said, not sounding sorry at all. "About the doughnut. I didn't mean to upset you."

"It's fine." The whole doughnut thing felt like it had happened centuries ago. Screw the doughnut. We had bigger things to discuss.

I took a deep breath. *Do it, Elizabeth. Just do it.* "Tristan, can I talk to you? Alone?" Simone took a half step back in surprise, her eyes widening so much I could actually see them through her eyeliner.

"Okay." His eyes darted between his sister and me.

Simone didn't move. "Simone, get out of here," he said.

"I'm going, I'm going." With one last glare at her brother, she went inside.

A few girls smoking at the other end of the patio glanced over at us. Coral held court in the middle, telling a story that was eliciting shrieks of laughter. "Come on," I said, grabbing his arm and pulling him to the opposite end.

I spit it out before I lost my nerve, talking so fast that my words jumbled together. "I know you sent me those packages in the mail."

"What are you talking about?" He looked at me like I'd gone crazy. But I knew what I knew. Didn't I?

"The packages with the tons of stamps? The jar of sand? The poster?" I pulled the brass ring out from under my sweater and waved it at him. "This? The journal? It was you."

He just stared at me, his face blank.

"It was you," I said. "Wasn't it?"

"Not me. Sorry." He pulled out his pack of cigarettes but put them away without taking one. Maybe he really was trying to quit.

I tried again. "But you highlighted the journal—where it said 'college-ruled.' It *had* to be you. Nobody else knew about that."

He shrugged his shoulders.

I had a horrible sense of déjà vu. "Please, I—"

"Yeah, uh, no."

I held myself together by wrapping my arms around my chest. "But . . ."

"You're looking in the wrong place." Then, without even saying goodbye, he turned and walked, fast, across the patio.

I'd done it again.

# *34*

**I WENT TO MY ROOM. HOW COULD IT NOT BE HIM?**
It had to be.

I'd been so sure.

By dinner, I'd decided that Tristan had lied, and I was right. The clues were too obvious to ignore.

By evening snack, I'd changed my mind. I'd made a colossal error. Tristan wasn't the guy. I'd humiliated myself. Again.

By bedtime, only one thing was completely clear: I was a fool.


I didn't tell anybody what happened between Tristan and me. When I woke up the next morning, I had the luxury, for a second, of having completely forgotten what had happened.

And then I remembered, and the day passed in a daze, until right before my Mary session. That's when Simone caught up with me in the hall.

"Elizabeth?"

When I turned around, it was like Tristan's eyes were staring at me from Simone's head.

"This is for you." Simone held out a battered blue iPod shuffle with white earbuds.

I didn't touch it.

Simone held it out farther. "Take it. Please?"

"No." I sounded like a stubborn toddler refusing to eat peas.

She pressed it into my hand. "It's from Tristan."

Obviously.

Next, she handed me an envelope with my name on the front. The handwriting was familiar.

I'd seen it on all the packages. "What's going on, Simone?"

She ignored my questions. "Just listen. His playlists are really good. He used to make them for me all the time." Simone tucked her hair back behind her ears. Then she leaned in closer. "You were right, you know. Tristan sent those packages."

"What?" Relief flowed through me. I wasn't delusional. But he'd lied to me. What an asshole.

"Did he send you here to say that?"

"No. I'm actually not supposed to tell you anything. Look, I know he comes off as a grouch, but he's an okay guy."

"But why didn't he just say it was him? Did he send me all that stuff to make fun of me? Was Heather in on this? I mean, the things he sent—"

"I don't know, I guess he wanted to keep the whole secret thing going, but then when you figured it out, he kind of freaked and just denied it."

"Well, why me, then?"

She smiled a sad, tiny smile. "Why not you?"

I didn't respond.

She stood a little taller. "Look, I have to go. I'm going to be late for my nutrition meeting." And then she walked off down the hall, the heels of her Doc Martens scuffing with every step. At the corner, she turned around. "Give him a chance, Elizabeth," she said. "Underneath everything he's a good guy."

I opened the envelope right there. Inside were two folded pieces of lined paper. The first was a playlist, titled *J-Curve*. The second was a note.

> Elizabeth,
> Okay, so you're right. I sent those packages. I'm not always good with words but I thought these things— things that mattered to you—might cheer you up. You

just seem so . . . sad. And I don't want you to be sad.
Sad sucks. The world is tough enough already without
a bunch of sad people walking around in it.

So I made you a playlist. Even if you think I'm a
jerk, you should listen to it. Think of it as an anti-sad
playlist. Put it on if you're feeling low, or shitty, and
keep listening. It'll let you wallow for a few songs, then
it will cheer you up. Like the letter J.

And, oh yeah, sorry about yesterday. Also, I accept
your apology for not eating my doughnut.

—Tristan

With everything that was happening, I forgot about my session with Mary until she stuck her head out her door to look for me.

The minute I sat down, she said in a suspiciously perky voice, "Elizabeth, I'd like to talk with you about something."

"What's wrong?" I held my breath.

"Nothing's wrong, Elizabeth. I met with your team about your discharge date."

"Oh." I sat up straighter. I'd had a feeling this was coming ever since I'd gotten my period.

"We are really pleased with your progress. Your health has stabilized, and you've increased the range of foods you are willing to eat. You don't have as much anxiety. The fact that you've started to menstruate again is important. And your BMI is up. So, keeping all that in mind, we've set a date to get you home."

"How much weight have I gained?"

Mary looked at me for a long minute. "You are currently a hundred and four pounds."

"Oh." I felt the panic set in deep, at the bottom of my stomach. I took a deep breath. Fourteen pounds. I could live with 14 pounds. Right?

"Elizabeth, we're proud of you. You've worked so hard."

A hundred and four pounds. A nagging voice in my head kept saying, *Fourteen ugly pounds! Fourteen gross pounds!* But I ignored it the best I could, because, in a weird way, I did feel proud.

Maybe I was ready to go home.

I thought of my bed first. My wonderful, comfy bed. I'd get to sleep in it again!

Then I thought of myself back in the school cafeteria, everybody looking at me as I carried my tray. I had no idea what I'd eat or how much.

And what would school be like? What about Priya and Shay? Should I act mad at them for totally blowing me off? Pretend nothing ever happened? And what about Charlie? And Heather? And Tristan? Would we still be friends outside Wallingfield? Suddenly, right where I was felt like the safest place—the only place—for me in the world.

"When am I leaving?"

"We're looking at next Friday, November ninth."

One week. Holy crap.

Mary watched me carefully. "I know this can feel overwhelming. We'll take it a little bit at a time."

A little bit at a time. No matter how little the bits were, it was only a week away. A week!

"One of the first things we do to prepare you is make sure our patients have at least one real-world eating experience before they leave."

That's what Lexi had skipped before she left. Nurse Jill sometimes took girls out to eat at a local restaurant, Finch's Bar & Grille.

Unfortunately, it was the most popular dinner place in Esterfall.

"You're on the list for dinner next Wednesday, the seventh," she said with a big smile, like suffering through dinner with a bunch of other anorexics and a nurse was an honor.

"What? Do I have to go?"

"Elizabeth, we can talk it through. I think you're ready for this."

"Who else is coming?"

"Jean."

That made me feel a little better. "Is she going home soon?"

"It appears that's the case."

Good for her. She'd been here for so long. I wondered if she was scared out of her mind, too.

"We'll go over the menu ahead of time so that there aren't any surprises. You can do this."

No, I couldn't. "Please, Mary, I can't go. I'll see people I know at Finch's. It'll be really, really, really humiliating." Tristan, Charlie, and Heather ate there all the time. "And I . . . and I . . . I think it might make me less ready to go home."

"Why do you think that?"

"If I screw up and order the wrong thing, I might have a relapse."

"Well, if that happens, we can talk about it."

For the rest of the session, I dredged up reasons to not go out to eat, and Mary countered with strategies to "handle" my concerns. As I was leaving, she said, "Elizabeth, you can do this. You are going to be fine."

"Define *fine*," I said from the doorway.

"Okay." She set down her pen. "You'll be fine because you are tough and strong and have learned a lot while you've been here. You'll have support from all of us to help you with any negative thoughts. You'll already know what you will eat ahead of time because you and Sally will pick it together. And no matter how hard it may be, it is only two hours. Two hours."

Only two hours. Two hours could feel like a lifetime. Trust me, I knew.

Later that night, Simone found me in the common room. As she put on her wool coat, she said, "Tristan will be here any second. Will you come?"

I nodded and followed her to the foyer.

Tristan was already there, sitting on the bench with his legs crossed. He ran his hand through his hair like he always did. Simone turned to me, mouthed "Good luck," and disappeared back down the hall.

"So," he said, fiddling with a button on his navy peacoat, "I sent the packages."

"You told me that in your note."

"Right." He exhaled and looked around. "Well, what did you think of them?" For once his voice didn't sound defensive. It sounded hopeful.

"What? What was I supposed to think?"

"What do you mean?"

"What do I *mean*? You had to know how much the

stuff you sent would mess with my head. How it would remind me of Charlie. Why would you do something like that? Was it *funny* to you?"

He scowled. "What? No! Like I wrote, I just wanted to cheer you up."

"Cheer me up? You made me look like an idiot, Tristan. I called Charlie. Because of *your* presents. That's screwed up."

He sat straighter. "First off, that wasn't supposed to happen. And I never signed his name. You created the Charlie theory all on your own."

"Are you kidding me? You had to know I'd think that. I mean, look at what you sent."

Tristan's cheeks reddened. "That's not true at all. I sent you that stuff because I noticed you liked it. The brass ring? You used to talk about Flying Horses all the time."

Well, that was true, I guess. I *had* talked about Flying Horses a lot. Mainly because I was afraid Charlie would forget his promise to take me there. "The only reason I talked about that place was because Charlie said he'd win me a free ride someday, and I was excited."

"Look, all I remembered was that you talked about Flying Horses. And that brass ring was my lucky charm. I won it when I was twelve." He looked at the ring hanging from my neck. "I was trying to be nice."

I'd forgotten I was wearing it. I stuffed the red ribbon

inside my shirt. "Look, if you'd just signed your name, none of this would have happened."

He threw his hands up in the air. "I know! I know, all right? Believe me. But Simone said it might be sort of cool to get a mystery gift, like from a secret admirer. She said it might cheer you up. And I was only going to send that one thing. But then I was at the pizza place, and I saw those plastic rings, and I knew you collected them, and I . . . I don't know. I got one for you and mailed it."

"I only collected those rings because Charlie gave them to me."

"Oh." He rubbed the back of his neck. The tips of his ears were pink.

"And what about the sand? You knew Charlie and I loved the beach."

"Elizabeth, *everybody* loves the beach. Besides, I used to see you run there in the mornings."

"You did?" I sat down next to him.

"Yeah." He tapped his heel on the floor. It made the bench shake and I wondered what part of me would jiggle. *Don't think about it,* I told myself. *You need to focus on what is going on around you. Not on body parts.*

He jumped up and started pacing, his movements tense. "Sometimes I'd come down in the morning with coffee and there you'd be." Tristan's house had a private path to the beach. "And right before you headed back to the road, you always took a moment and climbed up onto the lifeguard stand and stared out at the ocean like you were meditating or something. I thought it was cool that you did that."

Back in the summer, before I got too weak to run, I ran the mile from my house to the beach every morning. I loved the briny smell and the sound of the waves, and when I sat high up on the wooden tower and focused on the horizon, my brain would quiet and I'd feel at peace.

Tristan sat down again, and his hand brushed mine.

I pulled it away.

"Tristan," I said, suddenly annoyingly shy. "Why me? If you wanted to do a good deed for some girl in here, why didn't you choose someone else?"

He stopped and stared at me then. He bit his lip for a second. "Don't you get it? I liked you, okay? I liked you. I might even still like you."

He couldn't like me. I was a mess on a good day. "Look, I appreciate everything you're saying, really. But I have to go. I just—I can't take this right now."

He stood up abruptly, his coat sliding to the floor. He picked it up and rammed his arms into the sleeves. "I'm sorry I made you so miserable. Don't worry, I won't send you anything else. I promise." He flung the door open and walked out.

Simone came around the corner, her black jacket in her hands. "You okay?" she asked.

"I don't know."

"Yeah, he didn't handle that very well." She sat down next to me.

"You listened?"

Simone shrugged and sighed. "If I tell you something, you have to promise not to tell anybody, okay?"

I nodded.

"Not even your friends. Or even your mom."

I would never tell Mom about this. "Okay, I get it."

She settled herself on the bench. "So remember when Charlie asked you out that day in Scoops?"

"Of course."

"Well, Charlie wasn't supposed to do that. He knew Tristan liked you. They were going into Scoops to check you out."

"What?"

"Yeah. Charlie was supposed to be Tristan's wingman. But then he asked you out instead. Tristan was super pissed, but he didn't say anything."

"Why not?"

"I don't know. Tristan was mad for a day or two, but then he let it go. He figured that Charlie would dump you or Heather would get to him like always. But then Charlie started to actually like you, and he was so different. He was *nice*. He actually apologized to Tristan, saying he was so sorry, but that he lov—" She stopped.

Charlie loved me?

"You were so into Charlie that Tristan figured he'd never had a chance anyway."

"Charlie never said anything about this."

"Well, why would he? You probably would have thought he was a jerk."

Right after it happened, maybe. But not much longer after that. I'd seen Charlie be an asshole to plenty of people, but he was never mean to me, and that was one of the reasons I liked him so much. He made me feel special.

A horn honked outside. Simone ignored it. "Anyway, he told me he was going to send you his brass ring, and I suggested that he make it a mystery. I mean, who doesn't want a secret admirer?"

"I can't believe this."

Simone continued. "Look, I didn't know the shit he chose had anything to do with Charlie. But I guess that makes sense. I mean, think about it. He only hung out with you when Charlie was around."

She was right. We were never alone. Except once. In July. And just like that, I solved the riddle of the umbrella, the one gift I hadn't been able to figure out.

I'd been walking to work on Route 127. A thunderstorm

had rolled in and the wind turned my umbrella inside out. As I tried to fix it, a car roared by me, drenching me in a tidal wave of puddle water. Dirty rivulets ran down my face and silt burned my eyes.

I was so in shock that I didn't notice Tristan's Jeep until he'd reversed all the way back to me.

"Hey," he said. "Sorry about that. You okay?"

I grimaced.

"You're soaked. Do you need a ride?" I could tell he wanted me to say no, but it was already 1:56. I had four minutes to clock in. Sharon, my boss, was going to murder me if I was late.

My wet white T-shirt clung to my chest like Scotch tape. "Okay," I said, wiping my eyes, "I'll take a ride," and I climbed in, shivering in the air-conditioning.

I'd only been in the Jeep once before, after a beach bonfire a couple weeks earlier. Charlie got wasted after too many drinking games, and Tristan drove us home.

Now water oozed out of my Converse and pooled on his rubber floor mats. Without looking at me, he passed me a plastic grocery bag from a ball of them in the door pocket. "Can you put this under your feet? I just got the car detailed."

"Oh," I said, startled, then annoyed. It was his fault I was wet in the first place. "Okay."

We rode the rest of the way in silence.

The Jeep clock read 2:07 when we pulled into the parking lot. Sharon glared through the Scoops window.

"Thanks for the ride."

He touched me on my forearm. His fingers were gentle and warm.

"Sorry," he mumbled.

I nodded and hopped out, trying not to notice that I left a butt-shaped wet mark on his leather seat. The second I'd closed the door he was gone, taillights winking.

Even though it was nothing—just a ride—I never told Charlie about it, and I guess Tristan didn't either. And then Charlie and I broke up, and Tristan and I didn't speak again.

Until now.

# 35

**ON SATURDAY MORNING, I PUT IN EARBUDS AND** listened to Tristan's mix. It was the least I could do, I told myself, since he'd gone to the trouble. I planned to listen to it once and be done with it. I listened to it twice, and during the second time through I found myself warming up to him a little. Not in a dating kind of way or anything. Just a friend way. The mix was really good, full of indie bands I'd never heard of. I couldn't wait to get home and look up the lyrics on my computer, to see if he'd put as much thought into the message as he had the music. I had a feeling he had. When the very last song was about to start—Kelly Clarkson's "Stronger," a totally old Top 40 hit that even I, a total music ignoramus, recognized—I heard a buzz of voices outside my room.

When I opened my door, I found my entire cohort

crowded around a narrow girl with dark hair and a Long Island accent I'd recognize anywhere.

Lexi was back.

She'd made it fourteen days. Fourteen stinking days.

"Elizabeth!" she called, a huge smile on her face.

I stiffened.

She walked over to me with open arms. Her face was waxy and her frame skeletal. She looked way worse than when we'd arrived together. I dodged her and she stepped back, surprised.

"What's wrong?" she asked, her profile all angles. "Are you mad about something?"

"Mad? Why would I be mad?"

"I don't know." She dropped her arms and looked uneasy.

"I guess I'm just surprised to see you here."

She placed her hand on my wrist. I stared at it like it burned and she removed it slowly. "Look," she said, "I didn't think I was coming back. It wasn't something I planned."

"Okay." I stared at the floor.

"Elizabeth, do you think I did this on purpose?"

I shrugged, still not looking at her. "No. I don't know." I looked her right in the eye. "Maybe." And then I shut my door right in her face.

She'd lied. In her postcards she'd made us think she was making it, that it was almost easy. And I'd believed her.

One thing was for sure: I couldn't share a room with her now. And since the bed next to me was still empty, there was every chance I'd have to.

Nurse Jill was already at the nurses' station window when I arrived. "What can I do for you?"

I cleared my throat. "Nurse Jill, I was just wondering if you knew who Lexi was going to room with yet."

"Are you asking because you would like to share with her again? That's fine. I'll let everybody—"

I didn't let her finish. "Actually, can I request . . . Well, I mean, she's nice and all, but . . ." This was harder than I thought. "I don't want to room with Lexi again."

She put down her pen and pursed her lips. "Elizabeth, we only have so many beds here, and unfortunately we cannot allow residents to opt out of having a roommate."

"It's just—" *Come on, come on . . . think of something . . .* "It's just that, well, living with her isn't good for me. I didn't realize that until she was gone. She made me want to not eat. She taught me all sorts of tricks to hide food and how to exercise without making any noise." I was a backstabber, but Lexi was a liar.

Nurse Jill studied me for a long minute. I willed myself

not to bite my nails or fidget. I needed to be calm and collected. Like I was telling the truth.

"All right," she finally said, "Lexi can room with Jean. However, this is not going to be a pattern, Elizabeth. You can't expect to have a single forever."

I nodded. *I'll take anybody,* I almost said, *except a traitor.*

# 36

MARY CALLED ME INTO HER OFFICE IN THE AFTER-noon and told me to take a seat. I kept my eyes on her black, ugly leather clogs. *Hideous,* I thought. We weren't supposed to meet today, and I was in no mood for surprise therapy.

"I heard you asked that Lexi not be placed in your room," she said.

"Yeah," I said, chewing on my nails. "Maybe it was mean, but I can't be around her right now."

"Elizabeth, it's not a matter of being mean. I'm sure you had your reasons. But the fact that you chose not to room with her might be worth looking at together." She leaned in. "I'm curious. When Lexi left, you said she was inspiring, that she made you feel good about your own recovery. Something has changed, yes?"

My eyes met Mary's for the first time. "Yes."

"What feelings did her coming back bring up in you?"

"It's that she came back at all. I'm so mad at her. I'm mad because she let herself down. But I—" I didn't want to say any more. I felt enough like an asshole already.

"It's okay, Elizabeth. You know you can say anything here. This is a safe place."

"Fine. I feel like she let me down too. She told me she was going to make it. She was so sure. And if Lexi can't do it, how do I know that I can? That last part of her treatment, she did everything right. Everything. And now she's here. Again."

"But you're not Lexi, Elizabeth. Just because she had a setback doesn't mean *you* will. Or that she won't get better this time. Recovery is a long process, one that's different for every person. Anorexia has a high relapse rate—almost thirty-five percent for people who have been hospitalized once. Sometimes, people need more care. They just do."

"What I don't get, Mary, is how in school, you work hard, you get an A. Instant reward. Here, you could eat every single pat of butter and bowl of pesto pasta they throw at you and *still* fail."

Mary sighed. "I don't know, Elizabeth. I've asked myself that, too. I always do when a girl relapses. Lexi might not even know. But Lexi isn't you. Let me ask you this:

What voice is winning in your head these days—the eating-disordered one, or *yours*?"

"I guess mine."

"Okay. And how does that feel?"

"Well, I feel like my head is clearer."

"That's good. What is it saying?"

"It's saying that before, I wasn't healthy. That when people said I was skinny, they weren't necessarily giving me a compliment."

"Okay. What else?"

"That if I want to be better I'm going to have to eat."

"Those are all great thoughts to be having. You are taking good care of yourself. Is it saying anything else?"

"Well . . ." I paused. "I'm not actually fat. But I guess I always knew that. It's just parts of me that are awful." This conversation was excruciating; every word out of my mouth felt like a betrayal, like I was revealing just how weak I actually was.

"Elizabeth, what would happen if you were to talk to Lexi about your feelings?"

"I can't!" I said, my voice breaking. "No way!"

"It's up to you. I understand if it's too much. But it might make you feel less twisted up inside if you speak to her. And I'm sure she could use a friend."

I nodded. I'd think about it, but that was it. Think, nothing more.

From Mary's office I went straight to dinner. I was early, but Lexi was already there. I paused. Mary's voice flashed in my head. *She could use a friend.*

I sighed. *Fine, Mary. You win.*

*I can do this,* I told myself. I walked over to Lexi and sat down.

"Hi," she said softly.

Lexi's tray was loaded; she had stir-fried pasta and grilled chicken (in oil!), chocolate pudding with a dollop of whipped cream on top, and a carton of milk. She must have lost a lot of weight in two weeks.

"Ten pounds," she said, watching me.

"What?"

"Ten pounds. That's how much I lost. I saw you staring at my tray."

I blushed.

"No weight talk, please," Kay said.

I stared past her shoulder and watched the other girls filter in and sit down. Some picked at their food. A couple of them looked miserable; others were chatting.

"I think you should know," Lexi said carefully, "that when I left I was determined to make it work. I had a plan all set up. I was going to go with Dad, because his refrigerator was always full. Mom's never was. What I didn't know was that his girlfriend, Lara, moved in while I was away. She's a total bitch. Always was. Lara has three girls—eleven, fourteen, and sixteen—who moved in, too. She told Dad I was a bad influence, that she didn't want them to 'catch' anorexia. So I ended up back at Mom's, with her empty fridge. And my friends were all away at school. It was just so hard . . ." Lexi speared a piece of chicken and put it in her mouth.

Okay, fine. That sucked. But still, she'd lied to me.

"But what about Smith?"

"Ha, yeah, Smith. I wanted to go back as soon as possible, but they told me that after, quote, careful consideration, they didn't think I was ready to come back. They said I had to wait until next fall, and then only if I was at a stable and healthy weight. And so now all my friends will be a year ahead of me."

I could feel my anger ebbing away. "But, Lexi, why did you send us those postcards? You made it sound like you were doing so great."

"Because I didn't want to let you down. I knew you were watching me. I felt like if I failed, you'd think you would, too."

"I wish you'd called me or something. We could have talked about it."

"I know," she said, slumping in her chair. "I should have. Well, I guess you can still use me as an example—of what *not* to do at home. Reach out for help when you leave, Elizabeth, or you'll end up a failure like me."

"Lexi, you can still recover. Mary says girls have set-backs all the time."

"A setback. That's what they always say. When someone says you've had a setback, do you know what they are basically saying?"

"No, what?"

She stabbed another piece of chicken and forced it into her mouth. Her nostrils flared, her lips locked shut, and she chewed it like she was eating trash. "That you're screwed. That's what." Then, gagging, she spit the chicken out into her napkin. "I can't eat this crap," she said, and burst into defeated tears.

# 37

MOM AND DAD SHOWED UP ON SUNDAY NIGHT TO
have dinner with me in the guest dining room. I didn't
tell them about Lexi. Mom choked down more than
usual; she ate almost half her bean burrito. She'd either
taken our last conversation to heart, or Dad had given
her a talking-to. I guessed maybe both because she kept
looking at him, like she was asking if she'd eaten enough.

Then Mom said, "Honey, I wish you'd wear something
other than that same ratty black sweater."

"But I love this sweater."

"I'm not saying you have to burn it. I'm just saying that
it might make you feel better if you wore your nicer clothes
from time to time. I've found that if you dress nice, you
feel nice."

I slammed my fork onto the table. "Thanks, Mom, for

the *fashion advice*. Next time I pack for inpatient treatment, I'll make sure to bring my prom dress." But behind my sarcasm was hurt. I'd let her down, again.

None of us said a word. Mom kept her eyes on her plate.

"Sorry I lost my temper," I mumbled.

She looked up. "I'm sorry, too. You're right. I shouldn't have said that. Old habits die hard." She took my hand. "You're beautiful no matter what you wear."

Maybe someday I'd believe her.

"Honey," Dad said, breaking through the awkward silence that followed. "I just want you to know that we can't wait for you to come home. We've been talking with Mary and she's going to take you on as a private client in her office in Grantham. Isn't that great?"

"That's good." I was glad I'd still see Mary. She understood me.

Then Mom chimed in. "Yes, and I am going to meet with your nutritionist and get your menus ahead of time."

"When do I have to go back to school?"

Mom and Dad exchanged glances. Dad cleared his throat. "Well, everyone agrees that it wouldn't be productive for you to sit home, so right now, since you're getting out on a Friday, we're all thinking Monday would be the best return date."

"Monday? That's too soon." I'd thought I'd definitely

be able to push it back by a week or so. "Do I have any say in the matter?"

Dad's face twitched. "This is what Mary recommends—"

"So you're saying that I don't."

"Don't what?"

He knew exactly what. "Have a say."

Mom leaned toward me. "Honey, Mary knows what she's doing. Wallingfield has helped so many girls transition back to home."

Yeah, right. Wallingfield was so far from perfect. "Lexi is back, you know. She lost ten pounds in two weeks. So I wouldn't totally count on Wallingfield for my full recovery."

Mom and Dad went quiet, and Dad paled a little. I'd unnerved them.

Good.

"Well," Dad said, his voice not quite as strong, "I still think it would be great for you to get back into your routine."

"I don't." I never wanted to go back to school.

Dad reached over for my hand. "Honey, that's enough for now. Let's not worry about this tonight. Let's just focus on dinner." I pulled my hand away, knowing there was no point in arguing. When Dad said *enough,* he meant it.

So it was settled. In one week, I'd be going back to school. And I had absolutely no say in the matter.

# *38*

**RIGHT WHEN I WANTED LIFE TO SLOW DOWN, FOR** the days to crawl, they sped up. It was Wednesday, dinner-out day, before I knew it. At five o'clock I climbed into the white van with the Wallingfield logo on the door. Nurse Jill and Jean were already inside.

None of us talked on the way. Nurse Jill put on the easy-listening station as she drove. The evening was clear and cold. It wasn't even Thanksgiving yet and Fierman's Hardware already had its twinkly lights up. So did the used bookstore and the coffee shop. I thought I saw a freshman from the high school walking into Sam's grocery store as we passed, but I couldn't be sure. I ducked down anyway, just in case.

Finch's had a bar at one end and a dark dining room on the other with low ceilings and cozy booths and tables.

The miniskirted hostess seated us at a big, old wooden table in the back of the dining room, the table surface soft and a little sticky from years of use.

We were their first customers for dinner, and seventies rock music blared. At first Nurse Jill tried to chat over the songs, but gave up and asked the hostess to turn it down. She turned it so low we could hear the distant clanking of dishes in the kitchen.

"So," Nurse Jill said. "What are you all going to have?" Her voice rang out across the empty dining room.

"The turkey sandwich," Jean said.

"Me too." I was glad Jean and I were in this together.

We knew because we'd seen the menu already. We'd each met with Sally, the nutritionist, in the morning to go over what we might eat.

At first I'd thought it would be easy. "I'll have the green salad, add grilled chicken, with oil and vinegar for the dressing," I'd told her. That's what I usually got when my family went to Finch's. It came with six thin slices of chicken breast, and I'd always eat exactly one-half of one and most of the lettuce, sprinkled with a little plain vinegar. I'd use the extra lettuce to try to hide some of my uneaten chicken in case anybody noticed.

But Sally didn't like that idea. "Honey," she said softly, "you have to order something as is from the entrée section."

I'd panicked. Hamburgers, pasta, fish. Fish! That sounded promising. I scanned the menu. There it was! Pan-fried halibut with panko breadcrumbs. My heart sank. No way was I ordering fried anything. The fish was out.

I kept searching. Salads—spinach and blue cheese and walnuts. Nope. Steak fajita salad with guacamole, cheese, and sour cream in a taco bowl. Nope. Sunrise salad with avocado, bacon, goat cheese, and creamy— Nope. I was getting desperate.

Then I reread the sandwich menu. Cheeseburger. Grilled cheese. Fried fish sandwich. Fried chicken sandwich. BLT. Egg salad. Cheesesteak sandwich. When I was younger I used to get the cheesesteak sandwich every time. It came with fries. I loved their fries. Correction—I *used* to love their fries.

I almost cried out in relief when I saw the turkey sandwich with cranberry sauce, lettuce, and tomato. "I'll have that," I'd said to Sally, pointing to it.

"Really? Okay, great. Done." Sally had taken back the menu with relief. "So tonight we really want you to try to eat at least half of your meal as is. This way, when you go out with friends and family, you'll be able to eat regularly, like they do."

"My mom doesn't," I'd said sharply, and then felt bad. Mom was right. Old habits died hard. I was trying to give

Mom the benefit of the doubt more, but sometimes it was tough.

"Well, most people," Sally said.

As much as I hated to admit it, Mary was right about one thing. Knowing what I was going to order in advance did make me feel better. In fact, when the waitress came over, I wasn't nervous at all. "Hi, ladies," she said with a big fake smile. "My name is Elaine, and I'll be your server." Finch's had an agreement with Wallingfield—they always reserved this same table when a group of us came. "Here are your menus." She placed them on the table fast, like she was scared of us. I didn't blame her.

Nurse Jill opened hers. "Shit," she muttered. She got out her phone, stared at it for a second like she wanted to make a call, then put it away. "Pass me your menus, girls." Confused, we did as she said. She stood and walked straight to the manager.

They spoke quietly, but the occasional word reached us anyway—"changed . . . I understand . . . winter specialties . . . We have an agreement . . . This won't happen again . . ."

The manager shook her head, made the universal nothing-I-can-do-about-it shrug, and said, "Sorry."

Eventually Nurse Jill returned and handed back our menus. "Girls," she said, clearing her throat, "it looks like we hit Finch's on the very night they are debuting their new winter menu. Isn't that exciting?"

My throat closed. Jean squeaked. I turned to the sandwich page. *Please be there,* I prayed. *Please be there.*

It wasn't.

The roasted turkey sandwich was gone. The only item even remotely like it was a turkey melt, which was listed with no description. My calorie radar spiked, but the other choices were worse: burgers, fried fish on a bun, grilled cheese.

Elaine returned. "So, ladies, what can I get you?" Nurse Jill ordered pasta, and then nodded to me.

"I'll . . . I'll . . ." I desperately scanned the menu. "I'll have the turkey melt, please." The words alone made my stomach roll. *I'll just peel off the melted cheese,* I thought. *No one will notice.*

Jean ordered a hamburger, well done, with a side salad. Nurse Jill said nothing. I should have ordered what Jean had. She knew what she was doing. A hamburger wouldn't have any cheese on it. And well done meant that more of the juices and fat would cook off. I opened my mouth to speak up and change my order, but Elaine took off before I got the words out.

I jiggled my leg. The table vibrated. "Elizabeth," Nurse Jill said, "would you like to process your feelings? You seem anxious. We'd be happy to support you." Jean looked at me and nodded.

I shook my head. "I'm fine." *Except that I am about to eat a freaking turkey melt!* For the next ten minutes I waited for Elaine to come back, to ask how we were doing—if we needed anything—so I could change my order. But she never did. Right when I'd decided to screw it all and go find her, she appeared, carrying our food. I thought I might be sick.

She put mine down, the plate smacking heavily on the wood table. I stared at it, horrified. On two of the thickest pieces of toasted, buttered bread I'd ever seen sat a mound of turkey buried under a massive mountain of melted orange cheese, steaming hot yet already coagulating at the top. Peeking out of the corners were pieces of avocado and bacon. Mayonnaise oozed out between the layers. I had to eat half of this? Half a sandwich this size was probably more than I ate in a day, and I'd already eaten breakfast *and* lunch *and* two snacks.

More people were coming to the restaurant now. Each time the door opened, I worried I might see someone I knew. The buzz of voices drowned out the music, which the owners had turned back up. I watched Jean chew a bite of her burger to paste. I tore my eyes away from her and mustered up the courage to take a bite myself.

The cheese and mayonnaise exploded in my mouth and made my lips feel like they'd been attacked by a can of cooking spray. The avocado was brown and tasted weird and stuck to the top of my mouth, making me gag. I could barely choke it down.

The only bright spot was the bacon, which was hot and crispy and salty. I hadn't had bacon in over a year. My entire body wanted more of it after only one bite.

Well, it wasn't getting any.

I kept my eyes on my plate while I chewed. When I looked up, I almost didn't believe what I saw. Heather was here with her family. I choked a little. Nurse Jill slid me my water glass.

Heather hadn't noticed me yet, probably because we were so far in the back that even the lights had trouble finding us. She checked out the other tables with minimal interest, twirling her blond hair, chewing gum, and looking incredibly bored. I froze as her gaze came closer to where we were. I slouched down in my seat as low as I could, but it was too late. Our eyes met. Hers widened.

I tried to not look at her and focused on my food instead. My sense of time became measured by the bites I took. I tore through the turkey with my teeth and licked the mayo off my lips with my tongue. And then I chewed. And chewed and chewed and chewed.

Six bites in, I was sure I looked like this python I saw

in a YouTube video once that ate a dog. You could see the entire outline and shape of the dog under the python's skin, and that's what I pictured my stomach looked like, except the bulge was shaped like a massive sandwich. I could feel my yoga pants stretch. Seven bites in, I saw a waiter put an order of chicken nuggets down in front of Heather. They had to be off the kids' menu, and if my jaw hadn't been aching and my stomach hadn't been distended and resting on my thighs, I would have relished that moment.

At bite eight, Jean touched my shoulder. "You okay?" she whispered.

I shrugged. She nodded. "Hang in there, friend. It's almost over."

After thirteen bites, or precisely half my meal, I put down my fork. I could stop now.

When the bill came a few minutes later, Nurse Jill picked it up. "Don't worry, girls," she said. "It's on me!"

Jean and I stood up at the same time, thinking the same thing: *Let's get the hell out of here.*

Heather and her family had moved on to dessert and now, eating a fruit cup, she watched us like we were a TV show.

"Take a seat, girls," Nurse Jill said. "We aren't quite done yet. I'd like to do meal support here, before we leave." Right then the music cut out for a moment. I swear the entire restaurant heard her say, "How are you processing your meals?"

I saw Heather's head snap up. She scooted her chair a little closer. She'd heard.

"Elizabeth, how are you doing?"

I gulped. "Um . . . great. Ready to go, actually."

Nurse Jill scrutinized me. "Really? I know that according to the notes Sally gave me, you were planning on having a roasted turkey sandwich. How did you deal with the menu change?"

"Fine." We didn't have time for me to be a teachable moment for Nurse Jill.

Heather's eyes followed our every move. I don't think she even blinked.

The only way to get out of there was to play along.

"Um, well, I knew that turkey is healthy protein, so I looked for something that had turkey in it. Obviously, the turkey melt had turkey so I ordered that." Heather's dad asked her a question, and for a second, she was distracted. *Please leave,* I silently begged. *Please be telling her that it's time to go.* They needed to exit first. Or we did. We just couldn't all get up at the same time.

"Yes, flexibility is important. Well done, Elizabeth."

I nodded.

"And, Jean, how was your meal?"

"Actually, aside from the buttered bun, it wasn't as hard as I thought it would be."

I tuned out again and scanned the room super fast to make sure I hadn't missed any other familiar faces. Thankfully, it was a slow night. Many of the tables were empty, and I didn't know the people sitting at the others.

"Well, you two, thanks for a successful dinner. Let's head back." I leaped up from the table. Jean stood up, too, and started putting on her coat.

So did Heather's family.

"Um, excuse me?" I said, sitting back down.

"Yes, Elizabeth," said Nurse Jill as she pushed her right arm into her coat.

"You know what? I think I *do* need more support. The cheese was, um, really greasy and I am panicking right now."

"Well, let's go to the van and we can talk there," Nurse Jill said, reaching over and patting my arm.

Heather's family was standing. They pushed in their chairs and began walking to the door.

"Wait! Nurse Jill! I think I lost a button!"

Now she looked annoyed. "What, Elizabeth? What button?"

"A button from my coat. I'm pretty sure it rolled under the table."

Nurse Jill sighed. "Okay, let's look for Elizabeth's button." Dutifully, Jean squatted down and studied the dark floor. It felt like the entire restaurant was staring at us now. I didn't care as long as Heather kept walking toward the door.

But then she turned around.

Heather's eyes met mine. She walked over.

"How are you doing, Elizabeth?" Her voice was just as I remembered—loud and raspy.

"Great, Heather. Just great. You know, well, as you can see, I'm out to dinner. I had the turkey melt. It was delish. I recommend it." The words poured out of me like water from a broken faucet. "How were the chicken nuggets? I used to get them from the kids' menu, too. When I was actually a kid."

She flushed. *Score one for me!*

She recovered fast. "Everyone at school," she said, narrowing her eyes just the tiniest bit, "will be so happy I saw you."

"Oh," I said. "Say hi for me."

"Don't worry, I will."

Jean crawled out and apologized. She had breadcrumbs stuck to her knee. "Sorry, Elizabeth, I couldn't find it."

"That's okay," I said.

Heather stuck out her hand to Jean. "I'm Heather. And you are?"

Usually when I looked at Jean I saw how her eyes crinkled at the corners when she smiled. I saw how gentle and kind she was every time she talked to me, how she often put a reassuring hand on my arm. But in that moment I saw her through Heather's eyes. She looked like a giraffe. She was tall and awkward and gaunt even though she'd gained weight.

"This is Jean," I said haltingly.

Jean smiled. She had no idea.

"Hi, Jean!" Heather said brightly.

"Hi." Jean zipped up her jacket.

*Please make this end,* I thought. *Right now.*

"Would you guys like me to take your picture?" Heather held up her phone.

*Oh no. Oh no no no no no no.*

Jean shook her head. "No, I don—"

"No!" I put my hand up. "I don't think we—"

"Say cheese!" Heather snapped a photo.

I opened my mouth, but nothing came out.

Before she'd even gotten to the door, the phone screen illuminated her face. "I'll tell everyone I saw you!" Heather called back to me.

That was exactly what I was afraid of.

# 39

WHEN I KNOCKED ON MARY'S OFFICE DOOR BEFORE
breakfast the next morning, she probably thought I wanted
to chat about the menu change. She told me I'd handled
the "challenging night" very well, which was nice of her,
but I wanted to talk about something else. "I ran into someone at dinner last night."

Mary leaned over her desk. "Yes, Nurse Jill mentioned
that you saw a friend from school there."

"She is not a friend," I said, my voice flat. "She is the
opposite of a friend. More like a nightmare. It was Heather,
the girl from school I've told you about before."

Mary remained calm. "I can imagine that running into
someone from home could be upsetting in a situation like
this." She obviously had no idea how bad this was.

"She pulled out her phone and took our picture. When

she left she was typing like crazy fast, probably sending that picture to everyone at school."

"I wonder if seeing her is bringing up feelings for you about transitioning home?"

Why did Mary ask such obvious questions? "Well, yes. Of *course* it does. I can't go home."

"So, Elizabeth, let's talk about Heather for a minute. I'm curious: What would you do if you saw her right now?"

"I'd avoid her."

"Okay," Mary said. "You could also lean on your friends a little to help you. You have good friends, and you can use them, you know."

"Friends? What friends? My friends have completely blown me off. Katrina is the only one who has called or visited."

Mary put on what I thought of as her sad face. She would scrunch her eyebrows together, pinch her lips tight, tilt her head, and nod. "You know, sometimes people don't know how to react to a certain situation. There could be many reasons your friends haven't called."

"Like what?"

"Well, sometimes they might be scared. It is incredibly hard to watch someone you care about suffer. Other times I've had patients for whom something like this touches on their own fears for themselves. I've also seen friends and family members who, if they haven't had experience with the illness, have trouble understanding it and therefore avoid it. And other times, they are just busy, or are dealing with issues in their own lives."

"Do you think that's why Priya and Shay have ignored me?"

"I don't know, Elizabeth. Maybe you'll have to ask them. We can work on how to do that as we get you ready for your discharge."

My discharge. Using that word made me think of bodily fluid, and at that moment, going home sounded just about as appealing.

# *40*

MARY WAS RIGHT. I STILL HAD FRIENDS—CORRECTION —a friend. Katrina. She could help me.

She answered on the second ring. "Hello?" I said.

"Hey, stranger!" Katrina's voice jumped through the line.

"K! I am so glad you picked up the phone." It was ten in the morning. I must have caught her at study hall. "What's going on?"

"Nothing. Just studying."

Ha! I knew it!

Before I could say another word, Katrina jumped in. "Mr. Roberts quit!" Mr. Roberts was our AP US History teacher. "He's going to be a fly fisherman in Georgia."

"Seriously? A fly fisherman? What *is* that?"

"I have no idea. Apparently he met some lady online and he's going to move to Atlanta with her."

"Yikes. Really?" I tried to muster up the expected enthusiasm.

"I know, right? Who would want to be with *him*?"

The idea was nauseating. Picturing Mr. Roberts kissing a woman was even more alarming than the fact that he taught with his hand down the back of his pants like his butt was a pocket.

"So who is his sub?"

"Oh my God, Elizabeth, he's twenty-two. One of the girls in class asked him. All the girls flirt with him. He's shockingly hot. His name is Mr. Shaw, but he told us to call him Tom. We watched *The Simpsons* in class the other day."

"Wow." I tried to sound appropriately excited. I wished I cared more. I couldn't believe all this school stuff would be important to me again, too.

"I know!" Katrina said, and then she paused.

"Anything else happening?"

Another long pause. Too long.

"Katrina, tell me." I steeled myself.

She hesitated again. "It's not good, Elizabeth. I don't want to upset you. Are you sure you want me to tell you?"

"I think I might already know. Does any of this have to do with Finch's?"

"Maybe." Katrina didn't say anything else.

"I ran into Heather there and she took a picture of this other girl and me. I assume she's done something horrible with it."

"I'm sorry, Elizabeth. It's pretty harsh. God, I hate her."

"I do, too. Did she show it to you?"

"She posted it online."

"What site did she post it on?"

"All of them, Elizabeth."

"Oh." I needed to sit.

If it was everywhere, anyone could see it. *Anyone.*

I couldn't go home tomorrow.

As I hung up the phone, Tristan and Simone walked into the foyer. Simone walked right past me, shooting me a sympathetic look. Obviously she knew.

Tristan stood nearby, kicking at a speck on the floor and looking everywhere except at me. "Hey, Tristan," I said, hoping my voice sounded normal. "Thank you for the mix."

"You're welcome," he said, still avoiding my eyes.

"Anyway, I love it. I've listened to it so much. It really does cheer me up."

He smiled a little. "I'm glad you like it."

"I'm sorry I got so mad the other day. I overreacted." I sat on the bench.

He sat next to me. "Nah, I probably should have left you alone."

311

"I'm glad you didn't."

He looked relieved. "Really?"

I nodded.

"Hey, can I get your number?" Tristan pulled out his phone. "So I can call you when you're out?"

I nodded. He handed me his phone and I made a contact for myself.

I handed it back and we sat for a moment in silence before he said, "So . . . have you talked to anybody from school today?"

"Are you talking about the picture?"

His body stiffened. "You know?"

"Katrina told me. Is it bad?"

"Pretty bad."

"They don't let us online in here. I wish I could, though."

"I don't know about that. Maybe it's for the best."

I was sick of everybody trying to protect me. I had anorexia, not wimporexia, for God's sake. "Tristan, you follow Heather on Instagram, right?"

"Yeah," he said. "Of course."

"Will you show me the picture?"

He took a deep breath and exhaled, making his cheeks puff. "I don't think that's a good idea." He put his phone in his pocket.

"Tristan," the voice came from behind me. Simone was back. I turned. "Show her the picture. She has a right to know." Her face was makeup-free. I'd never seen her without eyeliner before. She looked younger and softer and not as scary.

"I thought you went inside," he said.

Simone stepped next to me, arms crossed. "I forgot my sweater. And it's her photo. Show her."

"Don't order me around. And no. I don't think it's a good idea."

Simone rolled her eyes. "Tristan, she's going to see it eventually, and isn't it better that she sees it here, where there's doctors and counselors everywhere?"

"Hey!" I wasn't their little sister, but they were treating me like one. "Hello? I'm right here? Tristan, I need to know what I'm dealing with. If I don't see it on your phone, I'll find some other way, and I'd rather watch"—and here I paused, because I still wasn't sure what Tristan and Simone and I were to each other—"with friends."

With one last glare at his sister, he took the phone out of his pocket. "Fine."

I stood too and looked around. The nurses' station was empty. My hands twitched as I watched him scroll through the posts, stop, read something, frown, scroll more, frown more.

"Look, people are assholes," he said. "I think that might be all you need to know."

"God, Tristan! Just give it to her, already!"

*Thank you, Simone.*

"Fine!" Tristan shoved the phone at me.

And there I was. The photo caption read, **Skelorexics out to eat**. The too-bright flash gave Jean and me red-eye. Jean's collarbone peeking through the V of her shirt was so distinct it almost looked like there was no skin covering it at all. The phone's flash washed all color out of her face; she looked like a worried zombie.

My mouth was half open, like I was saying something, and my eyes popped out of my head. My hand was up in protest, and each knuckle bulged out like knots in a tree. In the background Nurse Jill leaned over, fork in her mouth. She was taking a bite of Jean's unfinished dinner.

There were sixty-two comments.

I read every single one. Tristan and Simone watched, the same wary expression on both of their faces.

People I didn't even know had posted comments, things like:

**nasty**

**freaks**

**eat something**

**someone get them some fries**

this shit ain't for human eyes

now I can't unsee this nightmare!!!!!!!!!!!!!!!!!!!!!!!!!!

And the worst: **THEY SHOULD KILL THEMSELVES.**

I couldn't breathe. How was I supposed to go back to school in four days with this out there?

Halfway down the page was a post from Katrina: **Leave them alone!!! People like you are the reason women today have so many issues with their bodies. A$$holes!**

*I love that girl.*

I saw a bunch of similar comments from Shay and a bunch of people I didn't even know, like **You guys are disgusting. Leave them alone.** Even strangers were coming to my defense. Some guy named Tripp wrote, **HEATHER I DON'T KNOW YOU AND I AM SO GLAD BECAUSE YOU MUST BE A TERRIBLE PERSON.** And then, posted an hour before, was the last one, from Tristan. **You all need to get a life. Don't be assholes.**

I handed the phone back to Tristan. "Thanks." I didn't know if I was thanking him for the phone, or the comment, or both.

He ran a hand through his hair. "Are you okay?" he asked.

Was I okay? I'd just been humiliated by the most powerful girl at school.

But so many people had defended me. Tristan and

Simone were here, as my friends. Shay had popped up after a month of silence to stick up for me. Even people I didn't know said nice things.

And Heather was just one girl being a bully.

So was I okay?

"You know what?" I said. "I'm hanging in there."

# *41*

DAY 40. GO-HOME DAY. UNABLE TO SLEEP, I WAS the first at weights and vitals. The night nurse said, all cheery, "Hey, Elizabeth! Congratulations! We'll miss you! Don't take this the wrong way, but I hope I never see you again."

I laughed and stood, my back to the scale like always.

The nurse clapped her hands. "Honey, you did it. We are so proud. Your body thanks you."

I watched her hand write down three numbers. I bet I was more than 104 now. I swallowed the panic thickening in my throat. *It's a good thing,* I repeated over and over in my head. *A healthy thing.*

Breakfast and lunch flew by in a blur. After lunch, I went to my room to pack. I tossed my suitcase onto Lexi's old bed. I'd hurt her feelings when I told Nurse Jill that I didn't want her as a roommate. We'd barely spoken since, and I missed her.

I peeled the purple-and-blue-pinstriped comforter from my bed, folded my sheets, and threw my yoga pants and all my other clothes into my suitcase. I rolled up my taped-together kitten poster, wrapped up what was left of my jar of sand in a T-shirt, placed the plastic ring in its little bubble container, and put it all with the umbrella and journal in my backpack. I wondered if Tristan would text me once I got home, or if it would be awkward at school next week.

Mary knocked on my door right before two o'clock. "Elizabeth, your parents are here."

"Be right out." I looked around. The room no longer felt like mine. In less than five minutes, I'd stripped it of all evidence of me.

Right as I was about to head out to the common room, my door opened and Margot slipped inside, wearing her usual getup—a faded black T-shirt and ripped, faded black jeans. I hugged her.

She stiffened but didn't immediately pull away. "Hey. I just wanted to tell you goodbye, in private, because I don't think I can do the whole group farewell thing."

I nodded. "That's okay. I understand."

She pulled at her sleeves and shifted from side to side, looking everywhere except at me. "I know I'm not easy.

Most girls wouldn't have given me the time of day, but you did. Thank you."

"Margot, anybody would be lucky to have you as a friend. Anybody."

She blushed. "Yeah, well, take care of yourself, okay?"

"Can we have coffee when you get out?"

She nodded doubtfully. "Sure."

"Margot, listen to me. I will call you. You're so smart. You're nice and funny. And sarcastic."

"You mean bitchy," she said.

Standing there, looking at her face, which wasn't as pasty as before, and her eyes, which to me were so full of life and smarts, I felt this huge rush of appreciation. "No, I don't. Well, okay, maybe a little. But in the best way."

She tucked her hair behind her ears and chuckled. "Okay, if you say so."

"I do. And we *are* going to meet for coffee." I put my hand on her shoulder. She didn't pull away. "I'll miss you, Margot."

"I'll miss you, too."

I waited for a last sarcastic comment, or a joke, or something witty. But all she said was, "Have a safe trip home," and closed my door on her way out. I missed her already.

Less than a minute passed before Jean and Willa came in, bringing along the smell of cinnamon. *Must be muffins for afternoon snack,* I thought, remembering the first day, when the same smell scared the crap out of me. Mary had been right. The chef made delicious muffins.

*Muffins I will no longer be required to eat.*

The thought caught me by surprise. I wasn't supposed to have thoughts like that now. A lick of fear crept up in me.

Jean and Willa took turns hugging me. We all stood in a circle by my door. I guess no one wanted to sit on the old plastic mattress cover. I didn't blame them.

Then Jean said, "Guess what?"

"What?"

"I'm going home too. On Monday. Three days from now."

Monday. My first day back at school. "Wow! That's great!" I hugged her. "Are you excited?"

"So excited," she said.

Next to me, Willa bit at her nails. My heart hurt for her. "Willa, you'll go home soon too. I know it. Just eat, okay? Eat and you'll be out of here faster than you think."

She nodded. I hoped she heard me. "Yeah," she said. "I'll try."

"You can do it if you want to," I said. I felt terrible leaving Willa behind. But I couldn't heal her. She needed to do that herself.

Jean nodded. "I agree, Willa. You'll be okay, you'll see."

Through the window I could see my parents' Honda

parked in the lot. "My parents are here," I said. "Walk me to the door?"

They both nodded. As we left I took one last look at my room, burning the beige curtains and walls and rug into my brain. *Goodbye, room.*

As we walked, Jean talked. "Elizabeth, I want you to remember. You are strong. Like, massively strong. When you go back to school, do it with pride and don't let anybody give you a hard time. You should hold your head up because you're amazing. I'll miss you."

"Thank you," I said, my voice wobbling.

We were almost to the nurses' station when Willa spoke. I could see my parents in the foyer, waiting. "I am going to miss you so much. I hope that you and Tristan get married and have babies."

"Ack! No!" I made a fake-horrified face and hugged her little body as hard as I could. "Get better, Willa," I whispered. "You deserve it."

"I'll try," she said.

"Hi, honey!" Dad and Mom waved from the foyer.

"I've got to go," I said. *Don't you dare cry!* I told myself.

"Hey, Mom. Hey, Dad." I turned to my friends. "I'll miss you," I said one more time. Then I turned toward my parents.

Dad took my bags and Mom squeezed me, hard. "I am so happy you are—"

She didn't get a chance to finish.

"Elizabeth! Wait!" Lexi hustled into the foyer, her face flushed. She panted a little and I wondered if she'd broken the rules and run.

"Can I talk to you for a second?"

My parents nodded. "We'll be right here," they said.

Lexi tugged me back to the main hallway. "I'm sorry I let you down." She spoke fast and her voice was hushed, as if she were telling a secret with a time limit. "I have to tell you something. First, you were—are—a great friend. Second, you are so strong and brave and you are going to do great out there. Remember when I was leaving and you asked me if I thought that we'd have a day when we didn't think about food? Well, I know we will. We'll just eat it and forget it, just like we talked about. I didn't want you to leave without knowing that I believe in you and that I'm going to miss you." And then, more quietly, "I already miss you."

I took a deep breath and tried not to get all teary. "I'm sorry I wasn't nicer to you when you came back," I said.

"I'm sorry I lied to you in my postcards." And then she squeezed me once, fast and hard, and disappeared down the hallway. I closed my eyes and tried to burn in my memory just how warm and safe it felt with my friends sending me so much love and light and hope. And I felt a little stressed, too, because now I had a huge responsibility.

For the first time, I understood why Lexi had lied on her postcards.

Standing there in the foyer, I wanted time to stop, just for a second. I wanted to remember everything—the way Jean's hand seemed to float when she brushed her bangs out of her face, the order of the earrings in Willa's ear (Winnie-the-Pooh, Tigger, and then Ariel at the top), the cut of Lexi's jaw. Even the way Allie's blond ponytail bobbed like the cheerleader she was, and the way Coral's ladybug barrette was always clipped in her hair in the same exact spot above her right ear.

On the chalkboard on the wall under the stairs, someone had written, *Welcome to Julia and Robin, arriving today.* Then, under that, the daily quote: *You must do the things you think you cannot do. —E. Roosevelt.*

After a final glance around, I walked out through the same doors I'd entered forty days earlier. Sleet fell from a slate-gray sky. The wind blew clammy and cold right through my wool coat, and I wanted nothing more than to go back inside, where it was safe and dry.

In the movie version of my life, I'd always imagined myself bursting through the front doors on a summer day, the sun on my proud face. I'd march down the steps, one victorious fist up like Judd Nelson when he walked across the football field at the end of *The Breakfast Club.* Oh, and I'd be supermodel thin. And tall, too.

In real life, Dad hit the wheelchair button and the door crept slowly open and I trudged out so loaded down with my suitcase and backpack that I could barely walk. It wasn't until I was outside, standing on the slippery stone steps, that it hit me that I was actually leaving, and it took all I had not to turn around and run back inside. And I didn't feel triumphant as I picked my way down the steps. I was freaking terrified. An entire WORLD full of meals and restaurants and grocery stores lay in wait, and I didn't know how I'd manage any of them.

*You can do this.*

I carefully crunched over the gravel. Dad took my bags and opened the car door. I turned around one last time. Willa, Lexi, Jean, and Margot watched me from a window. I stretched a smile across my face and waved. I might or might not have channeled Kate Middleton when I did it.

Then I dove into the stained fabric backseat of the Honda.

"You okay, kiddo?" Dad asked, turning around.

"Yes, are you okay?" Mom asked. "Want me to come sit in the backseat with you?"

"I'm fine. And no, Mom. Definitely not. Can we just go? Please?"

"Absolutely."

I kept my head high and my shoulders square until we rounded the curve of the driveway. When I was sure we were out of sight, I buried my face in my hands. The car rolled past the old stone pillars that marked the Wallingfield entrance. And just like that, I was out.

# 42

ON THE WAY HOME, DAD KEPT HIS EYES ON THE road. Mom spent the time telling him to "Drive slower, Brian! There's *ice* on the ground!"

I kept looking for changes as the landscape flashed by, like trees that had grown, or houses that had been painted, or stores that had morphed into different stores. I thought that the world should look different somehow, because I was different. But everything was the same. When we'd pass a car, I'd look at it and think, *Those people have no idea where I'm coming from, what I've been through.* Then I wondered if maybe all of us, on the road, were doing the same thing.

The streets grew narrower and more crowded with cars and houses as we left behind the estates on Sea Drive. By the time we pulled into our driveway, there was almost an inch of slush on the ground. "Looks like the sleet is freezing; I'll have to salt this afternoon," Dad said. "Watch your step."

"Okay." I picked my way up the walkway. On a big piece of white paper stuck to the front door, Mom and Dad had written in purple marker: WELCOME HOME, ELIZA-BETH! WE ARE SO GLAD YOU ARE BACK!!!!!

Dad unlocked the door and carried my bags up to my room. Mom went to make tea. I followed Dad upstairs. The hardwood steps creaked like always. The entire house felt small. It made me feel a bit claustrophobic.

"How's it feel to be home?" he asked once we got to my bedroom.

"A little strange."

He stood next to my bed, hoping to talk more. He wore a blue plaid button-down shirt and gray work pants. He looked too tall for the room.

I needed to be alone. "I'll be down soon; don't worry. I just want to unpack."

He turned slowly. "Aren't you supposed to have a snack now? It's time, right?"

"Oh, yeah, I was supposed to tell you. I had it before I left. Granola." I didn't mean to lie. It just slipped out, maybe because, for the first time in forty days, I could actually get away with it. Once it was out there, though, I didn't know how to take it back. And I wasn't sure I wanted to.

"Okay, then." He smiled. "I am so happy you are home."

He waited for me to say, *I'm happy to be here, too,* but I couldn't. I wasn't sure how I felt.

He left and I closed the door and sat on *my* bed in *my* room. Except that it didn't feel like my room anymore. It was tidy, and I was messy. It felt weird to see the floor, which was usually covered with clothes. My bed was different, too. Mom had made it up with gray sheets and a white bedspread, the spares from the guest room. Both of my sheet sets were in the suitcase at my feet. A fresh vase of white Gerbera daisies rested on my bedside table.

My cell phone sat on my desk, and when I turned it on, it lit up like an old friend. I almost cried I was so happy to have it. I'd forgotten how perfectly it fit my hand, and how much I loved the case, which was navy blue with little white elephants all over it. A group text from Shay, Priya, and Katrina on the day I left, sent an hour after I'd already checked in, headed the long list of alerts and notifications that popped up on the screen. **Good luck in there!** Priya had written. **I will miss you so much, but you are going to do great. Be awesome!!!!!** was from Shay.

And, from Katrina, **Make yourself better in there, friend. I am rooting for you.** I smiled, grateful for their love.

My fingers hovered over the Instagram button for a moment before I tapped it, at which point I came face-to-face with every little thing I'd missed since disappearing into the abyss of Wallingfield. Priya and Shay had gone ugly hunting. In one picture, Priya posed in a strapless dress, a wild mess of yellow-and-pink tulle complete with sequins, beading, and a scarily full skirt. She looked like an upside-down, bedazzled tulip. She vamped for the camera, holding her hair up and making kissing motions with her lips. I felt a pang of regret. I missed them.

I kept clicking. Up popped photos of people wrapped in wool blankets in the cold, sitting around a beach bonfire. I thought I saw Tristan's outline, but I wasn't sure.

Finally I went to Heather's feed. I scrolled down past her most recent selfies—in her mirror, in the cafeteria with Charlie, in sunglasses, and in Charlie's car. Finally I found the photo of Jean and me. It shocked me all over again.

I waited to feel angry, and I did, but more than anything I was homesick. For Wallingfield. I missed Jean and Willa and Mary and Margot and Lexi and even Nurse Jill. What would I do if I had trouble eating? What if I got mad about calories? What if I cried? Who would understand? Mary had agreed to keep me on as a patient; I was scheduled to see her at her private office, where she worked one day a week, but my first appointment wasn't for six whole days. I was on my own until then.

I started to text Katrina but stopped. She'd assume I was happy to be home, and I was, mostly. But I didn't want to talk. Not yet.

I tossed the phone on my nightstand and dumped my suitcase out on my purple carpet. Wallingfield's dusty-heat smell filled my nose, and I sat down on the floor. Then I lay back and stared at my ceiling, like I'd done a million times since I was little. I looked at my watch. Four o'clock. Everybody at Wallingfield would be finishing up their afternoon activities right about now. I wondered if they missed me. I wondered if Willa would eat her dinner for once, or hide it in her clothes like always.

My phone chimed. I sat up right away.

Tristan: **Hey.**

Me: **hey**

Tristan: **Are you home?**

Me: **yup.**

Tristan: **What are you up to?**

Me: **I might watch some TV later.**

Tristan: **TV is bad for you, you know.**

Me: **I know.**

Tristan: **How does it feel, being home?**

Me: **Not especially awesome. Not horrible either.**

Tristan: Well, hang in there. Glad you are out of prison, as Simone calls it.

Me: ha ha. You write very grammatically correct texts, btw

Tristan: I know.

Me: Why?

Tristan: Because no one else does.

Me: Oh.

Tristan: I'll be in touch.

Me: okay

Me: Tristan?

Me: Tristan?

I stared at my screen for a few more seconds, convinced he'd text again and ask to get coffee, or go for a drive, or even just explain his thing for grammar. Anything. But he didn't. I wondered if I'd ever figure him out.

The next thing I knew, it was 5:30 and I was still on the floor, tangled in my dirty clothes. I must have fallen asleep. I checked to see if Tristan had texted again—nope—and shook off my nap haziness. Then I went downstairs.

"Hi, honey!" Dad said when I entered the kitchen. "We were just about to start dinner. Want to join us?"

"Yeah, okay." I turned to Mom, who was standing near the refrigerator. "Mom, you got my menus, right?"

Sally and I had planned my eating for the first week.

Three meals and three snacks a day, just like at Walling-field. Dinner tonight was one plain chicken breast, broc-coli with 1 teaspoon of butter, 1 cup of brown rice, three gingersnaps, 8 ounces of low-fat milk, and, for evening snack, ½ cup of granola and a yogurt. *Doable,* I told myself. *Completely doable.*

Mom nodded. "Yes. I met with your nutritionist. I got everything, I think." I wondered what Sally thought of Mom, if she'd had the urge to map out Mom's meals, too.

I grabbed a glass, filled it with water, and leaned against the counter. "Can I help?"

They exchanged glances. Dad cleared his throat and said, "You just relax and let us enjoy you." He reached over and, hugging me tight, murmured into my hair, "I love you, kiddo."

I blushed. "Thanks, Dad." I felt guilty that I'd lied to him about my afternoon snack. But there was nothing I could do about it now. Besides, it was almost time for dinner. Too late for a snack anyway.

In the dining room Mom set the table with our fanciest placemats, candles, and red and yellow tulips. It looked festive and lovely and had obviously been set with the expectation that we'd be celebrating. But I couldn't. My stomach was in knots.

When dinner came out, I picked a single spear of broccoli

332

from the bowl in the middle of the table. Then I grabbed my knife, cut off a piece of chicken breast, and placed it on my plate. Then I took a dollop of rice. Both parents stared at my plate, perplexed, like I'd failed a test I'd studied for all night long.

I didn't blame them. Even to me, my plate looked pathetic. Empty. No one spoke as Mom and Dad helped themselves. Mom took more than she usually would.

In a voice just a little bit too perky, she said, "I saw Shay's mom, Carol, at the supermarket. She got a new car. A convertible! It's lovely. Brian, wouldn't it be nice to have a convertible?"

Dad gripped his fork a little tighter. "Sure, Karen, right after we buy ourselves that summer house on the Cape."

"I was just making conversation. I'm not saying we have to get one. I'm just saying that a convertible would be fun to have *someday*."

"And so practical." Dad sounded defensive.

"Brian, I was just making a comment," Mom replied, hurt.

I took a bite of broccoli. "Is something wrong?" I asked.

"Everything's fine!" Mom leaned over, gave my arm a reassuring squeeze, and sat up straight.

We went back to eating in silence. Well, Mom and Dad ate. I moved the food around on my plate.

Dad put his fork down and exchanged a concerned

glance with Mom, whose eyes kept flitting between him and me like she didn't know whose side to take.

I managed three bites. Mom *and* Dad followed every single one from my plate to my mouth. The pressure was too much. "May I be excused?" I stood up so fast I knocked my chair over. "Sorry!" I said, and bolted upstairs without waiting for an answer.

They followed me. "Let us in!" Mom said through my closed door. She sounded scared. I wished I'd managed a few more bites.

"Elizabeth, open this door." Now she sounded pissed. "We are not leaving."

"We'll stay until morning, if that's what we have to do," Dad chimed in.

I stood on the other side of the door and said, "I'm really tired, guys. We were up late last night saying goodbye." Another lie.

They went quiet.

"The chicken was really good, Mom," I said. "Sally said I could take it easy on my meals the first day at home." Lie number three. "She said you could call and ask her about it if you want." Aaaaand there was lie number four.

And yet I kept going. "I'll eat everything tomorrow." I didn't know yet if that was a lie. "Don't worry," I said in the perkiest voice I could whip together. "Tomorrow is a new day."

They didn't respond. I could hear them whispering.

"We need to call right now." Dad sounded stern. "I know she's lying. I just know it. They would never let her skip."

"Let's give her a chance," Mom said, her voice soothing. "Being home is a big adjustment."

"Okay, but I don't like it. I hope we aren't making a mistake." Then they went downstairs, the wooden steps complaining the entire way.

Sometime after midnight I slipped out of bed, pulled on my comfy fleece slipper socks, and crept down to the kitchen, where a manila folder of printed-out menus lay on the 1980s-era beige tiled counter. With the hum of the fridge behind me, I flipped through the pages and pages of calories meant for me. They sped by in the form of lists organized by day and then by meal: yogurt, chicken, granola, cheese, fruits, vegetables, cereal, milk, bread, pita, cold cuts.

It seemed so easy, like it was ridiculous *not* to do it. I dug through the junk drawer next to the stove where we kept a bottle of Wite-Out. All I had to do was apply tiny white dabs here and there and voilà! More manageable menus. And I wouldn't white *everything* out; I'd just trim the calories a bit.

Now, I'd used Wite-Out before. I *knew* it sucked. But it was like Rational Me disappeared and this stupid, impulsive person took over. Or, more precisely, my eating disorder took over. Maybe this act was her last gasp. I don't know. But whatever it was, the one thing it definitely wasn't? Smart.

The first meal, tomorrow's breakfast, seemed easy enough. I whited out where I'd written one scrambled egg, leaving me with one Yoplait yogurt (any flavor), one banana, and 8 ounces of low-fat milk. Much better.

And then I noticed a little bit of Wite-Out on the black line printed beneath the letters.

Cursing under my breath, I went back to our junk drawer and dug out a skinny Sharpie to fix it. I carefully drew in the line. But instead of writing over the Wite-Out, it went right through the blob and made a weird gray line.

I should have stopped right there. But instead I kept going like I was obsessed or something, blobbing and cursing and scratching my way through the next six days, whiting out one item from each meal.

And then I heard Dad padding across the living room in his slippers he'd had since, like, 1992.

I shuffled the papers together and bumped into a kitchen chair, which scraped on the floor.

"Hello?" Dad called, his steps coming closer.

"Um . . . it's just me," I replied, frantically gathering up the still-wet papers.

"Couldn't sleep?" Dad looked groggy.

"Yeah, sorry. Did I wake you?" I tried to look calm. I leaned back against the counter like I was just hanging out. In the kitchen. At midnight.

"No, I've been having trouble sleeping," he said. "I often come down for a late-night snack these days." He smiled and patted his belly, which had gotten soft since I'd been gone.

Great. I'd made Dad fat. The irony didn't escape me. "I'm sorry, Dad, about tonight. I'll do better tomorrow. I promise." It scared me how easily the lying came.

"Okay. Just remember, your mom and I are on your side."

"I know." I wanted him to leave, but he walked over to me and he held out his arms and I gave him a quick and efficient pat. I could practically feel the papers drying all stuck together in that horrible pile.

"You want anything?" He opened the fridge.

"No, I'm okay."

He nodded. "You know, I think I'll pass as well. Can I walk you upstairs?" He turned around, and I noticed little patches of gray around his temples and dark circles under his eyes. He slumped now, too, even when he was standing. He hadn't looked like this six months ago. It reminded me of how presidents are elected looking one way and, four years later, they look like they've aged a couple decades.

337

"Thanks, Dad, but I'll be up in a minute. I was just looking at a magazine."

"What one?" he asked, his voice suddenly sharp.

"Huh?"

"What magazine?" He studied my face. He knew I was lying.

"Uh, well, I don't know what happened to it. It was just here." I scanned the kitchen. There had to be a magazine somewhere.

It didn't matter, because he didn't buy it. "Elizabeth, you have a chance here. An opportunity to get better. Don't screw it up."

I nodded.

"We want to trust you, but if we can't, things will change around here. You know what I'm saying?"

I pictured Mom and Dad monitoring my every bite, forbidding me to close my bedroom door, be alone in the house, or take a walk. I shuddered. No. That couldn't happen.

"You can trust me, Dad," I said. And I wanted that to be true. But even more importantly, I wanted to trust myself.

"I hope so." He reached over and placed his hand on my cheek, like he had when I was little. It felt warm and solid and made me feel even worse for lying.

"Well, good night, then. Don't stay up too late." After

one last glance around the room, he left, the door swinging behind him.

As soon as Dad was gone I tried to scrape away the blobs and dabs of Wite-Out, but all I succeeded in doing was making even more of a mess, including a tiny hole in one of the papers, which I ended up trying to fix with more Wite-Out. In the end, completely defeated, I shuffled the scarred papers back into a neat pile and trudged upstairs, praying that tomorrow a miracle would happen, that somehow I'd wake up, and the Wite-Out would just be a bad dream.

# *43*

**THE FIRST THING I SMELLED THE NEXT MORNING** was coffee. Real coffee. Someone was grinding beans. I jumped out of bed, pulled on an old pair of cross-country sweats, and headed downstairs. I was literally salivating. It smelled like heaven. I couldn't wait to have a steaming, hot cup of real coffee, not instant decaf, in my hand.

It wasn't until I'd swung around the large, wobbly newel post at the base of the stairs that I remembered. The menus. *Shit*.

I heard the rattle of the dishwasher closing and for a moment fooled myself into thinking that maybe everything was fine. But when I walked into the kitchen, Mom was standing at the counter, one hand on a bottle of dishwasher liquid, the other flipping through the unruly stack of paper.

My body clenched up. I tried to inch my way out of the room without her seeing or hearing me.

"Elizabeth." Mom's voice was quiet. She turned around, and for a second I knew what Mom would look like when she got old. "Why would you do this?" And then, louder, "I don't understand."

She'd set the table for one with a white lacy place mat I'd never seen before and a bowl from the pink-flowered fancy china set we only used at Thanksgiving and Christmas. She'd filled it with my yogurt and on a matching plate had arranged banana slices to look like a flower, with one raspberry in the middle. She'd poured my required glass of milk in our finest crystal and even stuck in a paper umbrella, like the kind you get at a beach resort.

"Don't understand what?"

"Your menus. What happened to your menus?"

"I don't know. Did something happen?"

Mom looked at me for a long second.

"Don't lie to me."

I crossed my arms and glowered at the wall behind her like this whole thing was her fault.

"Explain yourself."

I didn't say a word.

"Explain yourself," she said again. "Now."

*It isn't what you think,* I wanted to say, but deep in my heart I knew it was exactly what she thought. She stared at me for a few seconds more, then dropped the wad of paper in disgust and left the room.

I was going back to Wallingfield for sure.

Back in my room I locked my door, pulled on my ear-buds, and put on the *J-Curve* mix. I closed my eyes and pretended I was anywhere but here. The music was loud but not loud enough to keep me from hearing Mom's knock. I ignored it. She texted me a bit after that. **Come out and talk to me.**

**I'm sorry,** I typed. **I made a mistake.**

I wondered if I'd get my same room when they sent me back.

I'd read once about how sometimes people who are re-leased from prison commit crimes just to go back to jail. Did I want to go back, too? I pushed my pillow against my face as hard as I could. For the first time in weeks, it smelled like home.

An hour or so later, there was a knock on my door. "Elizabeth," Dad said through the wood, "open this door right now."

When I opened it, Dad was standing there, holding a tray with my breakfast on it. He looked even more tired than he had the night before. "You have a two-thirty phone call with Mary." He put the tray on my desk and sat down on the corner of my bed. I could smell a hint of his cologne. I'd always loved that smell. It made me feel safe.

"Elizabeth," he said, voice tight. "What the hell were you thinking?"

I stared at my hands and didn't answer. *I don't know what I was thinking,* I wanted to say.

"Answer me. Why did you do that? We just spent thousands of dollars to try to get you well. And then you do this? What are we supposed to think right now?"

"I thought health insurance paid" was the only lame answer I could come up with.

"Health insurance covered two weeks; we had to pay the rest out of pocket."

I'd heard Wallingfield cost a thousand dollars a day. I'd been at Wallingfield for forty days. Forty minus fourteen was twenty-six, which meant . . . Holy crap. *Twenty-six thousand dollars!* That's why he was so mad at dinner when Mom mentioned the convertible.

"Dad, we can't afford that. What are we going to do?"

"Well, you got a scholarship, for one thing. That knocked the price down a little."

A scholarship? Ha. "I always thought it was weird that Wallingfield called them that," I said.

"I know, right? Terrible name for it." A trace of a smile appeared on Dad's face.

I remembered on my first day, when Willa had talked about Wallingfield scholarships, how she'd had a tantrum in the dining room. How scared I'd been.

He collected my tray and brought it to me. "Eat," he said. I noticed that they'd added the scrambled egg I'd erased last night. I picked up the spoon and took a careful bite of yogurt.

With my mouth full I said, "Dad, I wish you'd told me how much it cost. I would have come home."

"I didn't tell you so you would feel guilty. I just—I want you to know that we are seriously invested, with every part of us—whether it be money or our hearts—and we will do anything to get you better." He paused. "Your treatment is worth it, Elizabeth. Anorexia *kills* people, and if Wallingfield can help you recover, it'll be the best money we've ever spent. Hands down. But it's on you now."

Why did getting better have to suck so much? Usually, if you were getting better from a disease, you *felt* better, right?

"Dad, I want to be done with this. But it is so hard. So. Hard." I speared a banana slice and slowly put it in my mouth.

He just listened.

"I *liked* going into a store and having everything be too big, and I *liked* feeling my ribs, my hip bones, the muscles in my thighs, my Achilles tendons, and my wrist bones. I don't want to not feel them. And I *loved* that my stomach was flat. It made me feel special. I like my bones, Dad."

Once I started, I couldn't stop.

"Do you know what type of control it takes to *not eat*? To sit down with a stomach so empty it makes you dizzy and foggy and think about food every single second of the day and still skip breakfast, lunch, dinner, dessert? Every day? Do you? It is so hard. But it's amazing to know that no matter what your body tells you to do, you can control it." It was like I was describing an elite athlete, an endurance runner or triathlete pushing through normal physical limits, not someone slowly starving herself.

Dad looked horrified.

"Elizabeth, I wish I could understand better. But what I know is that people beat this all the time."

"But what if I don't want to beat it?" There. The words were out there.

He took my hand. "Listen to me very carefully. We are not going to let this disease steal you from us."

"I know, and a part of me does want to get well. I promise."

He nodded.

I so wanted to believe what I said next. "Okay, Dad. I'll try. I promise I'll try. For you guys."

Dad stood. "You know, Elizabeth, in the end, you can say you'll try for us all you want, but it won't mean anything unless you start trying for yourself."

He stayed with me until I ate every single bit of food on my tray.

At snack time I came down to the kitchen and ate my granola bar and yogurt like a good girl even though I was still full. I ate my lunch, too—a can of Progresso lentil soup, two slices of bread with butter, a cup of green beans with 1 teaspoon of butter, a cup of strawberries sprinkled with ¼ cup of granola, and 8 ounces of milk. I finished in an hour. Mom and Dad were super cheery, saying, "Great job on that one!" after almost every bite, or "Well, there you go! Almost done now!"

Honestly, it was a little ridiculous. I felt like a seven-year-old at a soccer game, being praised just for running in the direction of the ball.

At 2:30 on the dot, Mary called on my cell phone. I took it in my bedroom. She said I wasn't going back to Wallingfield. Yet. "However, if you decide you have no choice but to relapse," she said, "you will."

"I know. I don't want to." What I didn't say was that I still wanted to be thin. I still wanted to fit into the jeans and skirts in my closet. In my heart I knew that to get better I had to dump them all, but a part of me couldn't bear it. I had worked so hard for those clothes. Fitting into them had been my biggest achievement.

"So what am I supposed to do now?"

"Well, I know this is going to sound anticlimactic, but I think you are just going to have to trust that with time, things will change. The urges won't be as strong. And it can help to create a distraction tool kit for when you start to feel like you might give in. Do you remember when we talked about it?"

"Yes." Mary and I had worked on it at our last meeting together. A distraction tool kit is a list of things you can do when the anorexia voice in your head gets loud, like watch a funny movie, call a friend, go to the mall, listen to music, or do yoga. "But what if all that stuff doesn't help?"

"Well, then you can call us. We have counselors on duty all the time."

"Okay." I wasn't convinced.

"Elizabeth, what it comes down to is this. *Wanting* to get better, while important, isn't enough. You have to *work* to get better. This isn't a disease where you take medicine and then wait. You have to choose. Your recovery is one hundred percent up to you."

After we hung up, I burrowed under a blanket and took a nap. It was only 3:15, but it felt like midnight.


My parents were already in their places when I came down for dinner at 7:30. "Your mother and I have come up with a contract," Dad announced. "You agree to eat your meals. We agree to do everything we can to help you. If you break this contract, we will send you back to Wallingfield. Got it?"

Totally numb, I nodded and signed my name. Mom let out an audible sigh of relief as she went to the kitchen to get our plates. Mine was so full it looked like an entrée from the Cheesecake Factory. There was enough food on that plate for five people—the biggest chicken breast I'd ever seen, about five big portions of broccoli, and one massive baked potato, split with sour cream already getting all liquidy in the middle. I was supposed to eat all this?

My face must have given me away. Mom said, "This is what it said on your menu, honey. What's wrong?"

She was right, but so, so wrong. Mom, the queen of diet portions, had royally screwed up my dinner. Sure, the menu said one chicken breast, but it didn't say one chicken breast on steroids! And that potato—at Wallingfield they were never that big, and the sour cream was always served on the side. Always. And five pieces of broccoli with butter didn't mean five separate heads. It meant five little pieces of the same head!

I cut a tiny piece of chicken and put it on my tongue. I chewed, tasting rosemary, garlic, and olive oil. The chicken was supposed to be plain. Somehow, I swallowed. I cut another piece. Across from me, Dad's plate was as full as mine. Mom's plate, however, looked like it always did: little islands of food surrounded by a sea of porcelain.

At 8:45, my cold, congealed food looked like it had come from an all-you-can-eat buffet past its prime. The

Wallingfield kitchen would have gotten the portions right. I'd be done by now. At least the meals were timed there. At home we were on our own.

I took one more small bite of potato. "Do you think this is enough?"

"Honey, I'm sorry, but the agreement was that you'd eat everything on your plate." I could tell Dad wanted to end this as much as I did.

"But the portion sizes are huge! They're twice what we got at Wallingfield! I ate everything I would have there! I swear it!"

"You can't leave this table until you have eaten your whole meal. You signed a contract." Mom looked pained.

I stared at my plate. *You have a choice.* Mary's voice pinged through my head. *No one gains weight from a single meal.*

"Okay," I said.

"Okay what?" Mom and Dad looked at me at the same time.

"Okay. I'll try."

"Good!" Dad said. "Karen, would you like me to pour you a glass of wine?"

Mom nodded. "Yes, please."

Dad cleared their empty plates and returned with two glasses of red and a Pellegrino. "I opened the good stuff," he said. "For all of us." My fizzy water had a lemon tucked into the bottle top. "I think we all deserve it."

At 9:30, I was still struggling. "Just a little more, Elizabeth," Dad said, and I could hear the frustration in his voice. To his credit, though, he tried to hide it. "Just finish up and we can both go to bed." Dad rubbed his eyes. He never stayed up past nine. Mom had gone to bed.

A fat, salty tear ran down my cheek, and I wiped it away. I pictured myself under my covers. My warm, soft comforter, fresh out of the dryer. My fluffy pillow. I picked up my fork. I took another bite of chicken. I gagged but got it down. The broccoli was limp, the milk warm.

Dad stood up and stretched. "I gotta hand it to you, kiddo. Your self-control and resolve are impressive. I know I would have given in about thirty minutes after this all started. You're like your mom in that way. She's always been stubborn, too."

"The difference, Dad, is that I am trying hard to change myself. I'm working on my flaws."

"She tries harder than you think, honey."

I sighed. "I know."

Dad nodded. "She's always wanted an easy life for you, that's all."

It still stung a little that Mom thought I'd had to lose weight in the first place. Some things, it turns out, you can regret saying with all your heart, but all the regret in the world doesn't make them hurt less.

"Elizabeth, your mom has spent her whole life feeling

like she wasn't good enough. Did you know that she went on her first diet at age seven? Seven! A girl called her fat, and when she went home, she saw what that other girl saw. And she felt like a failure. Did she ever tell you that?"

She hadn't.

"Maybe Wallingfield would have helped her," Dad said. "I don't know. But if you beat this, she'll see that. She's already seeing it."

I could barely help myself; how was I supposed to help Mom, too? "I'm the kid, Dad. The kid. I shouldn't have to take care of Mom."

"I'm not asking you to," he said. "Just go easy on her. I'm going to go heat up your plate in the microwave. I'll be back in a minute. Don't go anywhere."

When he returned, steaming plate in hand, he said, "Come on, kiddo. How about one bite while it's still warm?" and set it down in front of me. "As Robert Frost said, 'The best way out is always through.'"

I picked up my fork. Mom would never have given in like this, I thought miserably, shoving a bit of lukewarm, rubbery chicken in my mouth.

Nine fifty. I choked down the last chunk of potato, skin and all. Dad gave me a high five. I was so tired I could barely return it. I couldn't even obsess about the ball of food in my stomach. But I wasn't too exhausted to make Dad promise, before I took my last bite, that he'd call Sally and talk to her about portion sizes. I didn't care how long I had to sit at that table, I told him. I would not go through another meal like that again.

"Nope. Not like your mom at all," Dad said.

I didn't have the energy to argue.

# 44

THE NEXT AFTERNOON, KATRINA SHOWED UP. When the doorbell rang and I saw her outside, I actually jumped up and down in excitement. Wonderful, beautiful Katrina. My friend. "Kat!" I squealed, flinging open the door and hugging her as she stood there in her black puffy coat and red hat. "Thank you for coming! Thank you, thank you, thank you!"

I was so ready for her arrival. So far, my day had consisted of: breakfast with Mom, a snack and coffee run with Dad, lunch with Dad, and four episodes of *Friends* with Mom; she'd apparently watched the show in college, when it was actually on TV. All this together time was killing me. But now Katrina was here.

"Jeez," she said with a smile as she extricated herself from my death grip. "Hi there."

Then I saw Priya and Shay behind her. They'd made me a sign: *WELCOME HOME, ELIZABETH* in bubble writing.

"Elizabeth!" Priya yelled, like she hadn't just blown me off for the entire month. She was wearing a brown fake-fur vest I hadn't seen before. "I have missed you so much!" She flung herself at me. "I have so many things to tell you!" She paused. "Oh my God, you look great. So great!"

Shay stepped up next. At least she had the decency to be a little sheepish. "Hey, Elizabeth," she said. "Can I give you a hug? It is so good to see you."

I shrugged. "Okay."

She gave me a quick squeeze.

"Why are you guys here? Katrina, don't you have"—I checked my phone to make sure I had the right day of the week—"your chem tutor this afternoon?"

"Yeah. I can't stay long. She changed our time because she had something to do. And I wanted to come and say hi."

"I'm so glad."

"Me too. These guys were dying to see you, too, so I picked them up on the way." Both Shay and Priya smiled and bobbed their heads.

"Wait!" Priya yelled. She wore a miniskirt and boots. She looked fabulous, all tan and tall. Her skin never looked pale, even in the winter. She was so lucky. "We forgot something!"

Shay patted me on the shoulder. "We'll be right back. Don't move." They walked back down the path to Katrina's car.

Katrina turned to me. Speaking in a soft voice she said, "Your mom called mine and told her to send me over." She stopped smiling. "It was sort of weird to have to hear from my mom that you were home. Why didn't you tell me?"

"I know. I'm sorry. It's just, well, I don't know." And I didn't. I'd meant to text her, really, but I didn't know what I'd say when she asked how I was doing. I wasn't sure myself.

"Katrina, why are Priya and Shay here?"

Katrina glanced at the car, nervous. "I told you at Wallingfield. They missed you."

Maybe. Maybe not.

Katrina kept making excuses. "They've been super busy lately, you know—"

I stopped her. "You don't have to keep covering for them."

"I'm not! They're just deep into junior year, you know?"

"I guess."

She put a hand on my arm. "Well, they're here now. Give them a chance, okay? I've missed it being the four of us."

I had, too.

After Shay and Priya bounded up the front walk again, Shay holding a bag, we all went into the living room and sat down. Mom peeked in and smiled so wide I thought her head might explode. "Well, hello, everybody! It's really great to see you!"

"Hi, Mrs. Barnes," they all said.

"Can I get you anything?"

We shook our heads.

"No? Okay, well, I won't bother you. Stay as long as you'd like!"

I pretended not to see Mom mouth "Thanks" to Katrina before she left.

"So, we have something for you," Priya said. She pulled a box out of the bag and handed it to me.

"Oh?" I wanted to be mad. But they looked so goofy. "Okay?"

They'd wrapped the box in pink paper and tied a big white bow. I opened it, knowing there would be some sort of silly joke gift inside. Priya loved giving joke presents. For my birthday she'd given me "the perfect man," a man-doll keychain who, when you pressed his belly, said things like, *Okay, honey, whatever you say,* and *Honey, what I really want to do is go to Bed Bath and Beyond.* So totally sexist, I know, but it cracked me up anyway. I still had it somewhere.

But this wasn't a joke. Inside was a pair of the prettiest, softest turquoise pajamas I'd ever seen.

"They're silk," Shay said.

"They're beautiful." I got a little teary. I fingered the white lace at the neckline. The same lace lined the cuffs of the pants. "Thank you."

"We bought them for you a couple of weeks ago, but we weren't organized enough to actually mail them. We're sorry," Priya said.

"Really sorry," Shay added.

"It's true," Katrina mouthed.

I was still mad. Don't get me wrong. They'd totally blown me off. But Katrina was right. The whole thing— me being in Wallingfield—was weird. *I* didn't even know how to address it with other people, and I was the one who'd been there. "It's okay," I said, and I meant it.

"So," Katrina asked, clearly relieved. I could practically see her checking us off her mental to-do list. "When are you coming back to school?"

"Tomorrow."

"That's awesome!"

I wasn't so sure.

"What else is going on?" Katrina asked. "Who have you talked to?"

I wasn't sure whether to mention Tristan or not.

But these were my friends. "So, I'm sort of friends with Tristan McCann now."

Katrina looked at me, face blank. "Tristan?" She furrowed her brows. "Tristan *McCann*? Charlie's Tristan?"

I nodded.

"Wow. How did that happen?"

Priya squealed a little.

I told them everything. When I finished, I pulled out the brass ring from under my clothes.

"Holy crap. Are you going to go out with him?" That was from Shay.

"Tristan is pretty hot, in his own dark and brooding way," Priya added.

Katrina just waited for me to actually answer the question.

"No! No. I mean, I don't think so. We're friends. He just sort of gets me."

"Wow. So, just friends, huh? You sure about that?" Katrina raised one eyebrow.

"Yes! Totally. Just friends." At least, I thought we were friends.

"Okay, if you say so."

An alarm went off on Katrina's phone. "Damn it. I have to go. Mom will kill me if I'm late for my session. Come on, you guys."

They couldn't leave. I wanted us all to curl up on the sofa and talk until it got dark. "Do you have to go?"

"I'll text you later." Katrina hugged me and stepped out into the sunlight. Priya squeezed me, too, and so did Shay. "I'm really sorry about not calling," she whispered in my ear. "But I'm so glad you're home."

"Me too," I said back. And for the first time since leaving Wallingfield, I meant it.

# 45

**MY MENU CALLED FOR CHICKEN STIR-FRY WITH**
fresh veggies for dinner. I was almost looking forward to
it. Mom made a mean stir-fry. She used almost no oil. As
she cut the chicken, she weighed the pieces on the scale
Dad had picked up that afternoon after his conversation
with Sally. I loved that thing, even if I was forbidden to
touch it.

I got a text right after I'd sat down. My phone was on
the counter, just past the table.

I stood up to get it, but Dad frowned. "No texting until
you finish dinner."

It was pointless to argue, so I ate as fast as I could, only
struggling with the last bit of white rice. If I'd had more
time, I might have enjoyed it even more. I'd missed vegetables so much at Wallingfield.

The last bite was still in my mouth when I asked, "May I be excused?"

"Maybe we should have people text you more often," Dad said, clearly astounded at my eating speed. To tell the truth, so was I. "You're excused."

"Thanks!" I jumped out of my seat and pretended not to hear him ask me to clear my plate. In my room, I flung myself on my bed, opened up my phone, and found a text from Tristan:

**You surviving?**

It had been thirty minutes since he'd sent it. I hoped I hadn't missed him.

Me: **You there?**

Tristan: **Yes, I'm still here.**

Tristan: **What are you doing?**

Me: **just finished dinner**

Tristan: **I'm going somewhere. Want to come?**

Me: **Where?**

Tristan: **Does it matter?**

Me: **I guess not.**

Tristan: **Good. I'll be there in ten minutes.**

Me: **Where are we going?**

Me: **Hello?**

Me: **Tristan?**

I threw the phone down and jumped off my bed. I had nothing to wear. Everything was so small. I had larger clothes that I'd boxed up a few months ago and put in the attic, but there was no freaking way I was going to drag them down now. What if they actually fit? Just the possibility made me want to go downstairs and throw away all the food in the fridge. Besides, there wasn't time to try anything on now, and even if there was, they'd probably smell weird from being up there—like attic, all dusty and old. And who wants to smell like that? Not me.

I'd just dumped my clean laundry bin out on the floor and was about two seconds away from total meltdown mode (tears, general hysteria) when Mom appeared at my door. "Elizabeth, honey, what are you doing?"

I dug through the pile of T-shirts and sweatpants in frustration. "I don't have anything to wear. What am I going to do?" I could hear the shriek in my voice. "I'm going to look awful. I should never have agreed to go."

Mom didn't ask any questions, like where I might be going, or who with. She just said, "Take a deep breath. I have something for you. I was going to give it to you tomorrow, but maybe now is a better time."

She disappeared and returned a minute later with a large Urban Outfitters bag. Inside were four pairs of the same jeans, in different sizes. Bigger sizes. Same with four pairs of green corduroys, two cute black dresses, two blue sweaters, and two white long-sleeved shirts.

"I didn't know what size to get, so I got a variety. I thought maybe you'd prefer to try them on in private and not have to deal with the whole store dressing room thing." Mom looked a little nervous, like she was afraid I'd hate everything she'd picked out. "I can just return whatever doesn't fit." She cleared her throat and rubbed her hands on her pant leg. "What do you think?"

I touched her arm. "Thanks, Mom." I wanted to hug her and cry at the same time. Hug because she'd done this for me, and cry because all these clothes were sizes that, just a few weeks before, I'd have gladly dismissed as too huge for me.

She took a deep breath and nodded, relieved. "I'll give you some privacy," she said, and slipped out my door.

I dumped the bag out on my bed and pulled on a pair of dark skinny jeans with zippers at the ankle. They were way too tight. They were my pre-Wallingfield size. I kicked them off.

I shook off the depression lurking in my corners. I'd deal later. Tristan was going to be here in, like, five minutes. I pulled out another pair, bigger this time. They buttoned easily. I avoided the label. Then I put on the bigger white shirt and the smallest blue sweater, which was thick and warm. I brushed my hair and then, as an afterthought, put on lipstick. Real lipstick. Pale, skin-colored lipstick, but still. It was a step up from ChapStick.

I opened my door and took a deep breath. *You can do this,* I told myself. I stepped in the hall, hyper-aware of how the jeans hugged my legs. *They're supposed to fit that way. That's what skinny jeans do.* I breathed in again. Tristan was going to be there any second. *Get yourself together, Elizabeth!*

I hustled down the stairs and into the living room, where I could watch for Tristan through the picture window. "Mom, Dad, I'm going out!"

Mom came in and her face lit up. "Oh, wow! You look great! I am so glad some of those things worked." She seemed genuinely pleased, and I felt better.

The voice in my head came out of nowhere. *Tristan is going to think you look so fat.*

I shook my head, as if that would make a difference. *Shut up,* I pleaded with myself. *Just shut up.*

I got my fleece out of the closet. Mom helped me into one of the sleeves, like when I was little. "Now, what are your plans?"

"I'm going to hang out with Tristan. You know, from school? He's picking me up."

"Tristan McCann?" Mom asked.

I nodded, heart sinking. I'd totally forgotten that Mom had worked on the school fund-raising committee with his mother.

"When did you get to be friends with Tristan McCann?"

She looked so pleased. Too pleased. I picked my words carefully.

"At Wallingfield. His sister is a day patient. I hung out with them sometimes."

"Oh? That's right. I'd heard his sister was having some problems. How is she doing?"

"Fine, I guess."

"I should reach out to her mom."

"Please don't."

A car pulled into the driveway, its headlights cutting through the dark room like flashlights.

"I gotta go. Bye, Mom." I grabbed my purse and made for the door, hoping to escape before she asked the inevitable.

"Isn't he going to come in and introduce himself?"

And there it was. "Mom, this isn't a date, okay? We're just friends."

She hesitated before answering, so I bolted, making it all the way out the door and down the steps before she said, "Elizabeth! Your snack! Come get your granola and cheese!"

Ugh. For once I wished that I could just leave my anorexia behind. I turned around and grabbed the baggie and red wax–covered cheese out of her hand. I shoved them both in my purse.

Tristan stood next to the Jeep, holding my door open for me.

"Hey. How's it going?" he said as I hopped in. The car smelled like cologne and for a second my eyes watered. Tristan's hair was a little damp; he must have just showered. The ends curled over the collar of his coat.

"Hey," I said, settling in and clicking my seat belt. "Where are we going?"

"You'll see." He threw the car in reverse and backed down my driveway, and we were on our way.

My thighs spread out across the seat. I hated the way that felt. Before I even realized what I'd done, I pointed my toes, which lifted my thighs about an inch off the surface. They looked a little slimmer that way.

Tristan turned on the radio. "This is a great song," he said. "I love Radiohead." I didn't recognize it. I wished now I'd paid more attention to Margot when she talked about music. Maybe I would have had something to say.

Traffic was light, and we flew down the highway. When Tristan took the exit for Route 60, a two-lane highway lined with oil change shops, used car dealerships, strip malls, and the occasional Dunkin' Donuts, I knew where we were going. "Are you taking me to the airport?"

He kept his eyes on the road and nodded.

"Are we going to the Bahamas?" I said, trying to joke. "I should have worn my bikini!" He didn't laugh.

"I was just kidding," I said. "I didn't really think you're taking me to the Bahamas."

"I know," he said.

God, this was so awkward.

We passed a sign officially welcoming us to Logan International Airport. Tristan pulled into a parking garage and didn't say anything as we wound our way up through the middle of the concrete maze, passing spot after open spot as we went. "You're missing a lot of open spaces," I said, and immediately winced. I sounded like Mom.

"I see 'em," he said. One last ramp and we were on the roof, which was nearly empty. He pulled into a spot facing the runway and killed the engine and headlights.

In the sudden dark, the lights of the airport, the inky black ocean, and the lit-up Boston skyline stretched out in front of us. The air filled with the white noise of distant plane engines, taxiing and landing and taking off.

"Why are we here, exactly?" I asked.

"To watch planes. Come on."

I followed him out of the car and around to the front. "Let's sit," he said, and helped me up onto the hood. The engine was warm, which dulled the feel of the cold November night air through my fleece. I wondered why we couldn't have gone to the movies or coffee or something else like regular people did.

"You're cold?" I hadn't realized I was shivering. "Here," Tristan said, taking off his wool coat and wrapping it around my shoulders. "Wear this." It was still warm, and

367

despite the strong cologne-and-cigarettes smell wafting out of the navy fabric, it felt heavy and cozy. I snuggled into it.

Tristan sat next to me and I figured we'd talk then, but he pulled out his phone and started tapping instead. Had he brought me all the way out here to check messages?

"Ready?" he said after a minute, his eyes on the screen. "Look out at the runway."

I heard the roar first. The massive thunder rumble of a jet engine. As the noise got louder, the lights got closer and a plane—"It's a 747!" Tristan yelled over the noise—accelerated down the runway like a giant white bullet. The engines screamed and blocked out my thoughts and then the nose lifted, the rest of the plane following, its lights flashing. When the plane was safely in the air, it banked left, and I could see its entire wingspan, stretched like an eagle's.

"Wow," I breathed. "It was so close."

Tristan half smiled and consulted his phone again. "That one's either going to Dublin, Amsterdam, or Frankfurt."

"How do you know?"

"There's an app that tells you the takeoff schedule." He paused for a second and then asked, "Which plane do you want it to be?" He lay back flat on the Jeep hood and stared up at the sky. I did too. The ground was too lit up to see stars, but now that I knew what to look for, the sky was full of lights—plane lights, blinking and regular, full of people coming home and going away.

"Dublin." I shivered. "I would love to see Ireland. What about you?"

"I don't care. Anywhere but here."

"Do you do this a lot?"

"Yeah. I've sort of been obsessed with planes since I was little."

"So you can recognize the different types of planes?"

He nodded and crossed his arms, squeezing them tight. I wondered if he was cold. "I know. It's totally random. I mean, who sits around and watches planes?"

"I think it's cool," I said quickly. Because it was, sort of. And who was I to judge? My only hobby was starving, and look how that had turned out.

A light turned our way in the distance. "Oh! Here comes another plane!" I jumped off the hood and leaned against the concrete barrier. "Where is it going?"

Tristan checked his phone. "Either Paris or Detroit," he said.

"I hope it's Paris," I said.

The plane was smaller than the last. "It's Detroit," Tristan said loudly, over the plane's engine. "A Boeing 757. International flights are the ones with the big planes."

Big or small, when its front wheel lifted off the ground,

it looked impossibly massive. I stretched my arms in the sky and looked up at the dark night.

"Don't you wish you could get on one of those planes right now?" Tristan said.

"Totally." And I did. How great would it be to just hop on a plane and end up somewhere exciting and new—like Paris, or London, or Bangkok? Heck, I'd even take Miami.

"How does the eleven-fifty flight to Iceland sound?"

"Ha. I wish." It *was* tempting. No more Esterfall. No more angst.

"Come on!" Tristan hopped off the car and held out his hand. "Let's do it." His eyes found mine and held them.

"Too bad I don't have a passport," I said.

"Ah, that is a problem." He dropped his hand, but just for a second. "Let's drive, then. Let's just point my Jeep west and get out of here. Go to California or something. You'd never have to think about Wallingfield again."

Looking at him standing there, ready to take my hand, I could picture us. I could hear the music playing, see the Jeep flying past mountains and ocean and fields of corn, and feel my feet out the window, the air rushing through my toes.

*BEEP BEEP.* My reminder on my phone went off. Nine thirty.

Reality called. "It's time for my snack, Tristan."

"If we go away, you could eat whenever you want. You wouldn't have to be the anorexic girl ever again."

It all sounded so lovely. Except for one thing. "Tristan, thousands of miles won't stop me from counting calories in my head."

"How do you know that?" he said. "How do you *know*?"

"I just do." Sighing, I ate some granola, the chunks crunching loudly in my mouth. "Want some?" I asked.

Tristan shook his head. We got back on the hood of the car. Tristan took my hand and we lay there, side by side, staring at the night sky.

I didn't know how long we lay there. It felt like hours. All I know is that I felt closer to him than I ever had to Charlie. And then, just when things felt really right, Tristan slid a little bit closer to me.

I dropped his hand.

"It's late," I said hurriedly, hopping off the hood.

"Wait." He took my arm and gently pulled me toward him. He had long, beautiful eyelashes. I'd never noticed them before. He grazed my cheek with his pointer finger. "Thank you, Elizabeth Barnes," he whispered, "for coming here with me."

Gently, he ran one hand over my hair, and then it was like the Elizabeth I knew wasn't in control, like a new version—Elizabeth 2.0—had taken over. This Elizabeth let her fingers drift up toward Tristan's hair like girls did in the movies. When he moved his finger under her chin, lifted it up, leaned in, and kissed her, she kissed him back, no biggie.

But when his arms slipped down around her rib cage and his fingers rubbed over each individual rib, Version 2.0 disappeared like a ghost sucked into a vacuum.

I pulled away.

He took a deep breath. "I like you, Elizabeth."

"I like you, too. But I can't do this. I'm sorry."

"Is this about Charlie?"

"No. This is about me."

"You sure?"

"I'm one hundred percent sure. I just—I think I need to focus on getting better." I didn't add that I also needed to be able to look at my body in the mirror before I let anybody else see it. "But I do like you," I said. "Please don't be mad."

"I'm not mad." But the way he slid off the hood and stood with his back to me, studying the sky, indicated otherwise.

I slid off too. "You know, I'm not saying no forever. Just for right now." I tried to catch his eye, but he wouldn't look at me.

"Okay."

We climbed into the Jeep. He didn't open my door this time.

He started the car and let it idle. The headlights illuminated a blue Nissan Sentra parked down the way a bit. Then, after a minute or two, he put his hand over mine.

"Your hand is freezing," he said. "I'll warm it up."

I exhaled. "I'd like that." By the time we got home, my fingers weren't cold at all.

# 46

**ON MONDAY MORNING, I WOKE UP AT 4:59 A.M.**
My alarm was set for 6:47, like it had been since sixth grade, but I couldn't sleep. I lay in bed for a few minutes, hoping I'd fall back asleep, but it was no use. I was up.

My worries followed me down the hall and into the shower. I'd missed weeks of classes and homework. Would I be completely lost? Was I going to fail everything? If I failed, how would I get into college? What if the teachers made me make up *all* the work I'd missed? How would I manage that? Midterms were last week; would I have to take them?

I needed a mantra. Or a song. The Kelly Clarkson song on my mix from Tristan came to mind. The song thrummed in my head. As I lathered up my shampoo I tried to sing, but I'd never had a good voice and I couldn't remember all the words, so I ended up half humming, half rapping the same few words over and over as I shaved my legs and conditioned my hair.

The house was still dark when I turned off the water, wrapped myself in a towel, and padded back down the hall to my room.

"Good morning!"

I whipped around, almost losing my towel in the process. Mom was sitting on my bed in her cotton pajamas.

"Sorry, did I startle you?"

"Yeah, a little. What are you doing up?" I said, fumbling to cover myself.

Mom's eyes flitted over me, starting at my shoulders and ending at my ankles. She cleared her throat. "I couldn't sleep."

"Oh." My hair dripped water onto the floor.

"What are you going to wear today?" she asked. My heart sank a little. She always asked me this, and I always disappointed her.

"Well, I thought I'd wear those new jeans you got me."

"Great. They might go well with this. I thought you could borrow it if you wanted." She handed me a cashmere cowl-necked sweater the color of raspberries. It was my favorite sweater of hers; she'd never let me borrow it before.

When I took it I was struck, like always, by how soft it was. I rubbed it on my cheek. It smelled like her perfume. And all of a sudden I remembered smelling the same smell on my *Blue's Clues* T-shirt my first day of kindergarten, after Mom had left. I'd buried my nose into my shoulder all day, breathing in her scent whenever I got sad. I'd missed her so much. It was sort of nice to think I could do the same today. "Thanks, Mom. It's perfect."

She looked relieved. "I'm glad it will work. Honey . . ." She paused and looked at me, almost desperately. "I know today is going to be hard, but I want you to remember that I'll be thinking about you all day, okay? *All day.* And I know you might be worried that kids are going to stare or gossip. But you're tougher than they are. You keep your head up and look for your friends. And think of me, here, cheering you on."

I pulled my towel tighter. "Thanks, Mom."

She grabbed my hand. "You have been through a war, and you've won. You are stronger than you think, Elizabeth. I am so proud of you. I love you, honey."

"I love you too," I said. And I meant it.


Dad dropped me off fifteen minutes before the first bell. I had hoped it might be early enough that I could slip up the front steps of Esterfall High relatively unnoticed, but no such luck. Kids stood around the grassy front lawn wearing puffy coats and other types of warm jackets.

Trying to get my body out of the car felt like working up the courage to dive into an icy-cold pool. I knew it would hurt. "Everything will be fine, honey," Dad said quietly. "People are going to be so glad to see you."

*You are strong,* my mom had said, but what if she was wrong? I scoured the clumps of kids to see if Katrina was around; she often wore a red knit hat on cold mornings. Lots of red, lots of hats, but not one of them was hers. If she were with me I could do this. I should have told her to meet me here. I pulled out my phone and shot her a text. **At school. You here?**

"Elizabeth," Dad said, placing his warm hand on mine, "the best way out is through. Go on, honey, it will be fine. I just know it." Then he ruffled my hair, leaned across me, and opened the door. My hands flew up to smooth my hair the second he finished. I checked my phone. No response from Katrina. I was on my own. I lifted one leg up and watched it float over the car threshold; the other followed.

I ignored the girls who stared and the groups who whispered about me behind their cupped hands. *I've been through a war,* I told myself as I pulled open the ornate wooden doors of the school. *A war that I won.* But honestly, I didn't know if I believed it.

# 47

WHEN THE BIG DOORS CLANKED SHUT, THE sudden quiet of the hallway surrounded me like warm water. Two teachers talked down the hall, the murmur of their voices mixing with the muted sounds of outside. One laughed. For the first time in my life, I was jealous of teachers. No one cared what they looked like; no one whispered about them.

The front door flew open behind me and a girl stumbled in, her face hidden by a ginormous hood. When she pulled it off and shook out her hair, my heart dropped.

Heather.

We locked eyes. *You didn't break me,* I told her with my glare.

"Welcome back, Elizabeth," she said, almost meekly. And then, without another word, she walked down the hall.

Maybe I could get through this day.

I headed to my locker with its familiar dings and scratches. Everything was where I'd left it: my brown brush, a bottle of Pantene hair spray, and my red cross-country sweatshirt—turned inside out from the last time I'd worn it.

From behind, Katrina practically tackled me.

"Hi! Oh my God, hi!" I said, my voice cracking a little.

We hugged for a long second before she pulled back to look at me. "So, how are you?"

"Okay, I guess."

"Well, you look great. I love your sweater."

"Thanks," I said gratefully, rubbing the soft fuzz of it. I thought I caught a whiff of Mom.

Katrina looked at me for another second, as if deciding how to continue. "So," she said, "are you ready for history? Ready to meet Tom?"

"Yes! Do you still think he's hot?"

"No. Sadly, his personality came out, and that pretty much wiped out all the attraction. I think *The Simpsons* phase was just a ploy to get us to like him. He gives us so much work that it's like he thinks his class is the only one we have."

"That sucks," I said. Figured that I'd miss all the fun and return for the hard part.

As we walked down the hall, voices ricocheted off the

walls around me and into the classrooms, but I kept my head low, avoiding eye contact, like if I couldn't see people whispering about me, they weren't. *What doesn't kill you makes you stronger,* I repeated to myself.

Katrina looked at me funny. "Are you singing Kelly Clarkson?"

Oops. "Maybe?" I smiled apologetically. "Sorry about that."

"Don't apologize," she said, putting her arm around my shoulders. "It's as good a theme song as any for this place." And then, with that, we went off to history.

# 48

**BEFORE I KNEW IT, THE BELL WAS RINGING FOR** lunch. The sound of the cafeteria at lunchtime was terrifying, loud voices pouring out like club music. The air was humid with the smells of school lunch—something with bacon—and I could practically see molecules of liquid fat floating through the air and sticking to my skin. Thank God I didn't have to eat in there.

When Mom called the school on Friday to let them know I was coming back, she'd asked—no, demanded—that someone supervise me eating. I'd gotten mad, told Mom it wasn't necessary, but she'd insisted. "You are going to be under a lot of stress the first few days you go back. I want you to have support." So I'd promised my parents I'd eat lunch in Nurse Keller's office. That way she could sit with me and check off what I ate. At the time

I was pissed. Now I said a silent thank-you to Mom under my breath.

Nurse Keller wasn't there when I arrived. In the quiet of her office, I took a deep breath for what felt like the first time all day. The morning had gone by fast. English and math hadn't changed a bit, but Katrina was right about Tom. He was cute, sure—tall, with a face that looked a little like Ryan Gosling's. But he spent the entire period lecturing us on the War of 1812. He never even asked questions—he just talked the entire time.

After five minutes, Nurse Keller still wasn't there. "Excuse me?" I said, opening the door to the front office. Ms. Linda, one of the secretaries, saw me and sighed.

"Hello, Elizabeth," she said. "I assume you're here for your lunch." She looked annoyed. "Nurse Keller called in sick today, and I'm in the middle of some business in the office. Can you handle this by yourself, or do you need me with you?"

Sick? Today? That wasn't part of the plan.

"No problem," I lied. "I'll be okay."

She looked at me, her eyes narrowing. "Are you sure?"

"Yup. I'll be great," I lied again. "I have homework to keep me company." Not exactly a lie, since I did have homework, but I could never focus on it when food was in front of me.

"Okay," she said. "Keep the door open. If you need

anything, I'll be in the next room. Let me know when you're done."

"I will." I sat down and pulled the lunch box from the bottom of my backpack. It was new and covered with flowers in pink, yellow, orange, red, and green, like something you'd send to school with a first grader. A note from Mom was inside.

*Thought you might like a new lunch box for your fresh start. You can do this! Take one bite at a time. Call me if you have trouble. Love, Mom.* And, hurriedly scribbled below it, *and Dad too!*

Beneath the note were a number of small Tupperware boxes, clear with green plastic lids. Too many, it seemed. I looked at the included lunch list: *turkey sandwich on wheat bread w/ 1 slice American cheese, lettuce, 2 tsp. mayonnaise, ½ avocado, and tomato slice (1), apple (1), Greek yogurt (1), granola bar (1),* and *milk (1).*

For the first time since checking into Wallingfield, I was alone at mealtime. No one would see if I wrapped that turkey sandwich up in a napkin, put it in my backpack, and threw it away in one of the trash cans around school. Same with the apple, Greek yogurt, and granola bar. So much of my brain was telling me to do it, to toss the food. I stared at the sandwich. In my head I heard Mom. *You are stronger than you think.*

I bit my nails. I shook my foot. I got up and paced. The

sandwich just sat there on the table, refusing to eat itself. The secretary's face popped up at the window. She didn't bother to open the door. "Good?" she mouthed. I gave her a shaky thumbs-up. She turned back to her paperwork, which seemed to consist of eating a doughnut and looking at Facebook on her computer. I had ten minutes left. Ten minutes. I thought of the jeans in my closet. I thought of the tiny-size clothes in my drawers, the teeny T-shirts, skirts, and yoga pants. I thought of what they would look like if I put them on now. I thought of Wallingfield, of the girls who were on their second or even third trips into residential treatment. I thought of how, over time, the ones who refused to get better seemed proud of their illness, like they thought they were tougher than the rest of us, better even, because they'd mastered the whole eating disorder thing. I thought of Lexi. Did I want to spend my life bouncing in and out of treatment centers, having bone scans and waiting for the bad one? I thought of Margot, who didn't have what I had—parents who loved and supported me.

If I skipped lunch I'd find a way to skip dinner. Then breakfast, and lunch, and dinner again. It wasn't a slippery slope. It was a straight free fall, and I knew it.

I picked up my sandwich and took a bite. Mom had bought my favorite French bread from the bakery downtown. It was soft and delicious. I chewed each bite to paste, but I ate it. Same with the yogurt, the apple, the granola bar, and the milk. I finished, exhausted, just as the bell rang.

When the secretary came in, she glanced at my containers, said, "Good work! You're free to go," and opened the door. I wanted to shout at her, *Do you know what I just did?* and for her to at least give me a high five, or a fist bump or *something*, like they would have at Wallingfield. But she wouldn't get it, so I kept my excitement and pride to myself.

She held the door with her hip and picked at her fingernails.

After the quiet of the office, the hallway was overwhelming, a rush of kids moving and dodging and making their way to their next class. I hesitated. I was so tired. I didn't think I could fight my way into that chaotic flow of traffic. It was too much. I wanted to go home.

And then, there he was. Tristan. He stopped and smiled, the only kid wearing a messenger bag instead of a backpack. "Hey, superstar, ready to go?"

He made it sound so easy, like it was a no-brainer. I lingered in the doorway.

And then Mom was with me again. Her voice ran like cough syrup through me, coating my nerves. *You have been through a war, and you've won.* I took a deep breath. The war wasn't over. I had so much more work to do. But

Mom wasn't totally wrong. I'd won a few big battles, and that counted for something.

"Okay, so we'll see you tomorrow," the secretary said.

I put the straps of my backpack on one shoulder at a time. *Yes, you will,* I thought. *Yes, you will.*

# Acknowledgments

BACK IN 2012, WHEN I SAT DOWN TO WRITE FOR real for the first time, I had no words. Then I joined a writing group and they started flowing. Thank you, Mary Hill, Janine Kovac, Jill Dempster, and Joanne Hartman, for sharing your worlds with me, inspiring me, and believing in me before I did.

Kent D. Wolf, thank you for plucking me out of the crowd and caring about Elizabeth's story as much as I do. You are the best agent a writer could have, and I am grateful.

Joy Peskin, from the minute I met you, I knew that we were a match (Camby Hall 4-eva!). Your editorial vision, kindness, and all-around smarts made my book come alive and make every phone call and meeting a treat.

I super appreciate the teamwork over at FSG. Elizabeth H. Clark, Maya Packard, Nicholas Henderson, and Nancy Elgin, many, many thanks for everything.

Lisa Staton, thank you for listening and allowing me to be the fourth triplet for all these years. Abby Smith and Jacqueline Caruth, you fill my bucket when I need it the most. Jean and Raleigh Ellisen, someone in the universe was looking out for me when we moved next door to you. Thank you for the e-cards, the lemon curd, the daily hugs, and the love. Rachel Sarah, you read every single page of this book multiple times and probably know Elizabeth better than I do. Thank you for your friendship and your wisdom. I couldn't have done this without you.

So much gratitude also goes to: Authoress, whose name I will never know, but to whom I owe so much; the Renfrew Center, for its expertise; Alison McCabe, for keeping me together; Write On Mamas, for companionship and inspiration; Kate Chynoweth and Keely Parrack, for their CP skills; SCBWI, for the inspirational workshops; Litcamp, for making me feel legit; Michele DeMarco, for writing advice and lifelong friendship; Kimberley Gregg, for her enthusiasm and positivity; my twelfth-grade English teacher, Liz Moon, who looked into my eyes and told me that I was a good writer and who, with those few words, changed my life; my students—at Bentley School, the Clinton School for Writers and Artists, and I.S. 98—who inspired me with their writing and stories; and all the others whose generosity, love, and support made this wacky dream of mine come true.

And lastly, I'd like to thank my family. So much appreciation goes to my in-laws, Roberta and Phil Ballard, for their continuous love, cheerleading, and writing retreats at the ranch; my sister (in-law) Angela, whose wise counsel and support mean everything; and my brother-in-law Dustin, for his medical expertise and friendship.

My parents, Marlene and Doug Cann, sacrificed and worked harder than I ever have to give me a childhood full of wonderful memories. Thanks, Mom, for being my best friend and confidante, and Dad, thank you for the creativity gene and for being my biggest fan. I love you both and couldn't have done this without you. Thanks, also, for giving me a brother like Max, whose friendship and occasional couch tackle have carried me through the years. And Max, thanks for marrying Caitlin, who finally got my head out of the cake and in general just gets it.

Callie and Eliza—my smart, strong, amazing girls—thank you for cheering me on with hugs, snuggles, trampoline shows, stories, baked goods, homemade signs, and stories of your own. I love you both more than anything.

And to Chris, my brilliant husband. Thank you, thank

you, thank you for knowing that writing was what I was meant to do even when I had my doubts. You're my best friend and an amazing partner. I love you and can't wait to spend our springs in Paris, writing in coffee shops.

Finally, no thank-you would be complete without including the dog. Thank you, Riley, for always sitting at my feet.

# About the Author

**ALEXANDRA BALLARD HAS WORKED AS A MAGAZINE** editor, middle-school English teacher, freelance writer, and cake maker. She holds a master's degree in journalism from Columbia University and another, in education, from Fordham University, and spent ten years in the classroom, beginning in the Bronx in New York City and ending up in the hills of northern California. Now she writes contemporary YA fiction and spends her days delving into the magic, heartbreak, and everything else that comes with being a young adult. She lives in northern California with her husband and two daughters. You can visit her at alexandraballard.com.